Pr:

"Finding Hope, The Highway of Tears, is a fictional depiction of a true real-life horror story. Gagnon tells us the story of Hope Lachance, who goes missing along the notorious Highway #16, in northern BC, and is sought by retired Detective Norm Strom.
Engrossing plot, engaging characters, and superb imagery make this a hard story to put down. This well-written and timely account of a truly heart-wrenching problem, is well worth the read."
—*Christine Hayton - Author, Samhain Publishing Ltd.*

"Fix yourself a cup of tea and settle in for a great rainy-day read. You're not going to want to put down "Finding Hope." The author takes you on a haunting ride up western Canada's Highway #16, from Calgary to Hyder, Alaska. Along the way, retired Detective Norm Strom meets Hope Lachance, and then helps the RCMP try to find her, after she's gone missing. Digging into the case, Strom learns why the aboriginal people call the route, The Highway of Tears."
—*Caroline Hartman - Author of Summer Rose*

"Ed Gagnon weaves fiction and reality into an exciting story about the Canadian women who have gone missing along The Highway of Tears, in northern British Columbia. More than a book about crimes against women, and the lack of attention from law enforcement, Finding Hope is about prejudice, despair, and the courage of one woman named Hope."
—*Ben Vandongen - Co-Author of No Light Tomorrow*

Copyright © 2016 Edmond Gagnon

ISBN: 978-1-63491-408-6

All rights reserved. No part of this publication may be reproduced, stored in a retrieval system, or transmitted in any form or by any means, electronic, mechanical, recording or otherwise, without the prior written permission of the author.

Published by BookLocker.com, Inc., Bradenton, Florida.

Although this book was inspired by real events, the characters and story told are fictitious. Any similarity to real persons, living or dead, is strictly coincidental and not intended by the author. Any opinions expressed in this book are solely his and do not represent the opinions of the publisher or others.

Printed on acid-free paper.

Booklocker.com, Inc.
2016

First Edition

Finding Hope

The Highway of Tears

Edmond Gagnon

Author of:

A Casual Traveler
Rat
Bloody Friday
Torch

Authors Note

Although this novel is a work of fiction, the story and characters were inspired by real people, and events that have taken place in the Canadian Northwest. 'Finding Hope' is limited to Northern British Columbia—more specifically, Trans-Canada Highway #16, known as The Highway of Tears.

The violence against women in our country is comparable, if not worse, than the atrocities taking place in other places like Juarez, Mexico. In British Columbia, police have arrested and convicted Cody Alan Legebokoff for four of the Highway of Tears murders.

An American, Bobby Jack Fowler, is suspect in at least two Highway of Tears murders, but he died before he could be brought to justice.

Aboriginal women continue to be molested, abused, and murdered in Canada at an alarming rate. The matter has recently gained national and some international attention, but there seems to be no end to the violence.

Dedication

Between 1980 and 2012 there were 1,017 Aboriginal female victims of homicide in Canada, which represents roughly sixteen percent of all female homicides—far greater than their four percent representation in Canada's female population.
                                                    RCMP Statistics Canada

****

To the Memory of the Victims of the Highway of Tears:

Lana Derick
Nicole Hoar
Tamara Chipman
Shelly Ann Bascu
Monica Jack
Leah Alishia Germaine
Gloria Moody
Gale Weys
Delphine Nikal
Alberta Williams
Aielah Katherina Saric-Auger
Destiny Rae Tom

Roxanne Thiara
Natasha Montgomery
Jill Stuchenko
Cynthia Maas
Bonnie Joseph
Ramona Wilson
Pamela Darlington
Monica Ignas
Micheline Pare
Maureen Moise
Colleen Macmillan

Acknowledgements

"A novel is a story told
The story, words written
Words are thoughts revealed
Thoughts are limitless"

If writing a novel simply consists of putting thoughts into words, and telling a story, why doesn't everyone do it? To write a novel the author must consider more than the topic to cover, or how to tell the story. We have to consider what shape we are in, as a writer, and what kind of support we have, to help us complete the task.

In my endeavors to become a good novelist, I've had to learn how to be a better reader, as well as a writer. I had to dig into grammar books, read other author's work, and join writer support groups. I know I've gotten better at my craft, but I also know I have room for improvement.

My best writing aid has been the feedback from my readers. Honest critiques have helped me get to where I'm at. After listening to what my readers think, I learn from my mistakes. I rely on help from others in the trade, who are better than I am at things like grammar and editing. A professional editor can cost thousands of dollars. That is not feasible for me, as an independent author and self-publisher.

To get this book into print I enlisted help from Rachel Pieters, Ben Vandongen, Christine Hayton and Lydia Ure, who've all done their own writing and know what's involved in making sense of a bunch of chapters and pages of words.

While this book was being written, I reached out for input from Kathy Martinides, Michael Carter, Caroline Hartman, Carole Ruttle, Gary Pepper, and my wife Cathryn. Finding Hope has been my most ambitious undertaking so far. I truly appreciate the valuable time and support that everyone has contributed.

Table of Contents

Prologue - The Stone Orchard xiii
1 - Going Home 1
2 - The Alaska Trip 9
3 - Bear Country 16
4 - Snakes & Ladders 22
5 - He 29
6 - Hyderized 35
7 - Special Deliveries 43
8 - The Hunters 50
9 - Trophies & Treasures 54
10 - Bad News 58
11 - Reaching Out 67
12 - Stepping Up 75
13 - A Quickie 83
14 - The Cougar & The Fox 88
15 - A Ray of Hope 95
16 - Leg Work 104
17 - Fishing 112
18 - Getting Along 120
19 - Dakota 127
20 - Tag Team 134
21 - Searchers 140
22 - Natural Order 148
23 - Follow the Leader 153

Finding Hope

24 - Wings & Whoopee	160
25 - Secreted	166
26 - PTSD	174
27 - Well Laid Plans	177
28 - On the Road Again	184
29 - Booty Calls	191
30 - Hijacked	197
31 - Nagging Thoughts	205
32 - Body Count	213
33 - Sad Stories	220
34 - Trading Company	225
35 - Trapped	231
36 - Thunder & Enlightening	234
37 - Swap Meet	245
38 - Getting the Girl	251
39 - Little Things	257
40 - Finding Hope	264
41 - Loose Ends	270
42 - Crispy Killer	277
43 - New Horizons	286
Author Bio	295

Prologue

The Stone Orchard

He considered the dark road ahead of him, where the headlights landed on a curtain of black. The empty stage hosted his thoughts, and he replayed the previous sexual encounter in his mind. It was her eyes that first caught his attention—one brown and the other hazel. Peach fuzz ran down the sides of her neck, her skin subtle and breasts perky. A warm, tingling sensation spread from his loins through his entire body. He basked in the afterglow.

Trying to focus on the road, he watched for the Devil's Pitch Fork, what the locals called the ominous figure that marked his turn-off. It was all that remained of an old hardwood tree after a lightning strike.

The secondary road took him into the foothills of the Caribou Mountains. He knew the narrow and winding roads like the back of his hand. Mimicking a game he once played with his father, he closed his eyes to see how far he could travel without leaving the pavement.

He shifted the transmission to four-wheel drive and turned onto the old logging road. It was rarely used, with the exception of the odd hunter or Forest Ranger. Stopping, he removed the rusty chain that hung across the road. A 'No Trespassing' sign dangled from it. Scarred letters and a group of small dents were evidence of a shotgun blast. Someone had used it for target practice.

Nearly half a kilometer into the bush, there was a fork in the road. He chose the branch that led to a cabin. The other went to a small lake. He drove the winding road up past the cabin then onto a worn path that ended on the crest of a hill. The tires kicked up loose stones as the SUV bounced along the rocky terrain. Hearing a thump behind him, he checked the mirror, and cracked a smile at the body in the back.

A clearing at the end of the path was marked by a decrepit picket fence—the boards barely visible in the tall weeds. In the far corner of the plot a massive boulder the size of a car sat as a stark reminder of the mighty glaciers that carved the landscape.

An old orchard full of dead and withered trees surrounded the enclosure. Stepping out of his vehicle, he switched his flashlight on and swept the area with its beam of light. The trees looked sinister, standing as guardians to his netherworld, the stone orchard.

A ghostly figure stood tall in the center of the fenced property. The light came to rest on the solitary monument, sole representative of his forgotten family. He stepped up to the hand-chiseled slab of marble that marked his parents' grave. They rested there side-by-side, closer in death than they had ever been in life.

With one hand on the cold stone, he stood in thought, trying to recall any fond memories of his mother and father. There weren't many. He remembered how his father taught him how to hunt and shoot. Those early lessons in life proved to be valuable, regardless of the way they were drilled into him. There was never a kind word from his father. He didn't miss him.

He crouched and traced the carved letters in his mother's name with his forefinger, remembering the warmth of her hands on his face, the smell of her fresh-baked bread when they returned from hunting. She had sad-looking eyes, like a dog's when it's left alone. She had a beautiful smile, but it quickly faded when she laid eyes on his drunken father. She never drank alcohol; it didn't mix well with her blood. That's how it was with aboriginals—the reason they called it firewater.

Moving the beam of light, he pointed it at the worn path that led to the cabin, his boyhood home. It was the place his mother had died, something he was haunted by and could never forget. It caused a tightness in his chest like a strong hand gripping and squeezing his heart.

His father was killed in a car wreck a few years before his mother died. He was drunk at the time. His mother buried him in the stone orchard on the crest of the hill. At her own request, she joined him there later. To her, it was the proper thing to do. Startled by a fluttering sound above him, he snapped his head back and pointed the flashlight up into the abyss above. A bat darted after insects, navigating its way through the old fruit trees.

He looked back to the ground and waved the beam of light across the damp grass. It illuminated a pile of dirt twenty feet away. He walked to the SUV, opened the back hatch, scooped up the body bag and threw it over his shoulder like a sack of wet cement. After trading his flashlight for a battery-powered lantern, he carried the body to the pile of freshly dug soil.

Standing in front of the grave he'd prepared earlier, he let the bag slide from his shoulder and drop down into the hole. It hit bottom with a dull thud—like the sound his father's fist made when it rammed into his stomach. The noise was lost in the silence of the night.

He took a hand full of loose earth and held it up in the air, slowly letting the granules fall into the grave. He had seen his mother's father do it once, but he couldn't remember the words that were uttered at the time. It was a language he never understood. He slipped the other hand into his pocket and fondled the silver bracelet he had taken as a memento.

Finding Hope

After shoveling all the dirt back into the hole, he laid and tamped the sod back in place. A slight mound in the earth on a hill in the stone orchard, was the only reminder of a life that had once belonged to a young girl named, Mandy.

He stood in silence for a moment, using the shovel for support. Bending from the waist, he stretched out the muscles in his lower back. He felt fulfilled, but tired. Anxious to sleep, he headed down to the cabin where fond memories and sweet dreams of his new family awaited him.

1

Going Home

"All of the women who went missing along Highway 16 were aboriginal except for one. We're told by the RCMP there are no connections in any of these cases, but it's quite obvious there are."

—Beverly Jacobs

Hope Lachance asked the confused Asian couple, "Would you like anything else, dessert perhaps?"

They shook their heads in unison.

"Okay, I'll be right back with your check."

She looked up at the clock on her way to the cash register and thought, *only two more hours to go.*

Hope was anxious to get home and see her daughter. It had been two long weeks since she had seen her little angel, Charitee. The busloads of tourists that came to the Pro Sports Bar & Grill wore her patience thin. They didn't tip well, and most couldn't speak English. It was her last night before heading back home.

Her hard work usually resulted in good tips, more so with the regulars than the tourists, in Jasper, Alberta. Her appearance made a difference. The staff had to wear uniforms so Hope had hers altered to compliment her slim figure. She received compliments on her Cover Girl complexion and friendly smile, but they couldn't appreciate what hid behind her disquieted eyes. Men always gawked, but she had much more going for her, than her looks. She didn't like the attention, but if it meant bigger tips, she went along with it.

Hope wanted to head home to Stewart, BC early the next morning. She'd considered Jasper as her home, but had her reasons not to. The money was better there, but she preferred the anonymity in Stewart. The part-time gig in Jasper was strictly for extra cash. Otherwise, she would never stay away from her daughter so long.

Nick, the owner, had recruited Hope from one of his own barstools, while she was passing through town one day. Being a big hockey fan, she liked to stop there because of all the televisions that were mounted throughout the bar. He approached her with a job offer when he first laid eyes on her, pumping her fist in the air, and cheering out loud for the Montreal Canadiens.

After settling up with the foreign tourists, Hope asked the two goateed bikers at the end of the bar if they wanted anything else before she tabbed out for the night. The bigger guy was quite handsome. He and another man were watching the baseball game when he noticed she was checking him out.

He asked her, "Who's your team?"

"Sorry, baseball's too slow for me. I'm a hockey fan. Go Habs."

"Ha. When's the last time they won a Stanley Cup?"

Hope smiled. "I suppose you're a Canucks fan?"

Both men laughed out loud. The smaller of the two, who looked like a member of the Hair Club for Men, proudly announced, "I'm a Detroit fan."

"And what about you, big guy?"

"Me? I used to be a Habs fan, but I gave up taking hockey seriously after they expanded from the original six."

Hope listened. She liked the sound of his voice and the shade of his kind, blue eyes.

"Are you guys from Detroit?"

Hair Club guy answered. "We're from Windsor. It's a Canadian suburb of Detroit."

"That's a long ride!"

"We shipped our bikes to Calgary. Now we're going to visit my uncles in Prince George and Smithers. I'm Louie, and this is my brother-in-law, Norm."

"Cool. I'm Hope. You guys have got some beautiful road ahead of you."

Louie continued, "We froze our asses off coming out of Banff, and going through the Columbia Ice Fields. Great August weather you have here. We're going to a hick town in Alaska called, Hyder."

Hope grinned.

"I know it well. I work there too. Actually, I'm heading there tomorrow morning to see my daughter."

"You want a ride?"

"No. I'm good, thanks."

"Well, maybe we'll see you there. Where do you work?"

"There are only two bars in town. It's not hard to find me. Listen guys, I have to tab out for the night. Can we settle up?"

Louie paid his bill in cash. Norm opened his wallet to retrieve his credit card. Hope noticed something shiny; it reflected the light from above the bar.

"Is that a badge?"

He showed her his tin. It was chrome-plated and stamped with the words *Windsor Police - Retired Detective*.

"Yup, I'm a retired cop."

His words seemed to put her at ease. Maybe it was because she respected the law, or that she considered it an honest profession. Either way, she had a good feeling about him and she was drawn to his gentle eyes.

Finding Hope

"Maybe I'll see you guys when you get to Hyder. Have a safe trip."

They held their probing gaze another second. Then quietly, she turned and walked away.

Shortly after sunup the next morning, Hope walked over to the truck stop, only a few blocks from the house where she rented couch space from one of her co-workers. Joyce offered her the sofa bed for nothing, but Hope didn't believe in a free ride. She stocked the fridge with groceries when Joyce refused money.

When there was no bus service, the truck stop was where she went to hitch a ride home. Jasper is at the junction of Highways #39 and #16, a crossroads for trucks and trains, and the goods they haul cross-country. Hope had lived in Stewart, BC on the border of Alaska, for five years. During that time she had gotten familiar with some of the truck drivers who regularly ran the highways in the area.

She ordered scrambled eggs, brown toast, and coffee for breakfast. Hope was a cautious woman, she knew better than to hitch a ride with a total stranger. She'd heard stories of women who'd gone missing, and been found murdered. The locals had a name for the lonely stretch of Highway #16 that ran from Prince George to Prince Rupert. They called it the Highway of Tears.

There was only intermittent bus service in the area, and no service at all on the last leg to Hyder. She knew what she did was risky, but she took solace in the fact that she understood people. She was a perceptive person who learned a lot from working in the service industry. She was also of the belief that she knew men, or at least the difference between a good one and a bad one.

Hope scanned the room looking for familiar faces while she waited for her breakfast. She tried to ignore the poignant aromas around her that might spoil her appetite—stale cigarettes, diesel fuel and body odor. The grizzled and unkempt men looked and smelled like an old football team, who'd just finished a game in the greasy parking lot.

The only other woman in the diner was an old waitress who looked like Betty White. Hope smirked at the uncanny resemblance, and the fact that her name really was Betty. They weren't exactly friends, but the two of them often kibitzed about the motley crew of men who ate there.

A plainclothes cop sat a few tables over, a Mountie. He looked familiar. He stared over the top of his newspaper as he sipped his coffee. Once he saw that she'd spotted him, he smiled and winked. She hated that, it made her skin crawl.

She remembered why he looked familiar. He had picked her up hitchhiking on one of her trips down from Hyder. He lectured and interrogated her, trying to dig into her past, wanting to know why she lived in such a remote town. She thought he was just being a cop, but he was creepy.

Betty arrived at the table with Hope's breakfast in hand.

"Here you go, honey. You look nice today, are you on your way home? I bet you miss your little girl."

"Yeah. I'm done my stint at the sports bar—and yes, I can't wait to see Charitee. I miss her so much on these trips, but we need the money. Hey, have you seen Big Lonny this morning?"

Betty motioned to a customer that she'd be there in a minute.

"No. I heard he's laid up with his back again. Dale should be in this morning though. If he's done his fish run, he should be on the way back up. I'm not sure which smells worse—him or his truck."

Hope laughed out loud.

"I know exactly what you mean."

She had hitched a ride with Dale before, but he was never her first choice. He ran fresh fish down the highway from Alaska, then produce on the way back up. It wasn't the smell of him or the truck, she just didn't like him.

She surveyed the room once more before she re-arranged and assembled the food on her plate. She liked to put her scrambled eggs on the buttered toast, with a bit of ketchup, to create a fluffy egg sandwich. The cacophony of scraping silverware, and clanking coffee cups faded as Hope's thoughts drifted off. She stared into the empty space that hung above the hungry bobbing heads, while they sipped and gulped and chewed.

She wondered what her daughter was up to. On Saturday mornings, Charitee and her friend Hanna, liked to share their breakfast with the neighborhood chipmunks. Hanna and her mom, Laurie, lived next door and watched Charitee while Hope was away. Their girls were the same age, and went to the same school. She made a mental note to call Laurie as soon as she found a ride. She also wanted to tell Charitee that her mommy was coming home.

Hope snapped out of her trance when Betty stopped at her table to top up her coffee. She expertly poured the hot brew, and nodded towards the entrance. Hope saw Dale Strickland stroll in the front door with a newspaper tucked under his arm.

She blew a sigh of relief.

"Thanks Betty, can you add his breakfast to my bill?"

"No problem, sweetie. You have a safe trip home."

Betty patted Hope's arm before she walked away. She finished the last bite of her egg sandwich, and washed it down with a big gulp of coffee, burning her tongue. She had forgotten that Betty had just given her a refill. Charitee was still on her mind. She thought about the long ride with Dale: his rudeness, his smell, and the honky-tonk music. She studied the room one more time. He was her only choice.

Hope left enough money on the table to cover her and Dale's bill, and to give Betty a nice tip. Working in the same profession, she'd discovered that wait staff took care of their own, tipping each other well. She glided through the narrow aisle between the rows of tables, ignoring the stares from the horny truck drivers. She felt as though she was walking through an airport x-ray machine.

Dale had his head buried in a newspaper when she stopped at his table. He looked up when she slid into the chair across from him.

"Well now, if it ain't my only Hope."

"Hey Dale, how far are you going today?"

"I go all the way, baby. Do you?"

Dale always teased and talked dirty, but she liked to think that he was all talk. The first time that she rode with him, his wife was along for the ride. When she got into the passenger side of his truck she was greeted by a sticker on the glove box that said, *Gas, Grass, or Ass, nobody rides for free.* After he saw that Hope had read it, he pointed to his wife in the back and said, "She's all paid up."

Hope leaned back in her chair and rolled her eyes at Dale's comment.

"I'd like a ride Dale. I've already covered your breakfast. I know your rules."

"There's other ways to pay, darlin."

"Ha-ha, you're so funny, Dale. What about your wife?"

"She didn't marry me for my money, must be cuz I'm well hung."

Dale liked to brag about things like his looks, his penis, and his truck. In reality, he couldn't see his penis because of the overhang of his beer belly. His wife told everyone that he was hung like a budgie—a big man with a bird's dick.

"Can I hitch a ride or not Dale?"

"Sure, darlin. I've already got another passenger though—he's asleep in the back. His truck is in for servicing, so I agreed to drop him off at home."

"That's cool, Dale. I'll meet you out at the truck. I want to use the phone before we leave."

"Okay. Hey, clean the windshield when you get out there?"

"Sure. No problem."

Hope used the washroom, and then stopped at the payphone by the door. She called Laurie and told her that she was hitching a ride home with a trucker that she knew.

"I should be home some time Sunday morning, I can't wait to see my baby girl. Can you put Charitee on the phone?"

She could hear her daughter giggling in the background while Laurie told her to come to the phone. She heard the voice of her little angel.

"Hi mommy. I miss you!"

"Hey, baby girl. Mommy's coming home!"

2

The Alaska Trip

"We travel, some of us forever, to seek other places, other lives, other souls."
—Anais Nin

It was Wednesday, boys night at the Hook & Ladder Club, in Windsor. Every week Norm Strom joined his dad, brother, and a few buddies for beer and wings. His brother-in-law, Louie, joined the group about once a month when his wife wasn't home to cook for him. The family couldn't figure out what she saw in Louie, but they took him in anyway, as if he was stray dog.

He bought his obligatory round of drinks and plopped them on the table. He said to Norm, "Let's take the bikes to Alaska this summer."

They both owned Harley Davidson's and had ridden together locally, a few times. Norm took a gulp of his beer and pondered the proposal. Having just gotten back from two months in Southeast Asia, there was nothing stopping him from going on another trip. He was newly retired, after putting in over thirty-one years with the Windsor Police. Travelling was at the top of his bucket list.

"That's a long ride, Louie. It's gonna take us at least a week just to get there."

"I wasn't planning on riding all the way there, I don't have time off like you do, ya' retired bastard. We can ship the bikes to Calgary, and then start riding from there. I've got uncles and cousins in Prince George and Smithers. One of them is not far from Alaska."

Norm was impressed. Louie was a master embellisher and bullshitter, but it was obvious he'd done his homework.

"Tell me more."

"I looked into it—we can stay with them. It'll cost us about seven hundred bucks each to crate and ship the bikes to Calgary. The truck will pick them up at my shop. We hop on a plane a few days later, and pick up the Hawys there."

Louie and his brother, Giovani, owned a tool and die business; he was able to get a deal on shipping, through the company. Norm appreciated the discounted fare.

"So how long were you thinking? There's a lot of road to cover in northern BC"

"Well, the first day would be a write-off, flying. Then it's about five hours to Jasper and another five to Prince George. It's roughly the same to Smithers and Alaska—one day for each leg. So, I'm thinking we'll spend the first night in Jasper, then a couple days in Prince George, visiting my cousins. We'll need a few more days to get up to Smithers, then Alaska, and then back. All together we can do it in ten days, so I won't need to take much time off work."

"Will your boss give you the time off?"

Louie laughed. He was his own boss.

"So when do we leave?"

"I was thinking the end of August, before it cools off out there."

Norm had no job, wife, or kids to worry about. He raised his beer bottle to Louie.

"Cheers to Alaska!"

The Highway of Tears

After spending the night in a noisy airport motel in Calgary, Louie and Norm took a taxi to the warehouse where their bikes had been shipped. The jitney driver dropped off the two crates marked "fragile" on the loading dock. All they needed was a screwdriver to open one end panel on Louie's crate. He had packed an electric drill with his bike.

While they tore down the crates, a cold front crept down from the Rockies, bringing rain with it. They had to don their rain gear before they hit the road.

Riding in the rain was nothing new for Norm, but Louie was a little uneasy. He was a fair weather rider, with very few wet miles under his belt. Both bikes had windshields to help with visibility, but riding on wet pavement means less traction for the tires. As if that wasn't tough enough for Louie, he was born vertically challenged, so his feet barely touched the ground when he tried to hold his bike up.

He was terrible with directions, so it came as no surprise to Norm, that he made a couple of wrong turns before finding the Trans-Canada Highway. Norm had previously driven a portion of the highway—to Banff and Lake Louise, back in the early eighties when his family all lived in Calgary. They had followed the oil boom and bust out west, but eventually moved back to Windsor.

It's only an hour and a half from Calgary to Banff, but in that time the bottom fell out of the thermometer. They had to pull off the road to add another layer of clothing. Louie's smile looked like an over-stretched elastic band, as he took in the amazing alpine view. The temperature wasn't as impressive; it was forty degrees Fahrenheit—not quite normal weather for August in any part of inhabited Canada.

Norm walked over to the fence that separated him from the sprawling landscape that only Mother Nature, herself, could have created. There were more shades of green than in a deluxe box of crayons. The slope was covered with long grass, laced with white daisies and purple phlox. Rapids in a serpentine river, marked the bottom of the valley below. A lone spruce tree stood as sentinel on a tiny island, in the middle of the waterway.

On the far side of the river, an army of Christmas trees marched up the mountainside and off into the distance, where they became one solid mass. Shadows cast from the bruised clouds looming above, appeared as dark spots on the coniferous landscape. High above the trees a row of lofty mountain peaks stood vigilant over the awesome vista, as they have for thousands of years. Their true height couldn't be appreciated, because of the swollen clouds that sagged on their tops, like wads of wet cotton.

Norm took a final gander, and sucked in one last deep breath of the fresh air, satiating his senses. He chuckled to himself how he didn't miss working for a living; there was so much more to life.

He mounted his iron horse. Neither their stomachs nor the selection of restaurants in the town of Banff, beckoned loud enough to warrant an early lunch stop. Norm glanced back over his shoulder to Louie and shrugged. They throttled back and headed north into the Rocky Mountains.

Further up the road the dark clouds that had been scattered, huddled overhead, like a football team prepping for the next play. The sun went into hibernation and the damp, cool air, became cold precipitation. Their rain suits kept them dry for the most part, but the bitter cold pierced Norm's soaked leather gloves. The beautiful alpine scenery was no match for the discomfort of his cold and wet hands. At that elevation, the moisture-laden clouds looked like thick patches of fog, suspended in mid-air.

The lunch stop at a roadside service center was a welcome reprieve—a chance to thaw and dry out. Louie laughed when

Norm wrung out his leather gloves and left a puddle of water on the floor. Instead of buying a tacky Rocky Mountain souvenir, he bought a pair of tight-fitting football gloves and a pair of heavy black rubber gloves to wear on top. It wasn't sexy, but it was warm and dry.

Overcast skies and dryer weather welcomed them to the Columbia Ice Fields. It was the kind of place that made you feel insignificant. A massive glacier stretched down the mountain valley, lapping at the tiny humans and their vehicles with its giant tongue.

Louie and Norm arrived in Jasper hungry and ready to shed their multiple layers of clothing. Norm suggested that they find accommodations before it got too late—that proved to be easier said than done. Every hotel and motel in town was booked.

Dusk was upon them. Norm felt a sense of urgency as they drove up and down side streets and knocked on the doors of every Bed & Breakfast that they came across. He sat on his bike in front of a Victorian style house while Louie took his turn, and went inside to inquire about a room. When the streetlights came on Norm added a little anxiety to his hunger and fatigue. He started to wonder if they would have to sleep in an all night laundry mat.

It didn't look good. Louie came out of the house shaking his head.

"They only have one room with one double bed in it, and they don't know of any other vacancies around here. I told them we'd take it."

"Okay, but let me tell you right now, brother, there will be no balls to buns."

They both laughed uncontrollably—probably because of their hunger and exhaustion, from being on the road all day.

Most of the restaurants in Jasper were within easy walking distance from the B&B. They chose the Pro Sports Bar and

Finding Hope

Grill. Norm's stomach growled louder than the aftermarket exhaust pipes on his Harley. There was a line waiting to get in the dining room, but Louie weaseled his way through the crowd, and waved Norm over to the bar. "A smokin' hot waitress said we can eat here if we want."

"Seat, beer, food—I'm in."

Norm saw that the Blue Jays game was on behind the bar. He wasn't much of a TV baseball fan, but he sometimes watched the playoffs or World Series. It wasn't that he didn't like the game, he was an all-star when as a kid. He felt there were more interesting things to watch on television.

Louie looked like he was watching a tennis match—his head turned from side to side every time a waitress went by.

"Norm, did you see the one with the long black hair?"

"Yeah, I saw her. She's hot. Wipe your chin, Louie, you're drooling. I don't know how Lynn puts up with you. Don't forget, she owns half of everything."

Louie scoffed. Norm secretly enjoyed his own dirty thoughts. *Damn, I'd like to tap that ass. I can't remember the last time I got laid.*

"I know, I know. She says you'll help her spend all my money, after she kicks me out."

The boys got a chance to chat with the hot waitress before she cashed out at the end of her shift. She introduced herself as Hope, and told them to look her up in Alaska. Norm's eyes were glued to her ass as she walked out the door. He felt that there might have been a mutual attraction between them, and he wondered if she'd look back. He bet she would. Just outside the front door, she looked back over her shoulder. She smiled and waved goodbye.

That smile, and her pretty face, lingered in his mind. She reminded him of Cher, when she did her Half-Breed album, back in the day. He had a major crush on her. Hope had the same ripe olive skin, long black hair that tickled the cheeks of her ass, and what he liked to call, bedroom eyes.

After dinner and a few nightcaps, the boys headed back to their B&B. They both looked at the tiny bed and shook their heads.

Louie got undressed.

"I usually sleep nude."

"Well, you're *not* tonight."

They climbed into bed and fidgeted, trying to keep some space between them. Norm took a spare pillow and stuffed it between them, like a bumper cushion in a crib. He slept like a rock. The long ride, big meal and booze, surely contributed.

When he woke up in the morning he was face to face with Louie, barely an inch separating them. The sight of his big wet honker, jolted Norm awake. Afraid that Louie might blow snot on him, he jumped out of bed and into the shower.

3

Bear Country

The journey continued northwest from Jasper, on the Yellowhead Highway. After several miles Norm pulled off the road, and Louie stopped beside him. Norm pointed to Mount Robson in his rear-view mirror, the most prominent summit in North America's Rocky Mountain Range. It's the highest point in the Canadian Rockies and part of the Continental Divide.

Louie exclaimed, "Wow! You should get a picture of that."

"That's why I stopped. The snow-covered peak, framed by my mirror, would make a great post card."

As Mount Robson faded in the distance behind them, the Caribou Mountains appeared off to the west. The highway twisted and turned as it followed the northern branch of the mighty Fraser River. The fast water fractured the sun's rays, making it look as though millions of diamonds were scattered across it's surface. The air was heavy with the scent of pine and cedar.

Being a more experienced rider, Norm held the lead position. Louie followed slightly behind, on his right flank. Norm noticed a commotion up the road and signaled that he was pulling over. They parked their bikes on the shoulder.

"What's going on, Norm?"

"I dunno...they're all looking at something in the ravine. I thought it might be worth a look."

Tourists had gathered at the guard rail; some of them pointed down the pitch to a large bear that was feeding on berries. The animal was on a small island in the middle of the shallow river below the road. Japanese tourists, with camera's in hand, scrambled over the guard rail as they tried to get closer. Norm watched the bear from the road through his camera's zoom lens. Louie leaned on the guard rail beside him.

"Is that a brown bear, Norm?"

"That's a grizzly. Look at those morons—they think they're at the zoo."

Norm snapped a few pictures. The big bear was no more than a hundred yards away. It stood up on its hind legs, towering over the shrubbery.

"Louie, let's get out of here before those idiots walk right up to the bear and ask it for an autograph."

The weather gods finally smiled upon the boys, and the sun beamed overhead for the remaining ride to Prince George. Norm thought it was sad, seeing large brown patches in the normally green landscape, where hundreds of thousands of trees were ravaged and killed by the voracious pine beetle, an unprecedented forest-altering event.

When they approached the outskirts of Prince George, Norm noticed a unique tree that had been damaged and burned by a lightning strike. The black pitchfork marked a T intersection. The roads leading into the city were welcoming, lined with colorful flowers and manicured shrubs.

Louie had directions to the subdivision, where his cousin Loretta lived, so he took the lead. To Norm's surprise, he only made one wrong turn trying to find her house.

They arrived early in the afternoon, when Loretta and her husband Mark, were both at work. Norm used the down time to stretch out on the front lawn, and catch some rays. Louie wasn't one to sit still, so he used the garden hose to wash his bike. Norm had nodded off, but he was startled by a nudge from Louie, who was holding four cold cans of beer.

Finding Hope

"Where the hell did you get those?"

"Next door. The guy was higher than ten hippies—he even offered me a joint."

"I'll pass on the reefer, but the beer looks good."

It was typical for Louie, a social butterfly. He'd gone over to the neighbors' house and introduced himself, returning with their friendly offering. Norm was blinded by the sun reflecting off the chrome on his bike. He smiled.

"You washed my bike too...you're the best, Louie, I don't care what the rest of the family says about you."

Loretta got off work early and returned home with supplies for her house guests—more beer. Norm liked her right off the bat.

After returning home from work, and an being introduced to his house guests, Mark led everyone through his back yard, where they climbed the fence and went for dinner at the General's house. It's what they called Mark's mother.

Flora, another of Louie's cousins, greeted Norm with a beer and some antipasto. Like busy bees, the women carried food from the kitchen to the patio. They had been cooking for two days. *Mangia* became a new word in Norm's vocabulary. It was his cue to open his mouth and shove more food into it.

Appetizers and antipasto and alcohol flowed non-stop, like the Fraser River. There was beer before dinner, wine with it, and whiskey after. Food and famiglia, it's an Italian tradition. Shouts of *Salute!* rang out many times. Norm toasted to life with his new family. The story about how he and Louie had to sleep together in the same bed was a gut-buster.

Norm was the last one up in the morning, but he caught the tail end of breakfast. Loretta poured him a juice. "Louie said you don't drink coffee, and that you don't usually eat first thing, but I saved you a plate. You look a little rough, Norm."

~~Dave 6:00~~

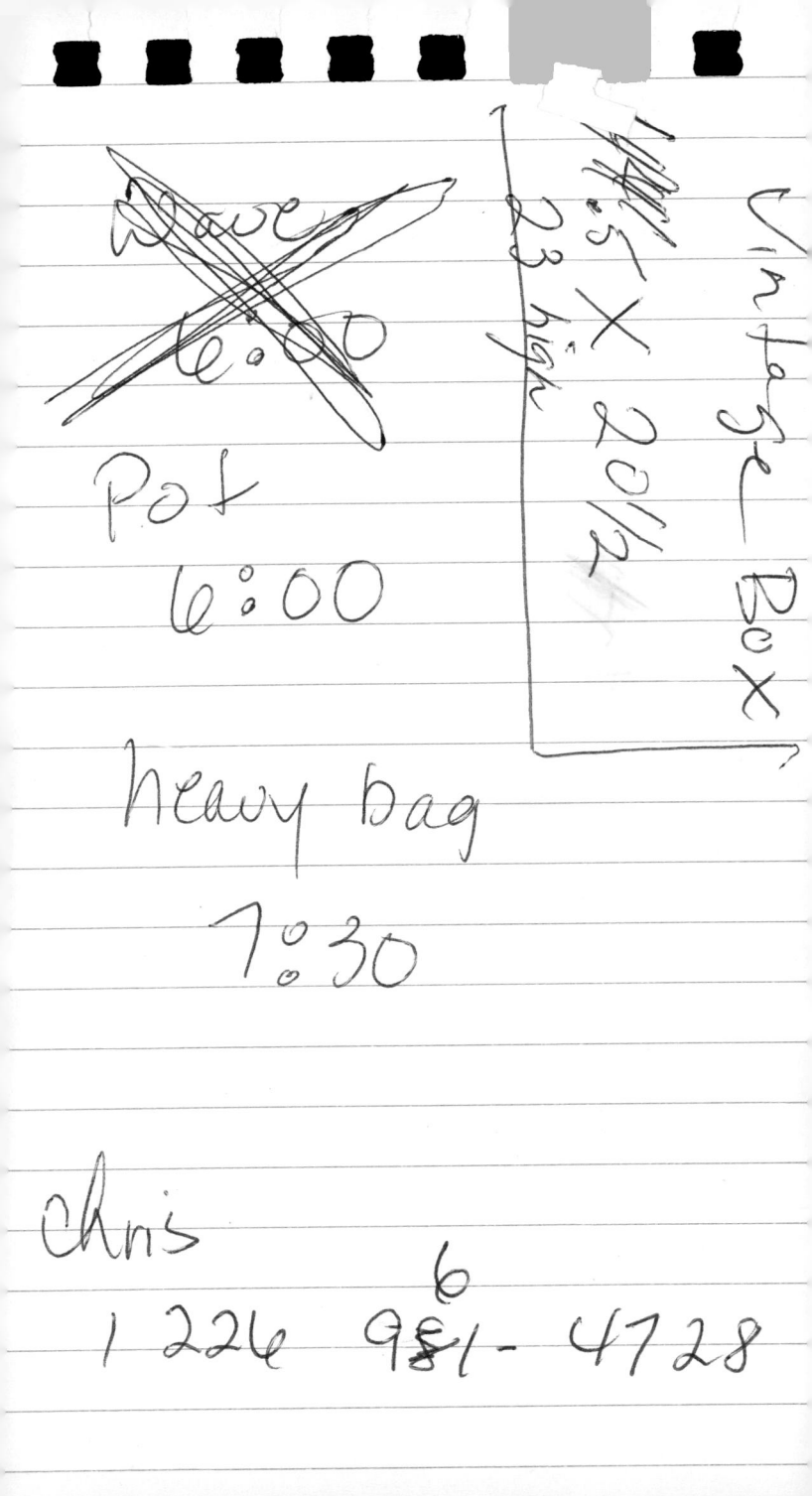

Pot
6:00

Vintage Box
14.5 x 20 1/2
23 high

Heavy Bag
7:30

Chris
1 226 981-4728 (6 above 8)

~~Vintage trunk~~
~~1:30 2:00~~
~~MATHEW~~

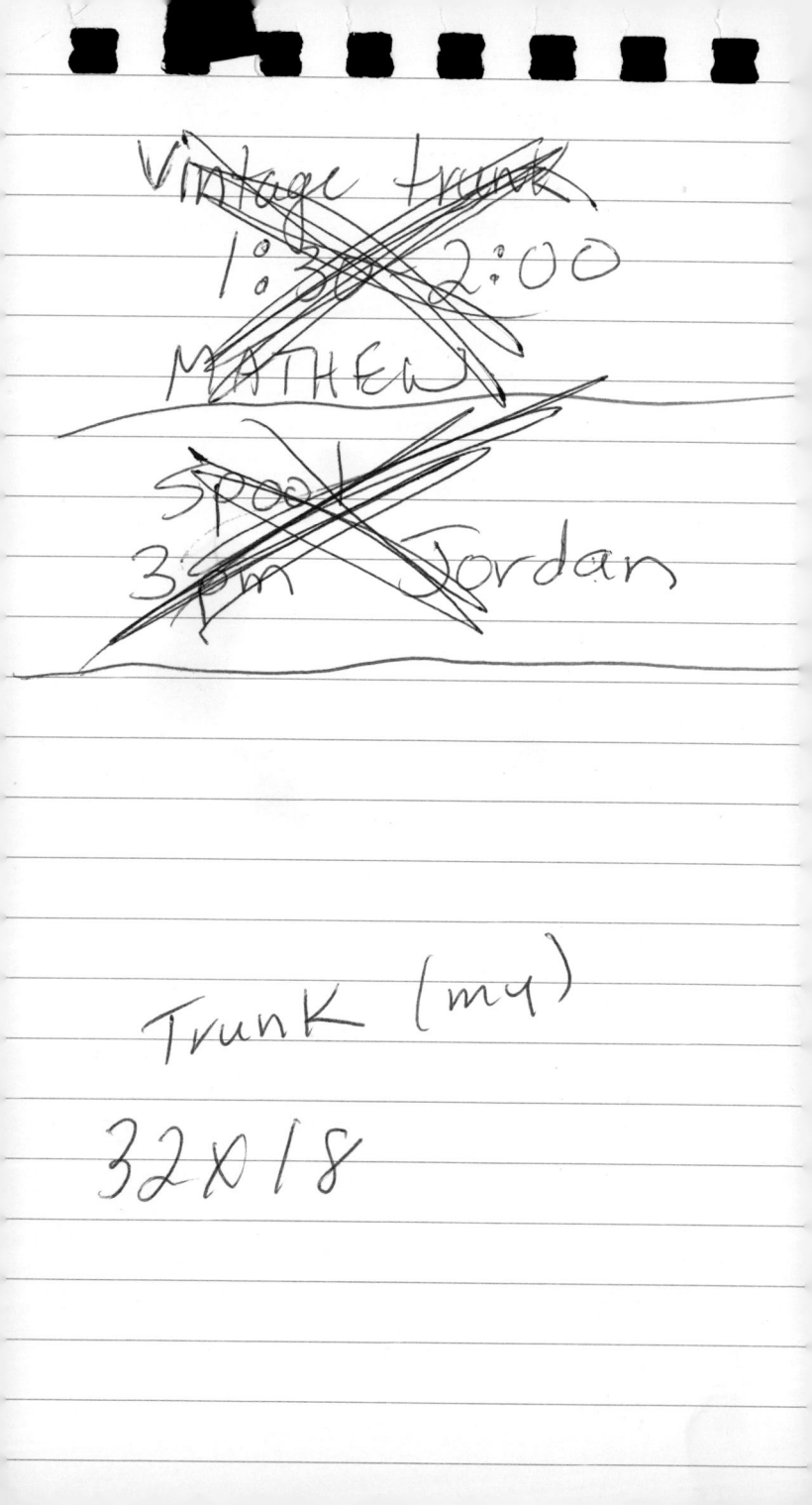

~~Spool~~
~~3pm Jordan~~

Trunk (my)

32 x 18

"You should see the world from my perspective; not quite as clear as the Sambucca we drank. I do need to eat something, then I want to go for a walk to burn off the fog in my head."

"You should go down to the park along the riverfront. There's a path halfway down the block that will take you there."

Houses along the street were colorfully landscaped. Brilliant yellow and orange sweet peas cascaded over a brick retaining wall, along the foot path that took Norm into a wooded area, and then a city park. There, a carpet of snapdragons and petunias, in a rainbow of colors, filled beds on both sides of the walkway.

The gardens brought back memories of Norm's home in Colchester, on the north shore of Lake Erie, where his entire back yard was an elaborate water garden. He had designed and built a stream, waterfalls, and two ponds, himself. It was surrounded by hundreds of perennials, that bloomed in specific colors for each season. A custom deck edged the lower pond, separating it from the house. Ducks, birds, dragonflies, butterflies, frogs, and fish called his backyard home.

One animal, that Norm wasn't familiar with, was a permanent resident in Prince George. While on the hike, he saw recently felled trees, victims of a local beaver. Timber, the size of telephone poles, had been gnawed off to a stump. The furry little munchers were as efficient as chain saws. In the summer, Prince George was a clean and colorful city. He shuddered at the thought of what it would look like under a thick blanket of snow.

Later that day, Louie and Norm treated their hosts to dinner out. Loretta and Mark were reluctant to except the invitation, but their house guests insisted. It was the least they could do in return for the hospitality that they had received.

Loretta had the next day off work, so she played tour guide for Louie and Norm. Mother Nature contributed to the outing.

She supplied an abundance of sunshine and warmth for their bike ride. The threesome meandered though the countryside, absorbing the pretty scenery of north-western British Columbia.

* * *

Darkness, then shadows. Her eyelids felt heavy, as though they were made of rubber. She used the tips of her fingers to massage them open. Some light, blurriness. The sound of her own breathing rang hollow in her ears. She sat up. More light, some clarity. There were fresh bruises around her wrists.

She tried to stand, but felt dizzy. Her memory was fuzzy and vague. She opened her eyes wide; there was a halo around the light fixture on the ceiling. She blinked hard and her eyes watered. It helped to clear her vision. There were birds chirping—the sound came from outside the room.

Colors and shapes took form around her. Wooden walls and furniture. She was sitting on a cot covered by a handmade quilt. It had pastel colored animals stitched into it. She turned her head and body to look at the rest of the room. Her knee banged into a nightstand beside the bed.

A bottle of water spilled all over the bible that was laying there. Being parched, she grabbed the container before it emptied, and gulped the water down. At first it hurt her throat, but the liquid was soothing, making it easier to swallow.

Her vision was almost clear. She focused on the walls, and saw that they were made of hewn logs. There were no windows in the room. Apart from the bed and nightstand, there was only a small table and chair. Eventually standing erect, she put one hand on the wall to steady herself. There was a door beside the nightstand; she hadn't noticed it, because there was no handle or knob.

On the table, there was a porcelain bed pan and a wash basin, half full of water. A folded white towel was beside the basin. She walked the perimeter of the room and guessed it couldn't have been more than eight feet square. Her vision was clear, but she was light-headed. Running her hand over the rough wooden walls, she surmised that she was in a log cabin. Thinking, trying to remember. *Where am I? What happened to me? Why am I here?*

Not being one to get rattled easily, she sat back down on the bed, trying to focus and remember. Her mind drew a blank. The birds stopped chirping. She heard a door close, then heavy footsteps outside of her room. Someone stood on the other side of her door, she heard the heavy breathing.

Hope Lachance jumped up and screamed at the door, "Let me out of here!"

4

Snakes & Ladders

"One's destination is never a place, but a new way of seeing things."
—Henry Miller

    Louie and Norm were each five pounds heavier when they left Prince George; three days of debauchery had taken its toll. Their plan was to return there after making the trek up to Alaska. Louie would ship his bike home and Norm would ride cross-country, all the way back to Windsor. Caressing his bulging stomach, he moaned to himself about the possibility of gaining yet another five pounds.
    A quaint town named Vanderhoof appeared next on Highway #16. North of it were the Fraser's—Fort Fraser, Fraser Lake and the Town of Fraser Lake. For hours, the scenic road hugged the edge of rivers and lakes, blazing a scenic path to Smithers. Off to the west, the rocky fingers in the peaks of the Coast Mountains reached up and tickled the underbelly of the big sky.
    Not knowing exactly where his Uncle Sal lived in Smithers, Louie waved for Norm to pull over at the Tim Horton's, so he could call him. He was there in about ten minutes. It was Norm's first time meeting Uncle Sal. He received the same warm welcome that he had from the relatives in Prince George, like he was one of the family.

Sal checked out the big Harleys, before he led his guests home. The drive took them up a winding road in the hills. To call the area a subdivision would be an injustice. The mountain homes are spread out on huge lots of an acre or more. The houses were built to aesthetically blend in with the forest. The quiet neighborhood was referred to as Regional One.

Sal's cedar-sided home fit perfectly into its natural surroundings. He had only removed enough trees to build the house. The manicured lawn was bordered by a split rail fence, hardly something that would keep a wandering bear out of the yard. The property was edged by purple coneflowers and yellow day lilies. Two pyramid cedars marked the entrance to the front walk.

The porch was accented on both sides by more flowers of the same color theme. A mature rhododendron, statuary, and a clematis-covered trellis added height to the garden. A raised deck wrapped around the side of the house.

Sal's wife Carol welcomed Louie and Norm into her home. They were shown to their separate guest rooms. Norm was happy that he didn't have to sleep with Louie again, as in Jasper.

When they came back downstairs, Sal was out on the deck holding a couple of cold beers. Sal and Carol's secret was revealed when Norm looked through the exterior wall of glass and sliding doors off the kitchen. It was the reason they built the house exactly where they did.

The view was absolutely breathtaking. In awe, Norm was lured to the deck's railing. He remarked, "Oh my god, your view is like a living post card."

Sal pointed and gave the travelogue: "Beyond that expanse of forest there...those two snow-covered summits are Hudson Bay Mountain and Mount Evelyn."

Finding Hope

Norm stared. The scenery was magnetic. A glacier lay nestled between the two peaks, as it had for tens of thousands of years.
"Those waterfalls are amazing."
"That's Twin Falls...from the glacial melt water."
The city boy was mesmerized. The waterfalls spilled down the mountain cleavage like a gleaming pearl necklace.

* * *

The response to Hope's demand for freedom was only met by a grunt from the other side of the wooden door. She pounded with both fists and yelled, "Why am I here? Let me out! Please...let me out!"
The door was made of thick tongue and groove boards. It didn't budge when she banged on it. A covered window, about one foot square, was cut into the center of the door at eye level. It wiggled a bit. She dug her fingernails into the crack and tried to pry it open.
Her efforts were useless and her demands went unanswered. She sat back down on the bed, thought about Charitee, and started to cry. She missed her so much. Hope remembered her phone call home, and leaving the truck stop with Dale. She remembered driving north to Smithers and having lunch there. *Oh yeah, the mountain man.*
It was there, while she was eating, that Dale had left the table and went to the bathroom. He was gone for quite a while. She saw him talking to a burly man, just outside the front doors. The man wore a soiled buckskin vest. His bushy brown hair and matching beard made him look like Grizzly Adams.
When Dale returned to the table, she asked who he had been talking to.
"That's the guy in the back—my buddy, Bear."

"The guy from the truck? I forgot all about him. He must have slept all the way here. Why doesn't he come in for lunch?"
"He's not much of a people person. Likes to keep to himself."
"He looks like a mountain man."
"That's basically what he is. He has a place in the bush up near Kispiox. We hunt moose together up there."
"Where's Kispiox?"
"Further north, past New Hazelton."

After lunch she noticed a stronger than usual stench of body odor in the truck. She sprayed on some extra perfume to kill the smell. She remembered reaching behind the seat for a Diet Coke. A giant hand appeared, offering her a freshly opened can. It looked like a thimble in his massive paw. That was the last thing that she could remember.

* * *

Uncle Sal took the boys sightseeing, the first stop was north of Smithers. Near Morice Canyon, he pointed out Moricetown, one of the five First Nation communities of the Wet'suwet'en people, who have thrived in northern BC for centuries. There, the main tourist attraction is the roaring Buckley River, where it tumbles into Morice Canyon.

From the road, Sal pointed to the fishing shacks used by the aboriginal people. Norm looked at both men, comparing Louie to his uncle as they stood side-by-side. They could have been brothers, but Sal had more hair and was taller.

Norm took an interest in the fish ladders that were built into the river to help the salmon upstream, for spawning. He knew that the people of the nations once owned most of Canada. It's the reason that they were exempt from requiring hunting or fishing licenses. The law says they must fish using traditional methods like fly rods or gaff poles, but that was not what Norm and Louie witnessed.

Along the river banks, in the shallows, thousands of salmon fought their way upriver. They swam along the edges where the current wasn't as strong. To make headway in the fast water, they swam and jumped up like popcorn from a hot pan.

One intoxicated native, fishing there, didn't believe in tradition. Instead of a hook or loop on the end of his gaff pole, he used a net. It was like a typical pole net, but about twenty feet in length. He only had to reach down into the water to scoop up the salmon.

It was fun to watch. The inebriated Indian could barely stand, let alone negotiate the rocky edge of the river. He was dressed like Johnny Cash. Wet strings of his long black hair stuck to his face and sunglasses—he was soaked from head to toe. Norm thought it would only be a matter of time before he fell into the river.

The salmon he netted were sold on the spot; they never made it to the roadside huts or any grocery stores. He made an exchange with a local red neck, who patiently waited by his pickup truck. It looked like a drug deal going down. The Indian threw salmon into the man's cooler, and in return he received a wad of cash. He stuffed the money into the front pocket of his pants. The redneck drove off, spinning his tires in the loose gravel.

Norm asked, "One of your neighbors, Sal?"

"I haven't seen him before. There's a lot of hermits like him up in the mountains. They live off the land and only come down for necessities. He'll probably smoke or jerk that salmon and eat off it all winter."

Next, he drove the boys up to New Hazelton, and the town of Old Hazelton. Sal could have easily been the local historian. He was well-versed on the history and folklore of the area. The boys thought the Hagwilget Canyon Bridge was pretty cool. It's one of the highest suspension bridges in Canada, perched two hundred and sixty-two feet above the Bulkey River. Norm got a little head rush when he looked down, over the railing. Like a big kid, he spit into the air and watched the gob fly all the way down to the water. *Fish food.*

The original town of Old Hazelton is miles off the highway, situated on the Skeena River. Norm loved anything Victorian. He marveled at how the town's buildings had been restored to their original condition. It reflected the glory days of the once booming mining town that was only accessible by riverboat, from Prince Rupert.

Sal drove Norm and Louie up into the hills outside of town, where he had grown up on the family farm. A small portion of the block foundation was all that remained of the old house. He pointed to a fenced-in graveyard where his parents had been laid to rest. A cement cross stood proud, the centerpiece in the tiny plot.

The top of the cross pointed to the taller monuments behind it, off in the distance. A cluster of prominent mountains stood watch over the grave site for eternity. To Norm, the tallest one resembled the Matterhorn, the iconic piece of rock in Zermatt, Switzerland. There was one puffy white cloud in the whole sapphire colored sky. It was snagged on the apex of the natural pyramid. The men stood there, in a moment of silence, gawking at the spectacle.

Just as amazing as the natural panorama, was Sal's story about his father's murder. He told Norm that he was only a child in 1952, when his father was killed. A transient robbed and killed him, while he walked home with his weekly pay cheque. Sal said the suspect was arrested and charged, but never convicted of the murder. He and his brothers looked into the case in an attempt to discover what really happened on that fateful day, but they never received satisfaction.

5

He

It was mid-summer in Prince George, the crisp evening air hinted at an early autumn. The orange glow from streetlights reflecting off an office building's windows, looked like teeth carved in a pumpkin. The railway yard across the street was ominous; the metal rails shined like strands of wire in the low light.

He came into the city on Highway #16. Familiar with the area, he cruised slow, searching the shadows along the roadside. Just as he had hoped, a solitary figure stood at the bus stop. Like a lone sentry on guard, a young woman stood curbside, smoking. The cigarette's glow illuminated her face.

Traffic was sparse and most people passed by without noticing the lady of the night. He pulled to the curb. A pigeon, leaving the safety of its perch, she approached the blue Ford Explorer and leaned in the passenger window. He recognized the young girl. She was no stranger to the street.

He offered a smile. "Are you working?"

"Sure, baby, are you?"

"Not tonight. I could use some company."

"I'm your girl."

She opened the door and jumped in beside him. He held his arrogant smile.

"So what's it gonna be, baby, a BJ in the train yard? I know a quiet spot."

"I was thinking someplace more intimate. I have a room at the Traveler's Inn."

His stare poured over her like hot wax. Working their way downward, his eyes explored her young body like fingers reading brail. His loins tingled.

"That's cool. It's fifty bucks for a BJ, double if ya wanna fuck me."

"Money's not a problem. It's Candy right?"

"Close, baby. It's Mandy—sweet like candy. Have we met before?"

"I have a good memory for faces."

Hers reminded him of a peach, ripe spots on her cheeks and fuzz at the base of her ears, along her neck. He yearned to take a bite of the juicy fruit.

"Aren't you afraid of being out here on your own? I read somewhere that Prince George is the most dangerous city in Canada."

There had been a recent string of nine murders. He knew for a fact that the actual number was higher.

"Yeah, I heard that, but I don't jump in the car with just anybody, and I know how to take care of myself."

His eyes glistened. He sucked his lower lip into his mouth while he drove and imagined the impending sexual encounter in his mind. She smiled back, revealing yellow stained teeth, probably caused by cigarettes or crack cocaine. She wasn't high, but her night was just getting started. Fake lashes and heavy eyeliner aged her; she was maybe sixteen—it really didn't matter.

At the motel he backed the SUV up to the door and told Mandy to wait a minute. He exited the driver's side and walked around to her door. She was puzzled when he opened it and offered his hand.

"I'm not a cripple."

"Oh, pardon me." He took a step back. "I was just trying to be a gentleman."

"That's a first."

He opened the motel room door, and waved his right arm into the opening, allowing her to enter first. The room was pristine. With the exception of a black leather duffle bag on the floor by the radiator, and what looked like a dark grey suit bag draped over the chair, nothing was out of place. The girl would know, she'd been there on more than one occasion.

"You can use the bathroom to freshen-up if you like."

She sat on the edge of the bed, staring at a velvet Elvis on the wall. He was obviously before her time.

"No, I'm good."

"Please, I insist. I'm very particular about cleanliness."

"If you insist."

Mandy slipped out of her sandals and shuffled into the bathroom. He cocked his head and watched her walk away from him. Her gait was so smooth that she could have balanced a glass of wine on the top of her head. His attention turned to the radio. He fiddled with the dial, and found a station that played classical music.

When Mandy returned from the bathroom the bed sheets were drawn back and he was naked, sitting with his back up against the headboard. His clothes were neatly folded and placed on the dresser. Thinking she'd seen it all, she was surprised he was masturbating.

He held a condom in his right hand, and he stroked himself with his left. He let go of his hard-on, and patted the bed beside him.

"Lay down here on your back, please."

"I see you've started without me—you horny boy."

She wore only a towel; it fell to the floor when she climbed onto the bed. Mandy was slender and her under-developed breasts revealed her youth. By the time her head hit the pillow he had slipped on the condom and was on top of her. She submitted as he fell in between her legs. He searched deep into her eyes as he slipped inside her.

To her, his stare was unnerving, but she wasn't worried. She knew how to escape from reality. Her mind blocked his piercing eyes, and she retreated to her safe haven. It was a magical place that she shared with no one.

He propped himself up on his elbows—the less contact the better, as far as he was concerned. She moaned. He guessed she was probably faking, but he didn't care. The friction from his thrusts, the glitter of life in her eyes, and the sound of her heavy breathing quickly brought him to the edge of climax.

He subdued his urge to explode, and slid his hands up and over her shoulders. He wrapped his fingers around the back of her neck, and used his thumbs to squeeze her wind pipe. Her eyelids fluttered, and she was yanked from her safe place. Panic was the first reaction to her difficulty in breathing, but she had experimented with erotic asphyxiation before. It was pleasurable if done right. She played along, since he was paying for it.

Her gasping and throaty sounds exited him more. He squeezed harder. Mandy's eyes watered and then bulged. Her body tensed beneath him. It was the moment of truth. She squirmed and tried to break his grasp, but he had let his full weight come to rest on her. She was pinned to the bed. She reached up, and tried to pull his hands from her neck. She swatted and punched and clawed at his face. He arched his back, his long arms kept him from her reach.

He was delighted at how the distant look in her eyes changed to surprise, then terror, and finally desperation. The process always intrigued him. The excitement was too much— he couldn't contain himself any longer. Mandy's arms fell limp at her side. Her body twitched, while her brain was starved of oxygen. He watched with contentment, as the light of life faded from her eyes. That was his cue. He came.

A violin concerto resonated through the motel room, adding a sense of sorrow to the death stare on her face. He took a deep breath through his nose as though he smelled something good in the kitchen. He savored the moment, letting it linger and become a sweet memory.

His pleasure was short-lived. Her haunting stare became his mother's. He rolled off of her, then cradled the limp body and carried it into the bathroom. While letting the tub fill, he removed the soiled bed sheet and rubber underlay he had placed there. He retrieved the body bag that was draped over the chair and laid it on the bed. He whistled softly with the music, while he bleached and scrubbed the body from head to toe, inside and out. A silver neck chain she wore was taken as a souvenir.

He slipped his fresh kill into the body bag, and checked the zipper like he was preparing a Ziploc baggie for the freezer. He returned to the bathroom, and climbed into the shower. He used bacterial soap to scrub every inch of himself, paying special attention to his genitals. The spray of hot water raining down on him, tickled his skin like the fingers that danced across the piano's keys, in the music that played on the radio. When the wind instruments cut in, he waved his scrub brush like he was conducting a symphony orchestra.

After using his own towel to dry himself, he returned to the living room to get dressed. He stood in front of the mirror, and turned from side to side, admiring his handsome physique. He flexed different muscles for effect and smiled with contentment.

He unlocked and opened the motel room door just enough to peek outside, and see if anyone was around. There was nothing but formless shrubs visible in the dark courtyard. He pointed the key fob at his SUV, and switched off the light outside the room.

After retrieving a handheld vacuum from the Explorer's cargo hold he left the back hatch open. He tossed the body bag into the vehicle like it was his hockey gear. He cleaned and tidied and sanitized the entire room. He bagged her clothes and the sheets, and would incinerate them later. As a final precaution he removed the drain covers in the sink and bathtub to retrieve any hair. Then he poured bleach down both drains and the toilet.

While standing at the door, he wiped his fingerprints from the knob and took one last look around the room, making sure that he had taken care of everything. The towels were re-folded on their racks, and the bed was remade. The room looked just the way it had before he used it. He left the key on the dresser.

Back inside the Explorer, he adjusted the mirror so that his view included his latest prize. He was delighted at the sight, feeling like a kid who had just won a big stuffed animal at the carnival. He drove out of the city the same way that he had come in, along Highway #16. He peered ahead into darkness, lathered in a state of euphoria. His was the only vehicle on the Highway of Tears.

6

Hyderized

The thrill of the kill was better than he could have ever imagined. Being able to act out his fantasies, fulfilled him more than just reading about others who shared his rapture. After he watched his mother die, he was consumed by guilt, and almost took his own life. He found salvation in the accounts of others who had committed the ultimate sin. Serial killers became the focus of his studies.

He lusted for sex and fulfilled the need, but his satisfaction was short-lived. The first time he took a life while sexually gratifying himself, he reveled in the euphoria. For him, it was like having multiple orgasms. He relived the experience in his mind, playing the scene over and over. Sadly, the memories weren't enough—he was insatiable. Homicide was his drug, and he was addicted to it.

He researched famous psychopaths, puzzled by how many of them there were who actually wanted to be caught. Not him. How could he exist if he couldn't satisfy his needs? He studied profiling and forensics so he could stay under the radar, and never be captured.

His job allowed him to move around the country, remaining anonymous. He preferred the northwest, where he was at home. He knew, from past experience, that it was prime hunting ground. For him, the pay as you go plan was the simplest way to meet women. Prostitutes were easy prey. A guaranteed fix, in more ways than one.

He hunted close to home, where he had the luxury of being able to bury his kill in the stone orchard. He fantasized about a cross-country trip to gather his dead, bringing them home to rest. He felt close to them—their faces were etched in his memory. They were the only family he had.

* * *

To Norm, the thrill of motorcycling across open country was difficult to elucidate and was better experienced personally. He thought it was about the freedom, not being wrapped in a cocoon. Without that shell, your senses were bombarded by Mother Nature. She gave you a natural high. He got hooked when he was only nineteen, during a summer trip from Windsor to Daytona Beach.

To a traveler like him, who enjoyed the journey more than the destination, mode of transportation matters. A motorcycle may be more dangerous than a car, but if you eliminated the safety factor, riding on two wheels offers a deeper driving experience. At times he felt as though he was a part of the scenery that surrounded him—like he could reach out and touch it.

Norm had thousands of motorcycling miles under his belt, and he appreciated what it was all about. He watched Louie's reaction to the stretch of road from Smithers to Hyder. He looked like a kid on his first bicycle ride without the training wheels. If his smile grew any wider, the chin strap on his helmet would have popped. The road was so desolate at times, they were able to ride side by side, in both lanes. Thumbs up and nods of appreciation were passed back and forth.

Norm chuckled to himself when he saw, what his father used to call the oasis, on the road in the distance. It's that shiny spot, up ahead on the road, where heat waves rise off the hot

The Highway of Tears

pavement. It drove him crazy as a kid—like searching for the end of a rainbow. It's something that you never seem to find.

He thought about the lack of wildlife in the area, and noticed a car stopped on the right shoulder up the road. The driver was out in the tall grass, photographing an animal in the bush.

Curious, Norm pulled over and stopped ahead of the parked car. There was movement in the brush a few hundred feet away. It was a black bear on all fours, foraging in the shrubs. It either heard or caught wind of Norm. The bear stood up on its hind legs, and looked directly at him.

Norm pulled his camera out and took pictures. Louie waved like a highway flagman, trying to get his attention. When Norm looked his way, Louie pointed to another bear on the opposite side of the road. Surprised, Norm stood still, and watched in awe. The bear waited for a car to pass, then it looked both ways before it crossed the road. It must have learned how in Cub Scouts.

The other bear remained standing. It looked at Norm, then at its furry friend, and then back at Norm again. Being dressed from head to toe in black leather and wearing a black helmet, perhaps the bear was confused, or it wondered if the man in black was another bear. It wasn't a mystery that Norm needed to solve. He jumped back on his bike, and drove off.

They stopped at a rustic little gas bar at the junction of highways #37 and #37A. When they paid for their gas, the clerk warned them to watch for bears. She said that two bikers had to be air-lifted to the hospital after they hit a couple. She didn't know if the bears were injured—they left the scene of the accident.

Pulling out of the gas station, Louie took the lead. A short distance later, he tapped his brake lights. Norm saw what he was looking at. A hitchhiker stood on the right shoulder. The young girl was wearing cut-offs, and a pink tank top. Norm disengaged the clutch and thought about it for a second, but he shook his head at Louie and they drove on.

Norm had an extra helmet, but he knew better than to stop and pick her up. There were a few good reasons. Louie wasn't experienced enough to carry a passenger, and Norm had his travel bag on the passenger portion of his seat, acting as a back rest. The other reason was the most logical—he just knew better. Picking up a young, female hitchhiker spelled t-r-o-u-b-l-e.

With her long hair and olive skin, she reminded Norm of Hope, the hot waitress back in Jasper. *She's taking a big chance out here on her own.* A short distance up the road, he noticed a big yellow billboard. The sign was a warning to women, not to hitchhike on the highway.

Highway #37A cuts through raw wilderness. The elevation alone caused Norm's ears to pop. The tops of the mountains got a lot closer, offering stunning views of turquoise glaciers that melted into beautiful waterfalls.

Some of the ice was so close to the road that he they felt the temperature drop, as if someone just opened the freezer door. Louie and Norm stopped for a photo in front of a scenic lake at the base of Bear Glacier. The chunk of blue ice could have been a wedge cut from the sky and dropped it into the mountain valley. Icebergs floating in the lake resembled a regatta of white sail boats. Louie was slack-jawed.

"Why are the glaciers blue Norm?"

He had paid attention in geography class and knew the answer.

"It's because the dense ice of the glacier absorbs every color of the light spectrum except blue, so that is what we see."

During lunch at a diner in Stewart, Norm saw pictures of Bear Glacier on the wall. There was a log house on the lake, and the picture was autographed by actors, Al Pacino, and Robin Williams. The movie, Insomnia, had been filmed there, and the house was built as a movie set. A waitress said the two celebrities kept the town abuzz while the film was being shot on location.

There were some cool buildings in Stewart, including the old firehouse, but the sleepy town was only the gateway for their final destination that day. Two miles out of Stewart, the pavement on Highway #37A ended abruptly at the border of Alaska. There were no US officials at the border. Hyder is the only unmanned crossing in that country. Ironically, there is a Canada Customs booth for vehicles leaving the US.

After some pictures in front of the 'Welcome to Hyder' sign, Louie and Norm cruised down the main gravel road in town. Buildings were scattered along both sides of the road—most were houses, some businesses. Besides one B & B, there was only one other place to stay in town, the Sealaska Inn & Camp Run-A-Muck. The boys parked their hawys alongside a row of four-wheel drive trucks, out front of the place.

When they walked in the front door of the Inn, they found themselves standing in the bar. A dozen gruff-looking men sat at the bar, and a couple of kids chased a dog around the tables. The barmaid eyed the two strangers, who looked like they were completely lost.

"Are you guys here for the wedding?"

Normally, that would sound like a strange question when you are in a bar looking for a place to stay, but it wasn't the first time that day that someone had asked them that question. About an hour back up the road at a rest stop, they took a pee break, and encountered a woman who had been asleep in her car.

The car had appeared empty, but the woman surprised Norm and Louie after they had relieved themselves in the bushes. She was a cute blonde wearing a white sundress and tan

Finding Hope

cowboy boots. Her bed head and wrinkled dress were telltale signs of her roadside nap. She didn't shy away from the two men when they returned to their bikes that were parked near her car.

She asked, "Are you guys going to the wedding?"

"We weren't invited." Answered Louie.

"If you're staying at the Sealaska in Hyder, you'll be part of it."

They weren't really sure what she was talking about at the time. Even though there was a wedding at the hotel, there was still a room available for the boys. The room itself was a plywood bungalow, adjacent to the main building. It was nothing to write home about, but it was clean and comfortable.

Before unpacking, Norm flung open the drapes to let in some light.

"Holy shit Louie—look at the view!"

It was worth the price of the room. The mountains were close enough to touch. After settling into the room, they went to explore the town, and to get *Hyderized*. It didn't take long to see it all, as there were only a dozen shops, and about eighty residents in Hyder.

The only other hotel in town, which was full, was called the Glacier Inn. It's the official place where people from all over the world go to get Hyderized. The bar was rustic to say the least. Every inch of every wall was plastered with paper money from every country you can think of. There had to be thousands of dollars on display. Aside from the currency, there were dozens of colored hardhats lined up on shelves, and orange life buoys hung in strategic places. The huge head of a mountain goat was mounted on the wall above the bar.

Norm ordered a couple of beers. The barmaid asked, "Are you boys gonna get *Hyderized* first?"

Louie answered. "I guess. What exactly does that mean?"

She grabbed a bottle of clear liquor and poured two small water glasses half full.

"One hundred and fifty proof, seventy-five percent pure alcohol," the woman smiled as she put the glasses in front of them.

It had to be two or three ounces of moonshine—way too much to swallow all at once. Norm thought downing it quickly would be best. He did it, and gulped his beer to dilute the firewater before it reached his stomach. Louie took his turn and tried to smile like it was nothing. His watery eyes told the truth, and he expelled only air when he tried to speak.

The barmaid lit the residue in both the glasses on fire. She took the certificates that they had each signed, and burned the edges with the blue flame. After proudly receiving their certificates, the boys bought some more beer and post cards, and then headed back to their room to relax on the deck and soak up the view.

Norm sipped his beer on the front porch. He watched a beat up reefer truck drive by, and then turn around in the lot, looking for a parking spot. The beefy driver had his arm out the window, with a cigarette in his hand. There was a stenciled sign on the door that looked like it was supposed to read, Strickland Transport. The letters t and r had peeled off, leaving "S--ickland Transport."

After the truck drove away, the blonde from the highway rest stop pulled up beside the bikes. She approached Louie, who was smoking a cigarette on the porch.

"Hey man, can I use your bathroom?"

"Uh...sure, go ahead."

Blondie with the bad hair and wrinkly dress took quite a while in the bathroom. Norm looked back into the room to see if the door was still closed. Louie was curious too, he went back inside just as she exited the bathroom.

"Everything alright?"

"Yeah, I had to fetch something I had hidden."

She sat on the edge of one of the beds. Norm went back into the room to see what was going on. She had a crumpled plastic baggie full of what looked like cocaine, in her hand. He had seen plenty of the stuff in his drug squad days.

"Do you guys mind if I smoke?"

Puzzled, Louie asked if she wanted one of his cigarettes.

"No, that's okay, I've got my pipe. I was nervous about bringing the coke across the border, it's for the wedding party tonight."

To their astonishment, she pulled a crack pipe out of her purse and used it to smoke a rock right there in front of them. Norm looked at Louie wide-eyed, silently mouthing the word 'wow'. Louie stared in awe as blondie inhaled the thick smoke, then blew it in the air, and laid back on the bed. It smelled like burnt Styrofoam. Norm shook his head and went back out to the deck.

A couple of minutes later blondie bounced out the room a lot happier than when she had went in. Norm knew the effects of crack cocaine, he'd seen some of his police informants high on it. It winds you up and has the same effect as downing ten coffees.

Blondie sung out,"Okay guys, I'll see you later."

Louie looked over at Norm.

"It should be an interesting wedding."

7

Special Deliveries

Dale Strickland didn't give a second thought when he watched Bear carry Hope down the laneway that led to his cabin in the woods. Dale's chubby cheeks pinched his smile as he squeezed the gold nugget in his right hand. *Good trade,* he thought to himself. The two men bartered for all sorts of things; Hope wasn't the first woman whom Dale had traded.

He didn't know much about her, but he guessed she wouldn't be missed by anyone. That was the way of the wilderness, as far as he was concerned. Man lived off the land. He took and used whatever he needed to sustain himself. Dale lived with his wife in an old trailer on the highway near Fraser Lake. He was too lazy to fend for himself or rough it on his own.

After he dropped Bear and Hope off, he made a few more deliveries of vegetables. His second-to-the-last stop was the Sealaska Hotel in Hyder, Alaska. The customs officer had his head down reading a newspaper. Dale snickered and thought, *if he only knew what I carry across this border.*

The Sealaska lot was full. Another truck was in the spot near the back door, where he usually parked for deliveries. He drove past and turned around at the end of the lot. Flicking his cigarette ash out the window, Dale glanced over at the bungalow where two bikers were drinking beer on the porch. The shiny chrome on the black hawg caught his eye.

After he delivered his last crate of vegetables to the Sealaska, Dale made his way to the old fishing pier. Hundreds of rotting wooden posts littered the harbor. They're all that remained of the original boomtown of Hyder, that was built on the water, like the city of Venice.

A faded blue fishing boat gently bobbed in the water near the launch. Dale pulled up along side the Seven Shees, where Sandor was busy working on one of the downriggers. His attire was as worn as his boat, but his physique, thick grey hair, and cookie duster mustache, made him look like a commander in the Russian navy.

Dale flipped him the bird when he pulled up—his way of saying hello. Once the truck was stopped and in park, he turned the heat control to the high position and pressed down on the brake pedal. It was the sequence required to electronically release the latch on the hidden compartment in the back of his truck.

Sandor was already at the rear door by the time Dale got his fat ass back there. The cargo hold of the truck was empty, with the exception of some wilted lettuce leaves on the floor, near the front. Dale grunted and groaned and struggled to lift his heftiness up and into the truck's box. Sandor peeked around the side to make sure that no one else was around. Dale opened the secret compartment and removed the cargo.

When he bought the truck, he had the cargo hold specially modified. A false wall was built, creating a hiding space that was invisible to anyone looking into the truck. Behind the secret door, was one hundred and twenty cubic feet of storage space. It was enough room to store dozens of pounds of marihuana or cocaine, or two young women.

On this trip, he delivered one hundred pounds of BC bud, that Sandor would smuggle into the lower United States. If the shipment was cocaine, it travelled in the opposite direction. The two men were part of a trafficking ring, whose business included drugs, guns, women, and anything else that they thought they could make money on. They were transportation specialists, who worked for the commodity brokers higher up the food chain.

After loading the last of the contraband on his boat, Sandor returned with a cooler full of fresh salmon, and two pounds of marihuana for Dale. In return, he gave Sandor a box of Cuban cigars. He smelled the box and smiled. He used his tongue to roll the soggy and stale butt that he had clenched in his teeth to the center of his pursed lips. While his hands fumbled to unwrap a fresh cigar, he spit the old one into the water.

The weed Dale received was his transportation fee. It was his to sell or to trade for something else. Even for a stoner like him, it was way too much weed to smoke on his own.

Sandor gave Dale the fish because he had more than he needed, and he knew the fat man was too lazy to catch his own. He happily accepted the cigars; he loved to smoke them, and they were illegal to buy in the United States.

* * *

Norm decided to take a shower before they went out to scare something up for dinner. He gazed down at his naked stomach and noticed the extra pounds he'd gained since he retired. Running his fingers through his thick brown hair, he took solace in the fact that he still had some, and there was hardly any grey in it.

Louie poked his head in the room. "Hey Norm, I'm gonna walk over to the campground and check out the wedding."

"Okay, bring me back a piece of cake."

After a shower, Norm felt as fresh and as clean as a spring morning. He cracked open another beer, and plopped back into his chair on the deck with the wondrous view. He proclaimed to himself. *Life is good.*

He had just finished his last beer, when Louie returned with a bag of more beer that he *borrowed* from the wedding.

"What, no cake?"

"You don't need it, Norm. Hey, you won't believe the redneck wedding that's going on—some guy just married his sister."

Norm spewed the gulp of beer he was trying to swallow.

"I'm not shittin you. The minister is wearing a baby blue polyester leisure suit, and one of those thin black ties. With his white hair and beard, he looks like a skinny Colonel Sanders."

Norm wiped beer from his chin and shook his head. A loud racket came from the direction of the campground; they couldn't believe their eyes. It was the bride and groom in their wedding limousine. It was one of the most bizarre things that Norm had ever seen.

The newlyweds were riding in the back of an over-sized pickup truck, painted in dark camouflage. Blue and white pom-poms were strategically placed around the exterior of the body and in the center of each of the wheels. There was a Just Married sign, with red and white streamers, hanging in place of the tailgate. Strings of empty beer cans that were tied to the bumper, bounced and clanked across the parking lot.

The bride and groom sat on turquoise plastic lawn chairs. They looked like they were riding on a redneck parade float. At their feet was a silver metal cooler, no doubt filled with beer. Since there was really nowhere to go in the tiny town, the truck drove by the motel and circled around the parking lot a few times, before returning to the campground. Norm laughed so hard he nearly pissed himself. Louie had tears in his eyes.

Invited or not, Louie and Norm found themselves in the bar, where the wedding reception eventually continued indoors.

The Highway of Tears

The same kids from earlier in the day, chased the same dog around the tables. Having been offered, and not wanting to offend anyone, the boys helped themselves to the food that was laid out on long tables at one end of the room. Satiated and bellied up to the bar, Norm noticed that there was only one thing missing. Hope.

The barmaid told Louie earlier in the evening, that she and Hope were the only single women in town. He joked that they were the only two with a full set of teeth. Norm thought that maybe Hope was working the nightshift. He asked the barmaid, Laurie, where she was. Laurie was evasive at first, she said that she should be coming in at any time.

As the night wore on, the crowd thinned out. At some point Louie wandered back to the room to pass out. Norm's powers of perception faded with the amount of alcohol he had consumed, but he sensed something was amiss with Laurie. She returned to his end of the bar after making a phone call, one of several that she had made throughout the night.

"What time does this place close, Laurie?"

"Depends on the crowd."

"You look upset—bad news from home?"

Her eyes said that she wanted to answer the question, but her lips didn't move.

"Hey, what happened to Hope? I thought she was coming in tonight."

The question hit home. Laurie's eyes watered and welled up.

"How do you know Hope?"

"We met briefly in Jasper, and I took a shine to her. She said she'd be here."

"I'm surprised that she talked to you. Nothing personal. It's just that she doesn't trust men—some shit from her past. Even I don't know everything that went on. That's why she's in Hyder, everyone here is *hiding* from something."

"So where is she?"

A single tear broke free of her left eye, and rolled gently down her cheek. When she reached for a napkin, her right eye followed suit. "I don't know and I'm worried sick. She called me before she left Jasper and should have been here by now."

"Maybe her car broke down and...have you tried her cell phone?"

"She doesn't have a car or a cell phone. When she can't catch a bus, she hitches a ride with truckers heading up this way. I keep calling my babysitter, but she hasn't heard anything. She's watching both of our daughters for the night."

"Hope has a daughter? She barely looks old enough."

"Charitee. She's a sweetie—pretty, like her mom."

"Does the father live around here?"

"No. Well, I don't think so. Hope never talks about him. He's the reason she came here. I don't think he knows where...do you think he's caught up with her?"

"I wouldn't know, Laurie. You know her better than I do. I'm sure she has a good reason for being late. Maybe the truck broke down. There's a lot of road between here and Jasper. Anyway, maybe I should pack it in for the night. It looks like the guys at the end of the bar are ready to go too. What time is it anyway?"

"It's a quarter to four."

"Holy shit! Louie likes to wake me up at seven-thirty, I gotta get some sleep."

Norm pulled out his wallet, fumbling for his credit card. Laurie saw his police badge.

"You're a cop?"

"Retired."

"Really? We don't have any cops here in Hyder."

"What do you do when there's trouble?"
"We call the Mounties from across the border, in Stewart."
"Do they have *jurshdition* here?"
He slurred the word badly. Alcohol and fatigue had taken their toll.
"We all chip in to take care of each other up here—like me and Hope."
Norm pulled one of his old business cards out of his wallet.
"Take my card. It has my phone number and email on it. I was hoping to talk to Hope...hey, that kinda rhymes. Oh yeah, I need to go. "Night Laurie, nice talkin to ya."

8

The Hunters

Henry Jensen hated hotel rooms; he thought they were disgusting. His room at the Ramada Inn looked clean, but he was repulsed, wondering about the previous guests' activities. Regardless of appearances, he disinfected the phone, TV remote, light switches and doorknobs, before he unpacked.

The hotel was in downtown Prince George, a city Jensen was familiar with. The morning sun infiltrated the gap in the curtains, its rays bathing the room in amber light. Standing in front of the dresser, in only a bath towel, Jensen admired his own physique. He pinched both sides under his ribcage, trying to see if any body fat had gathered there.

He loosened the towel around his waste, letting it fall from his hips. Opening the top drawer, he removed a pair of neatly folded underwear. He liked how the white Jockeys clung to his genitals and buttocks. Six pairs of black nylon socks were perfectly lined up beside the underwear. He removed a pair and slipped them on.

Jensen walked over to the closet and removed a pressed white dress shirt from its hanger. He had ironed it the night before. The smell of brewing coffee was enticing. He poured some in a cup that he had washed out when he set the timer on the coffeemaker. He inhaled the aroma, like a sommelier.

Returning to the closet, he ran the back of his hand across his five suits, one for each day of the workweek. He hung them in order, black was for Monday. He wanted to make a statement, get noticed on his first day. Tan, navy blue, brown and grey finished off the week. His ties were pre-selected to complement each suit with only a hint of a contrasting accent color.

The Italian black leather shoes got a last minute inspection and buff with a soft cloth. He slipped them on, looked in the mirror, then tugged on the lapels of his single-breasted suit to adjust the fit. Jensen grabbed his nine-millimeter Beretta and holster from the nightstand, and slid it onto his belt. He drew the pistol, checking the action to ensure that it was ready to rock. Satisfied, he re-holstered it.

The gold badge glittered in the sunlight that spilled across the top of the dresser. On it was a wreath of gold maple leaves wrapped around the embossed head of a buffalo. A red and gold crown topped the wreath. Written in gold on blue around the buffalo's head were the words, Maintiens Le Droit (Maintain The Right). On a blue and gold banner under that were the words Royal Canadian Mounted Police. The badge was mounted on a black leather belt clip; he slipped it on in front of his gun.

He walked into the banquet hall at precisely 7:40. The meeting was scheduled for 8:00, but Jensen believed in punctuality, arriving early if he could. To the right of the door, he saw a hoard of men hovering around the coffee and delectable treats, as if they were a wake of vultures. He expertly weaved his way through the gauntlet of other cops to get to the table.

Happy to see that they had evolved from donuts, he chose a multi-grain bagel and some apple juice, then stepped over to the nearest wall to get out of the breakfast traffic. A typical cop, with his back to the wall, he scanned the room checking faces for anyone he might know. He only recognized two of them; the investigators had been brought in from all over the country for the task force.

Jensen was impressed with how they turned the banquet hall into a functional office. At the front of the room was a line of portable wall partitions, lined with rows of photographs. On the left were images of women, and on the right were men, most being police mug shots. Set up along both walls were makeshift office cubicles. A telephone and laptop sat on each desk. Every office had a number posted on the wall above it.

Banks of filing cabinets and stacks of file boxes stood on both sides of the picture wall. In the center of the room were long tables loaded with boxes of equipment—flashlights, batteries, office supplies, portable radios and raid jackets. Jensen felt exhilarated.

A deep voice boomed above the others in the room.

"Ladies and gentlemen, if you haven't already, please pick up your briefing packages from the table to the left of the back door. It contains your desk assignments, along with the material you'll be briefed on. Once everyone takes their seat, we'll get started."

Jensen had already retrieved his package, he was assigned to desk number one near the front of the room. *Perfect,* he thought, *the location gives me a clear view of the entire room.* He went straight to his make-shift office, and arranged the desk exactly the way he liked it.

The officer in charge stood behind the podium, flipping through his notes while everyone got settled. There were thirty cops in the room, most dressed in plain clothes, a few in uniform. The majority were male, the exceptions being one investigator, and one uniformed officer who were females. Jensen scoffed at the woman in plain clothes, *who did she blow to get here?*

"Good morning everyone, I am Inspector Nickerson. Welcome to project E-Pana, better known as the Highway of Tears task force. A quick background for you new people in the room...this task force was started in the fall of 2005 when E Division took over a series of unsolved murders linked to Trans-Canada Highway #16. At this point of the investigation, we are looking into nine separate murders that we know about. Since 1969, there have been documented reports of several hundred missing women."

With the exception of a couple of hushed gasps, the room was quiet. Jensen had done his homework; he knew what E-Pana meant. The E was for the RCMP "E" Division. Pana is the Inuit word describing the spirit goddess that looks after the souls before they go to heaven or are reincarnated. The original investigators chose the name.

"What you see behind me on the wall are the victims, suspects, and persons of interest associated to the on-going investigations. The file cabinets contain information on missing women, some who, I have no doubt, been murdered. I don't think I have to explain to you the challenges that we all face, in any investigation so massive and complex.

In the hundreds of missing women's cases, there are over a thousand persons of interest. We believe that there is more than one killer involved. Consider the numbers along with the vast area and terrain involved. Then consider the number of people you see in this room, you'll get the picture.

Some of us have been here since the beginning. Our numbers have been as high as fifty, with sixty open investigations going on at one time. This is a monumental task that we are burdened with. Your briefing packages contain an outline of your specific cases and the zones that you are responsible for. Now get to work."

9

Trophies & Treasures

Daniel Grayson loved being a mountain man, living off the land—he was in comfort zone. His childhood in the big city of Calgary, was not that memorable. He recalled the other boys picking on him, because he was smaller and more shy than them. He was only nine when his father lost his job, and moved the family into the wilderness.

By the time he was seventeen, Bear had grown into a strapping young man. His father gave Daniel the nickname, because of his passion for tracking and hunting bears. He bagged his first black bear at the age of fourteen. His trophy was the skin rug that sprawled in front of the fireplace.

Bear sat in his chair by the window. The view was stunning. A natural opening in the fir trees offered a glimpse of the stream at the edge of his property. The view brought him mixed emotions. It was where his father drowned after a slip and fall, when he was out checking traps. Bear found him in the water, but it was too late. It was a lesson about survival in the wilderness he never forgot.

Natural light from the window brought life to the article he was reading in National Geographic, about wildlife in Madagascar. He'd read it several times over the years. Bear's father had provided an assortment of books and magazines to be a source of knowledge and educational material for home schooling. A faint knock came from the room where he held

Hope captive. Bear dog-eared the page he was reading, went to the door, and opened the little window.

"I'm hungry, can I have something to eat?" She asked him politely. Hope knew better than to yell or scream. If the mountain man was anything like her ex-husband, it would only piss him off. She had to play nice. "Hey, what's your name? You're Dale's friend right?"

Bear didn't answer, but he treasured the pretty young woman he had locked in the room. Staring at her, he remembered why he didn't trust women. His mother had left when he was young, she couldn't handle living in the wilderness. All women left—even his last girlfriend ran away. He left the window open, then walked over to the stove and a pot of chili.

Hope stuck her face into the opening, and looked around the cabin. It was one big room with a wooden table and chairs in the middle, close to the stove. Two willow rockers sat by the window near the fireplace. Floor to ceiling bookshelves lined both sides of the mantle and hearth. Her mind raced, while she tried to absorb every detail in the room. There was no telephone or computer, not even a television.

Bear's hulking body suddenly blocked her view. He handed her a bowl of chili with bread, through the window.

"Thank you."

"Bear. Everyone calls me Bear."

"Thank you, Bear. Can I have some more water too? I spilled mine."

She handed him the empty bottle and went to her table to eat the chili. She had gobbled down half of the bowl by the time he returned to the window with her water. "This is really good, what's in it?"

"Venison."

Finding Hope

Hope took the water bottle from Bear, and he closed the window.

"Hey, don't you want to talk? Are you gonna let me outta here?"

She only heard a mumble from the other side of the door.

Bear went back to his chair and picked up the magazine. Staring out the window he thought to himself, *this has to be the one*. He wanted what his parents once had. If only the last girl stayed—he never thought she would run away with his money. He was trying to help her.

Bear lost interest in his book. He remembered Dale telling him how women go missing all the time along Highway #16. He never thought he'd end up with one of his own. *Maybe if I'm nice to her, she will love me. It would be great to have a son, to teach him how to be a mountain man. She is young and pretty—will make a good wife...and mother.*

Hope sat down at the table and finished her chili. She stared at the door, wondering what would become of her and her daughter. She thought back to her previous life in Truro, Nova Scotia, on the other side of the continent. She had a good childhood. Her alcoholic father was the only bad thing in her life, but he was hardly ever home. She really didn't miss him, after he drank himself to death.

The worst man in her life had been her psycho ex, Robbie Chambers. And now, a guy named Bear, had her locked in a room. *What the hell?*

Granted, Robbie was the cutest and sweetest boy in town when she met him. Marriage and alcohol changed that. Abused by one man, now imprisoned by another. *Why does this keep happening to me?*

With her stomach full, Hope felt a calmness settling over her. She felt sorry for herself. As far as she was concerned, none of it was her fault. Obviously, hitching a ride with Dale was stupid, but how was she to know what would happen. Just like Robbie; how was she to know he would lose his job and become an abusive alcoholic. How does someone who says he loves you, belittle and smack you around? How can he want you to give him a baby, and then resent you for giving him one? Life was always difficult for Hope, but she appreciated what she had accomplished on her own. Her mother was never any help—she thought Hope was stupid for having a baby. She wanted nothing to do with it. Running away was the best thing Hope could have done for herself, and her daughter. *Poor Charitee—what would she do without her mother?* Hope felt depressed. *What will I do without her?*

She stared at the last two bites of chili and small clump of bread in the bottom of the bowl. Using her spoon she played with the leftover food, knowing she wouldn't finish it. She had to stop thinking so negatively. At the moment there was nothing positive to think about; sorrow consumed her. Her eyes watered. She grew tired.

Hope left her lunch on the table, then sat on the bed. The comforter was bunched up at the bottom end. She pulled it up, holding it to her chest. Tears streamed down both cheeks. She was tired of trying so hard and being beaten down by life. She wiped the tears from her cheek with the back of her hand, then laid down. The tears didn't stop, just like the bad things that continually happened to her.

She pulled the comforter up higher, trying to absorb the flow of tears. Loneliness crept over her. She wanted to get up and pound on the door, demand to be let out, but she was tired. She was so tired.

10

Bad News

"When life gives you a hundred reasons to cry, show life that you have a thousand reasons to smile."
—Unknown

    Norm couldn't remember the last time he was hung-over so badly. He sucked it up, wondering if he was still drunk when he climbed onto his hawg. Louie laughed. He had already been up for an hour, had two coffees, three smokes, and wiped both bikes down. Fog as thick as soup, hung in the air. Norm rubbed his eyes, trying to clear the cobwebs that clouded his cranium.
    Leaving Hyder, he gazed out at the old harbor, the leafless trees along the road lurked like phantoms in the mist. Rocky pinnacles breached the top of the fog shroud. The roads were slick. The moist air became water droplets on Norm's moustache. He rolled his shoulders and stretched his neck, settling in for the long ride ahead. Experience told him that the hangover would subside, eventually.
    He hated backtracking or travelling the same route twice, but there was only one road back to Smithers, the same one that they had come into town on. Any new scenery would surely be hidden by the haze.
    A big greasy breakfast in Stewart helped to settle Norm's stomach. By the time he and Louie finished eating, the sun had dried up what was left of the fog outside. Louie paused in thought, before getting back on his bike.

"Hey Norm, did you see anyone in the customs booth at the border?"
"Nope, the guy was probably sleeping. Why, did you want to declare something?"
He shook his head and laughed.
"How's your hang-over?"
"Like Hyder - slowly fading into a memory."
"That town was different. Hey, did you ever find out what happened to that Faith chick?"
Louie was terrible with names.
"If you mean Hope, no, she's MIA. She never showed up and her friend doesn't know why. An Alaskan mystery I guess. Too bad—she was hot."
"I think the bar tender wanted me."
"I know, Louie, they all want you. I just don't know why my sister does."
Later that afternoon, Louie and Norm arrived at Sal and Carol's place in Smithers. They were greeted with an offering of cold beer, and a plate full of sandwiches. Norm politely refused the beer, asking for a diet coke instead. After sampling some of the sandwiches, he shyly excused himself and slipped upstairs for a nap.
He fell into a deep sleep and dreamed of Hope. She was being chased by someone. It was weird, like dreams normally are. At first she was being chased on foot by a faceless man, big and burly, like a bear. Norm was watching. Then she was riding on the back of a horse with him, fleeing the burly man. The horse became the Harley. Hope had her arms around Norm, squeezing hard to hang on. He reached back with his left hand, lightly patting her thigh to comfort her.
Her leg felt tiny. Norm looked back and saw his little sister, Rhonda, sitting behind him. She was eating penny candy from a small brown paper bag. The burly man chased them with an old

rusty truck that had loud mufflers. Norm turned onto the street he grew up on, and saw his old house at the end of the block. The truck rammed him from behind.

He woke up in a cold sweat. The pillows were on the floor, and the bed sheets were tangled around him. He'd had a fight with them and lost. Thinking about the dream, Norm realized he hadn't thought about the day that Rhonda went missing in many years. He tried not to remember; his involvement in the harrowing experience haunted him.

Rhonda was only six at the time, five years younger than Norm. His mother had convinced him to take his little sister to the corner store, so she could spend the quarter that she had earned, as an allowance for doing her chores. He was reluctant, but he knew better than to argue with mom. The store was less than two blocks away; Norm rode his bike.

Banana seats were in style back then and there was room for two. Norm told his sister to climb on the back then they rode to the store. While Rhonda engaged the store owner at the penny candy counter, Norm dropped a nickel into his favorite pinball machine. It was a baseball game with mechanical men, that ran the bases after you hit the silver ball. It was the same with real baseball—he was good at it.

When the game was finished, Norm's nightmare began. His little sister was gone. The store owner thought she was with Norm, he thought she was with him. At least that's where she was before he got wrapped up in the game. He assumed she walked home on her own, so he rode back the way they had come. The feeling of being kicked in the gut came when his mother questioned him at home.

"Where's your sister?"

"I dunno. Isn't she here?"

"No. What do you mean you don't know? Weren't you watching her?"

"I was. She was taking forever picking candy—I played pinball."

"So where is she...Norman-Edward-Joseph-Strom?"

He would never forget the look of panic on his mother's face and the guilt that came with the burning sensation in his stomach. She told him to go back to the store, and not to come home until he found his sister. He saw his younger brother, Al, and his buddy on the way back to the store. A neighborhood search party grew from there. The store owner said that he had seen a strange car stop out front, it was possible Rhonda got into the car.

There was no such thing as Amber Alerts back then, the police weren't called unless it was a dire emergency. Family, friends, and neighbors searched the whole block, looking in bushes, garden sheds, and even garbage cans.

A few hours later, Rhonda came walking up the laneway, behind the Strom home. She was eating from her bag of candy, without a care in the world. She said that a nice man offered her a popsicle and a ride in his car. It was the only information that was ever revealed. Rhonda appeared unharmed, the identity of the stranger was never known.

Sal and Louie were relaxing on the deck, when Norm came back downstairs.

"Hey, it's Sleeping Beauty. How do you feel?" Asked Sal.

"Like a new man. Got a beer?"

They both laughed out loud. Sal went into the kitchen, returning with a beer, and Norm's cell phone.

"It was vibrating on the kitchen table."

Norm looked at the number. It was long distance, he dismissed it as a telemarketer.

"After you finish your beer, Norm, I want to take you guys for a ride, and show you the trailer park I manage. We can stop

Finding Hope

at the market, and pick up some steaks for dinner while we're out."

Norm downed the beer. "Sounds like a plan—I'm good to go."

The next morning, the boys loaded up the bikes and said their good-byes. Sal made a point of telling Norm he was now considered family, welcome back any time. They hit the road, heading back to Prince George. It was to be the last leg of the journey for Louie. He would crate his bike there, then fly back home. Since Norm had nowhere to be, and was in no hurry to get there, he planned to visit his youngest sister Brenda, in Vancouver, then ride cross-country back home.

They retraced their route to Prince George, always on the lookout for wildlife. They didn't see any bears, but a group of White-tailed deer darted across the highway in front of Louie, scaring the crap out of him.

During the ride back, Norm's phone buzzed two more times. The caller left a message the second time. He didn't recognize the number or return the calls. He thought he'd check the calls later, from Loretta's house. That way he wouldn't have to pay the long distance charges.

While the Dagostino women went to work in the kitchen preparing dinner for the clan, Norm used the phone extension in the den to check his messages. The calls were from Hope's friend Laurie, in Stewart. She said that Hope was missing, that she was worried. She asked Norm to call her back.

In thought, he pursed his lips together. Across the room Louie was sprawled out on the sofa. He watched Norm with narrowing eyes.

"What's up with the phone calls?"

"You remember the bartender that wanted you in Hyder?"

"You mean Linda?"

"Close, Laurie. She says that Hope is missing. She was supposed to show up there around the time that we did, but Laurie hasn't heard a peep from her. She's worried because of all the missing and murdered women."

Loretta walked into the room with a plate of thinly sliced prosciutto and friulano cheese, catching the tail end of the conversation.

"Someone you know, gone missing Norm?"

"Yeah, a young girl we met in Jasper. We were going to meet up again in Hyder, but she never showed up. In my drunken stupor, I must have given her girlfriend my phone number, cause now she's calling me, wanting to know if I can help."

"That's not unusual around here. There are hundreds of women who have gone missing and many of them have been found murdered."

"What? What do you mean hundreds? Is there some kind of epidemic here?"

"I'm serious Norm. It's been going on for years. They're mostly aboriginal women who have disappeared while hitchhiking along the highway that you guys rode here on. They call it the Highway of Tears."

"That's crazy. What are the cops doing about it?"

"Not enough, as far as the locals are concerned. What does she want you to do? Are you gonna call her back?"

"I dunno, I guess it's the least I can do. I don't know what she expects from me."

Louie chimed in. "You probably showed her your badge, Norm. She thinks you're a cop and you can help."

"I'm retired now. What could I do to help?"

Loretta held the meat and cheese platter under Norm's nose.

"You should call her. She's probably worried sick and could use the moral support. Most of the missing women are never found."

Norm stacked meat and cheese, making a sandwich, then shoved it into his mouth while he thought about the call from Laurie. Louie was falling asleep even though he was chewing a mouthful of food. He looked over at Norm with only one eye open.

"We're outta here tomorrow, what are you gonna do?"

"I was planning on heading to Vancouver to see Brenda. I guess it can't hurt to call the woman first...tell her I'm out of the game now."

"What the hell could you do, if you stayed?"

"Nothing that the cops aren't already doing."

Louie mumbled something in response, his eyes were closed; it looked like he was talking in his sleep. Norm hashed it over in his head. *What the hell can I do? I don't know my way around out here...I have no connections, no authority any more.* Then he remembered the dream about Rhonda. A small fire started burning in his gut. *Maybe I can call my old Mountie buddy, Steve; he might have some connections here.*

* * *

Hope was worried that she would lose track of time. She figured she had been in captivity for three days after being on the road with Dale for one. She wasn't sure when she had arrived at the cabin, but she believed it was day four since she left Jasper. She broke a tine off the plastic fork that she was given for dinner. If Bear noticed she'd simply say that she needed it as a tooth pick.

Finding a spot on the wall side of the bed that was out of sight, she scratched little lines on the wall to keep track of the days. Wondering how long she would be there, she doubted that anyone knew where she was—except for Dale. *The bastard! He knows.* Did anyone see me catch a ride with him? Betty—she would know. Maybe the cops will question her. Laurie must have reported me missing by now. But of course, they never find anyone.

Hope depressed herself with the negative thinking. She picked up the poetry book that Bear had given her to read, and flipped to the page where she had left off. It was useless, she was in no mood to read. She wondered about Charitee, but then tried to put the thoughts out of her mind. Her eyes started to well up. She needed a distraction, she needed to get out of that room.

Bear opened the little window, and passed Hope a plate with a bowl of soup and a half a sandwich on it.

"Hi Bear, you must be lonely out there. Do you want some company for lunch?" Hope knew better than to make it about her. She needed to use reverse psychology to let Bear think it was all about him. She smiled shyly, letting her eyelids flutter a few times. He scrunched his face while thinking about it. She heard the latch slide open on the other side of the door, then he slowly pushed it open.

"Can I join you at the table? We can eat together."

He grunted and pointed towards the kitchen table. Judging by the crumbs laying there, he had already eaten. He scooped himself a bowl of soup and sat down across from her. The soup was piping hot; her eyes browsed the cabin. She blew on her spoon to cool it down.

"It's very quiet here. What do you do all day?"

"Fish, hunt, chop wood."

Bear wasn't much of a conversationalist, he only talked when he was spoken to. Even then, his answers were short and abrupt. She wanted to make sure she played him right.

"Is there something I can do to help out? I'd like to earn my keep."

He shrugged.

"I can cook—not that there is anything wrong with your cooking. Or I can clean and do laundry...whatever you need."

His eyes shifted, he looked her up and down. Those were the wrong words, she feared the inevitable. Surprisingly, he hadn't tried to force himself on her yet. As much as the thought terrified her, she knew she could survive. After all, it wasn't the first time that she had been locked in a room and raped. She was married once.

Finishing the last bite of her sandwich, Hope scanned the rows of books by the fireplace.

"Do you think I can have another book? I like the poetry one you gave me, but sometimes I like to flip through magazines or picture books."

Bear got up, going over to the book shelf. He ran his fingers across a row of Readers Digest magazines. He quickly glanced back over his shoulder, at the lock on the front door. He moved his eyes back to Hope, then back to the books. He pulled three magazines from the shelf, handing them to her. He nodded towards her room, gesturing her back to her cell. Hope complied, quietly slipping back into her private prison.

11

Reaching Out

"Life's most persistent and urgent question is, 'What are you going to do for others?'"
—Martin Luther King, Jr.

Norm made the call to Hope's friend, Laurie. She sounded surprised, but was grateful he made the call.

"I'm not sure what it is, that you think I can do, to help Laurie."

"I don't know either, but you impressed me as a caring and sincere man, when we chatted at the bar in Hyder."

"You *do* remember that I was drunk?"

"Yeah, but I can tell when someone is speaking from their heart. I've been a bartender and waitress for a long time. I know people. I think you're an honest guy, Norm. You also made it quite obvious you like Hope. You're a cop. I reported her missing to the Mounties, but they have a lousy track record when it comes to finding missing women."

"I'm a retired cop, out of the loop now. But I'll tell you what I'll do...I can try to reach out to a Mountie buddy of mine. He used to work out here."

"Anything you can do would be great, Norm. Hope's daughter is starting to ask questions I can't answer. I hate lying to her."

"I don't have any children, so I can only imagine. Can you email me a list of her friends and the places she works or stays?

Finding Hope

And some current pictures of her, if you have any. I'll look it over—maybe my buddy can hook me up with someone here."

"It won't be much of a list, she keeps to herself. Hope doesn't have many friends. The last time I heard from her is when she called me from the truck stop in Jasper. She said that she was hitching a ride home with a trucker."

"Okay Laurie, send me whatever you have, and I'll have a look at it tonight. I'm in Prince George right now. I'll make some calls and get back to you."

"Thanks Norm, this means a lot to me—and Charitee."

"Okay, I'll talk to you tomorrow."

Loretta hollered out from the kitchen.

"Dinner time!"

Norm looked over at Louie, who was snoring on the couch. His eyes popped open as though someone threw cold water on him.

"C'mon Louie, it's dinner time."

"We gotta eat again? We just snacked five minutes ago."

"That was over an hour ago, you've been sawing logs ever since."

"Really? I guess I can eat again."

They joined the rest of the family at the table; a smorgasbord was laid out in front of them. Norm surveyed the table-full of food, then looked down at his stomach, wondering if he should loosen his belt. Loretta was watching him. She smiled, probably knowing what he was thinking.

"I heard you talking on the phone about the missing woman. Can you do anything Norm?"

"I doubt it. I've been out of the game for awhile now, and I'm way out of my jurisdiction here—even if I was still in the game."

Mark passed a platter full of honey garlic spare ribs.

"You're right, Norm. Not that I know much about Windsor, but it's different up here on the northern frontier. There are thousands of miles of wilderness, with only a handful of Mounties to keep an eye on things. There are millions of acres of bush for someone to disappear in. The women that the cops *have* managed to find were already dead. I hear that a lot of them were victims of domestic violence."

The General joined the conversation. "I heard there's something like a thousand women missing, going back to 1969. That's crazy."

Norm let the bowl of roasted potatoes pass, but he grabbed the green beans on their way by.

"I can't believe those numbers. How can there be so many?"

"Did you get some salad Norm?" Flora asked.

She answered Norm's question. "The biggest problem is that nobody cares about most of the women, so they're not missed."

"What do you mean, nobody cares, Flora?"

"Well, almost all the women are aboriginal. Many of them are prostitutes, drug addicts, or runaways. They don't have caring families to notice or report them missing. It's not a new problem here. It's been going on for years, and it's been ignored. That wouldn't happen if all the women were white."

Norm washed down a mouthful of chicken Florentine with a gulp of Chianti. "That doesn't make any sense. No matter what creed or color they are, someone must know something about all those women."

The General tapped Norm's arm. "Have some more spare ribs. You're not going to solve the case on an empty stomach. Mark, do you want any more?"

"No thanks, Mom. Think about it Norm. Thousands of miles of open road, travelled by hundreds of truckers or perverts or whoever. They pick up a young hitchhiker, have their way with her then dump her in the bush somewhere. Who's to know? It's that easy."

"It sounds too easy Mark, maybe that's why it's happening so much. There has to be more than one person responsible for all those missing women."

Louie tried to stifle a burp with the back of his hand, but it slipped out.

"Sorry. My compliments to the Chef."

Everyone chuckled.

"So what are you gonna do Norm?"

"I don't know, Louie. I'd like to help, but it's not my job anymore."

"You gonna leave it up to the cops here?"

"Can someone pass the corn please? Even if I wanted to help, the cops here would scoff at me—a retiree from out of town, sticking his nose where it doesn't belong."

"C'mon, Norm, I've listened to you talk about your job for years. I know you're happy to be done with it, but I also know that you care about people...whether you're retired or not."

"Sure I care. I know a Mountie from back home, I'm gonna call him. Maybe he'll know what's going on, or he can connect me with someone who works here. I have to admit that I'm curious, and concerned for Hope. If my buddy can hook me up, I'd like to hear the cops' side of the story."

The women cleaned up the kitchen after dinner. Norm took his shot of Sambucca into the den so he could check his email. Escaping from the kitchen to sip the liqueur was better than staying there, doing many more shots of it. He used Loretta's laptop to check his email. Sure enough, he had received something from Laurie.

She was right in saying Hope didn't have any friends. There were a handful of names. Laurie did her best at describing

people she'd only heard about through Hope. She had compiled a list of names:
  Robbie or Bobbie - her abusive ex, back east somewhere.
  Nick - pervert owner of sports bar in Jasper, where she worked.
  Joyce - older waitress, Hope slept on her couch.
  Betty - waitress at truck stop that looks like Betty White. Works at post office in Jasper too.
  Big Lonny - trucker she sometimes hitches with. Nice guy.
  Dan or Dave? - another trucker, pervert, bad BO.
  In a separate email she sent some colored pictures of Hope. The images were grainy, they had been scanned into the computer. There was one clear photo of Hope with her daughter, Charitee. They had matching sets of brown eyes and long black hair. Looking at Charitee's eyes, Norm was reminded of his sister Rhonda. He printed a copy for himself.

After clearing his inbox, he sent a letter to his Mountie buddy, Steven Davis, explaining the situation and asking if he had any contacts in the area. Steve was originally from the east coast. After a tour out west, he was transferred to Windsor, doing a stint with Norm in the Drug Squad. He was a cool guy, for a Mountie.

The majority of Mounties Norm met, were a different breed; they were Canada's finest, maybe that's what set them apart from street cops in the city. They were like Dudley Do-Right and went by the book, instead of using their own good common sense. Lessons taught in the classroom could never stack up to lessons learned on the street.

Norm couldn't get to sleep that night, partly because of the food baby he was carrying. The other reason was he couldn't stop thinking about Rhonda and Hope. He knew that getting involved was the right thing to do, but logistics, lack of knowledge, Mounties, and other challenges made him think he might be in over his head. He tossed and turned throughout the night.

While he checked his email in the morning, Louie was outside having a smoke, loading up his bike. There was a reply from Steve—a contact number and a sarcastic note:
"Storm, you retired old fart,
I'm forwarding you the contact information for an old boss of mine. He's the guy in charge of a task force in Prince George. He's a hard ass, but we're from the same home town. I hope you play nice with Canada's finest while you're on their turf; you won't be able to push them around like you did to me in Windsor. Good luck Buddy.
Inspector Harold Nickerson - Cell phone number: 316-555-0345.
P.S. If you get lost or in trouble, don't call a cop."
Norm and Loretta stood on the front porch and waved good-bye to Louie. He followed Mark to his shop, where he'd crate up his bike. Afterwards, he'd get dropped off at the airport.
Loretta put her hands on her hips, gaping at Norm.
"You know you can stay here as long as you need to. Now what are you going to do about that missing girl?"
"I'm going to make some phone calls, then make a decision."
He went back into the house, and called Inspector Nickerson. Surprisingly, he answered on the first ring.
"RCMP Inspector Nickerson, how can I help you?"
"Hello Inspector, my name is Norm Strom, I'm a..."
"Retired detective from Windsor and a friend of Steven Davis. I just finished reading his email. Steve said that you are looking for a missing girl?"

"Yes sir. Hope Lachance...she lives in Stewart and was on the way there from Jasper when she went missing, a few days ago."

"Right. Let me bring up the file on my computer. Got it. Her friend reported her missing, says she was hitching a ride home. Unfortunately Norm, missing women hitchhikers is not unusual here. Have you heard of the Highway of Tears?"

"Not until recently, I rode a portion of it on my motorcycle. I had no idea about all the missing women. It's crazy, I never heard anything about it back home."

"Don't feel badly, Norm. People here have been up in arms for years, but they haven't gotten much press...some local rags mostly, nothing national to get anyone too excited back east."

"I'm just trying to help find a friend, Inspector. Is there anything I can do?"

"As far as I'm concerned, the more eyes I have in the field, the better. I'm sure you've worked with ethnic or minority groups back home, who don't trust the police. It's the same here with the First Nations people. They cry to the government that they want our help, but then they refuse to cooperate when we offer it to them. It's a real catch twenty-two. I wouldn't be offended if a civilian with past investigative experience wanted to do some snooping around."

"I don't know anything about your ongoing investigations, so I'm more than a bit out of my depth here."

"I'll tell you what, Norm. My man who has the Lachance file is out this morning interviewing a couple of witnesses on another case—a body we found yesterday. We're set up in the Ramada, in downtown Prince George. If you come in after lunch I'll introduce you to Henry Jensen, the officer in charge of your friend's case. I'll leave him a note to expect you, in the event that I have to step out."

"I can't tell you how much I appreciate your help, Inspector. Thank-you."

"Not a problem, Norm. Just remember you're a civilian now and only an observer while you're here. Jensen's a straight arrow, but he's experienced and knows the ropes."

"Thanks again, Inspector, I look forward to meeting you and your man Jensen, later this afternoon."

Norm caught Loretta as she was heading out the door for work. "Looks like I'm staying a while longer. What's for dinner?"

She smiled and waved.

12

Stepping Up

"Life is 10% what happens to us and 90% how we react to it."
—Dennis P. Kimbro

The only thing that kept Hope from having a complete breakdown was the thought of her daughter, Charitee. That look of innocence stayed with her throughout the day; she pondered what her little angel was up to. Hope tried pretending that she ate her meals with Charitee, instead of Bear. She tried to replace his face with hers. It didn't work.

Eventually, the inevitable happened. She'd never be able to forget his repulsive kiss, the way he slobbered with his mouth open. It was like a St. Bernard was trying to lick her whole face. He clumsily forced himself on her. As horrible as it was, she had to wonder if he'd ever had sex before. She found herself reliving the same vile treatment that she had endured from her ex-husband, when he abused her.

When she wasn't daydreaming about Charitee, she thought about her past relationships. She wondered if she would ever be with a normal man. That is, if she survived the nightmare she was living, or was able to escape. She'd schemed since the day she arrived, but could find no way out. There was never any noise from airplanes, trucks, cars, or even people. She had no idea where she was.

Survival was her only goal. She had considered taking her own life, but she wasn't a quitter. Besides, Charitee needed her.

Finding Hope

She had to live for her daughter—had to believe she would see her again. The question of *when* caused a tightness in her chest and she couldn't breathe.

* * *

Norm parked his blue Road King in front of the Ramada Inn, early in the afternoon. He thought he'd give the Inspector a chance to digest his lunch before he met with him. The small hotel lobby was quiet. The front desk clerk looked curiously at the big man wearing a black Harley shirt and faded jeans, his sunglasses flipped up on the top of his head.

She offered a friendly smile when he flashed his police badge, saying the RCMP were expecting him. The clerk wrote down four numbers on a piece of hotel stationery and handed it to him.

"You'll need this sir; it's the combination to the door at the end of the hall, which leads to the main banquet room. That's where your friends are. Is there anything else I can do for you?"

Her nametag read, Melanie. She was petite with rust colored hair. Her eyes blinked rapidly when she spoke. *Badge bunny*, he thought to himself.

"Not right now Melanie, but I'll make sure to stop and flirt with you on the way out."

She blushed.

Leaving the front desk, Norm looked back over his shoulder, to see if she was still watching. She was.

He wasn't sure what to think when he arrived at the banquet room door. There was an eight by ten sheet of white paper neatly taped to the door, with E - PANA printed on it in bold black letters.

Norm opened the door quietly, and stepped into the room. It was cavernous. There were desks, filing cabinets, wall partitions, and bulletin boards lined with pictures. It reminded him of the criminal investigations office at the cop shop back home.

There was only one person in the room. He was on the phone and gave Norm a look, like he had just walked into the wrong bathroom. The man could have been a poster boy for the Mounties. His brown hair, buzzed short on the sides and flat on top, made him look like a military recruit. Crows feat clawing at his eye sockets, said he was older.

He wrote something in his notebook, ended the phone call, then stood up. Norm put him at about six foot two. His custom tailored suit fit perfectly over what looked like a rock solid frame. He nodded to himself, as though he just remembered something, then waved Norm over to his desk.

"Corporal Henry Jensen. You must be the cop from Ontario. Inspector Nickerson gave me a head's up that you were coming in."

He reached out and shook Norm's hand, then pointed to the chair beside his desk. The firm grip was impressive, but he held it too long. *A control thing,* Norm thought, *trying to impress upon me that I'm on his turf.* The man forced a smile.

"Retired cop, Norm Strom. Thanks for seeing me...It looks like you guys are swamped here, with your project."

"Yes, it's overwhelming to say the least...there's no end in sight. Listen Norm, the Inspector got called to the morgue for the DB we found yesterday, and everyone else is scattered from here to Alaska or Alberta. I'd show you around, but I have to do a phone interview. Why don't you snoop around the room—Just don't touch anything on anyone's desk. Oh, and here's the file on the Lachance woman."

"Thanks Henry, don't let me get in your way. Go ahead and make your call."

"Call me Jensen, I hate Henry. They called me O'Henry when I was a kid."

Norm noticed Jensen's dark eyes, how they were set deep and close to the bridge of his nose. *Charlie Manson eyes*, he thought to himself.

"Okay, Jensen. I'll get out of your hair and read the file."

He sought an empty desk near Jensen's and was about to sit down when he spotted a vending machine at the front of the room. After getting to it, he put two quarters in and retrieved a Diet Coke. The coin return immediately spit the money back out. It was rigged to supply free pop, probably a perk offered by the hotel.

The file on Hope didn't contain much. Inside, was a copy of Laurie's telephone statement and a computer generated copy of the missing person's report. A photo of Hope was stapled to the top corner. It looked like the same one that Laurie sent him.

A follow-up sheet was stapled inside the back cover. Only a few things were listed:

- call Pro Sports Bar in Jasper, speak to owner (Nick), obtain list of friends, co-workers
- call truck stop in Jasper, interview waitress (Betty), get names of truckers (Lonny, Dan, Dave) who victim knew
- who is the ex? (Robbie, Bobbie)
- no criminal record or history on victim, dig deeper

None of the follow-ups had been completed. Norm shook his head, but tried to contemplate the magnitude of the project that the Mounties were involved in. He stepped over to the wall of photos, scanning the faces. They were all so young. It reminded him of the pages in a high school yearbook. To his surprise, many of the pictures were mug shots. The women had criminal records for things like prostitution, public intoxication, drug possession, and shoplifting.

The victims' names were typed on the bottoms of the photos along with the dates that they had been reported missing. Some had been gone for years. Norm glanced back over his shoulder at Jensen who was still on the phone, making notes. Hope had been missing for five days and the police hadn't done a thing to find her. He looked back up at the rows of young faces in front of him; *it was no wonder the locals were pissed off at the police.*

The sound of Jensen clearing his throat, made Norm turn around. He was off the phone, but still making notes. Using the edge of the folder he was holding, Norm scratched the bottom of his goatee. He looked at Jensen, thinking to himself, *these poor bastards must be pissed off too...most of these cases have been open and unsolved for years...it's hopeless.*

Jensen looked up from his notebook.

"What do you think of our little project, Norm?"

"Honestly? This is insane! You could spend the rest of your career here and never put a dent in this caseload."

"Sounds like a pretty accurate observation. Actually, I have some solid leads on one serial killer, and another random killer, but the cases are taking us longer to build than the Gaza pyramids. I apologize for the empty file in your hands. It was dumped on my desk while I was out of town working on something else. I've got five active and ten cold investigations on the go."

"What makes a cold case, here?"

"It gets that classification after it's gone unsolved for a year. I'm sure you know how important the first forty-eight hours are in these matters. Your friend has been missing longer that that. In reality Norm, time stands still up here. Hours quickly turn into days, then into weeks. You have to consider the ground we have to cover—the vast distances between cities and towns up here."

"I sympathize with you, Jensen, I really do. That's one of the reasons I'd like to offer my help. I know I'm not a cop anymore and I'm way out of my element, but I have eyes and ears, and I remember how to track someone down."

Jensen didn't respond, he reached out and took Hope's file. He flipped through the folder, then looked back at Norm.

"Well, my Inspector told me to size you up and make my own decision on whether we should let you in. I'll tell you what I'll do. Give me some time to think it over, and we'll talk some more later. Where are you staying?"

"With friends, on the other side of the river."

"I'm busy the rest of the day, but I can talk with you after dinner. Here's my card and cell phone number. Give me a call later on and we'll meet up somewhere."

"That sounds fair. Thanks for your time, Jensen. I'll see you later."

Norm left Jensen to his work and headed back to the front desk. Melanie had her back to him when he approached the counter, her face lit up when she turned around and saw him standing there.

"How'd your meeting go, Detective?"

"I'm not sure. We have to continue it later, after dinner. I'll be looking for somewhere to grab a few beers before then. Maybe you'd like to be my personal tour guide?"

The question appeared to embarrass her. There was no wedding ring on her finger, but her shyness and hesitance to accept the invitation said that she was attached. She bristled at the attention and answered politely. "Thanks, detective, but I can't."

"That's okay, Melanie. I only drink when I'm alone or with someone."

She thought about that for a few seconds, then laughed nervously.

"Thanks for the offer. Enjoy your stay in town."

"I will. You have a lovely day."

Norm walked to his bike parked outside the front doors and climbed on. After strapping on his helmet, he fired up the engine, giving the throttle a half of a crank. The exhaust pipes roared. He saw Melanie jump at the noise; she smiled and waved. Norm waved back and rode off.

Mark and Loretta were both working, so Norm drove across the river, up the hill to the pulp and paper mill, where Loretta worked. She must have been looking out the window and saw Norm pull up. She exited the side door of the building, lighting up a cigarette while Norm parked his bike. He met her at the bench, where the sidewalk ended at the parking lot, in a makeshift smoking area.

"How'd your meeting with the Mounties go?"

"Okay, I guess. They didn't kick me out of town yet. The cop I met might let me help out. We're gonna hook up after dinner and talk some more." Norm chuckled, "Like I really need his permission to look for a missing person." He sat down on the bench.

Loretta inhaled a long drag off her cigarette, then blew the smoke out the side of her mouth, away from him.

"It sounds like you've made up your mind to get involved. I'm glad. I don't know what the cops here are doing, but they don't solve many cases here."

"I'm not sure any cops could do better, Loretta. There's hundreds of women missing and only a handful of them to investigate. I saw the taskforce project room; it's mind-boggling."

"So what's your plan? You know you're welcome to stay with us. We consider you family now."

"Thanks, Loretta—you and Mark have been great. Do you have a spare house key with you? I'd like to park the bike at the house, freshen up, then grab a few beers while I wait for my new Mountie friend."

"I don't have a spare, take mine and make a copy. That way you can come and go as you please. Leave mine in the mailbox when you go out."

"Cool. I'm not sure how long I'll be in town—if I follow up on this, I'll be heading back to Jasper to question some people there."

"Can't you just call them?"

"Sure, I could do it that way, but I like to talk to folks, face to face. I'll get a better read on them, and a better feel for the area."

"You're the cop...I guess you would know."

Norm guffawed and scratched the bottom of his beard. "I'm just a civilian now—or so I've been reminded. Hey, where's a good place to grab some beer and wings, to meet the Mountie?"

"There's a pub on the left side of the road, right after you cross back over the bridge. It can get a little rough when the mill workers are in there, but the beer is cold and the wings are the best in town."

"Sounds perfect; I'll see you later tonight. I promise I won't be too late, Mom."

Loretta laughed. She put her cigarette out on the bottom of her shoe, then flicked the butt into the bushes. "I gotta go too—some of us have to work for a living."

Norm got back on his bike, rode down the hill and back across the river. He spotted Billy's Pub on the left, then continued on to Loretta and Mark's house. He planned to park the bike there and take a taxi back to the bar. He yawned, sucking in a mouthful of fresh air. *I feel like a nap—I'm entitled. I'm retired.*

13

A Quickie

His job wore him down, and the long hours took their toll both physically and mentally. He needed a fix, but he lacked the pure energy needed to properly track and acquire his prey. Hunting and killing and disposing of his victims took planning and time, a luxury his work schedule didn't always allow.

He cherished his time off, when he researched his competition, and scanned the media outlets for any hint of his handiwork. He knew, he wasn't the only killer on the loose. With so many missing women, there had to be others like him. His work was a distraction, but not a solution to his addiction.

In between the interviews and meetings he had the time. He just needed to find some relief. It was all he could think about on the drive into Prince George, but it was daylight—hunting would be dangerous and difficult, but most people were oblivious to streetwalkers.

A young girl stood alone at a bus stop, just inside the city limits. She turned away when a bus slowed and then passed her by. The cheeks of her ass peeking out of her shorts, and the bikini bathing suit top she wore, suggested that she was waiting for something other than the bus.

He preferred to scope out the area first, but he was more visible in daylight and didn't want to attract any unwanted attention. He was anxious and horny. The girl appeared at his door the moment he pulled to the curb.

There were no pleasantries exchanged, the conversation was blunt and to the point. They both knew it was a business transaction. She spoke first. "Hey honey, it's forty to suck, eighty to fuck."

"Wow, you're direct. How do you know I'm not a cop?"

"Does it really matter?"

He eyed the clock on the dashboard, knowing there wasn't enough time to be smart and follow his routine. To completely indulge himself he preferred a hotel room, but his loins burned and screamed to be answered. It wasn't the first time he'd had sex in his vehicle. It was risky, but exciting at the same time. He headed to a conservation area nearby.

"What's it gonna be, baby? I need the cash up front."

He pulled two twenties from his wallet and folded them in half twice. He reached over like he was going to slip the money in her top, but he popped the front clasp, exposing her breasts instead. He'd been ripped off before, and figured she'd be less inclined to bolt with her tits hanging out. Before she could protest, he tucked the cash in the visor above her head.

"Your money will be right there when you're done."

The lack of makeup revealed that she was a naturally good looking girl. Wavy brown hair, streaked with blonde, rested on her shoulders. She had a tattoo of a white dove on the back of her neck, just above her collar. The patina of her skin reminded him of chocolate milk. His foot grew heavy on the gas pedal; his anticipation accelerated with the vehicle's engine.

She held her bikini top over her naked breasts, and stared out her window. He didn't know her name and he didn't care to. Grabbing her left hand, he placed it on the bulge in his crotch.

"Wow, a little anxious Big Guy? Think you can wait till we pull over? I'm not into highway head—the last time I did it, the guy drove off the road and nearly killed us."

"Don't worry sweetheart, we're here."

The Highway of Tears

He barely had the SUV stopped and in park, when he grabbed her by the back of her head and pushed her face into his lap.

"Easy, baby, let me unzip you first."

Conditioned air blew on his forehead while he relaxed and thumbed the stereo's volume control on the steering wheel. She unzipped his pants and pulled out his throbbing member. There were no other vehicles in the parking lot. It was secluded, surrounded by trees.

He closed his eyes while she performed fellatio on him. Heavy organ music played on the radio. He preferred strings, but the throaty notes carried the moment. The piece wasn't familiar to him. Her rhythm and speed paced the music. He opened his eyes and brushed her hair back from her neck.

Knowing he was nearing the moment of truth, he massaged the back and sides of her neck, slowly letting his fingers inch their way around it. She knew he was getting close too, she started to back off. He tightened his grip around her neck and forced her all the way down onto his shaft. She started to gag, but he didn't care. He held her there and climaxed.

The excitement was too much—he couldn't stop himself. He squeezed her neck so hard he thought he could feel himself in her throat. She resisted and squirmed, trying to pull her head back. She grabbed the steering wheel with her right hand, trying to push herself away. She swatted and punched at his face with her left, trying to break from his grasp. Two of her fingernails scraped the underside of his chin. She reached for his eyes, but he leaned forward, using his chest to pin her arm behind her head.

Faces of all the others flashed in his mind, consuming his every thought, making him forget where he was at, and what he was doing. He wished he could see the look of panic and desperation in her eyes. She kicked wildly at the passenger window and door in a final effort to break free. The blows landed softly, she became weak and limp.

Curiosity got the best of him, he pulled her head back to look into her eyes. He was disappointed, they were tightly closed. There was no death stare to remember her by. *Shit! You idiot—this is how the other morons got caught. It should have only been sex, you shouldn't have killed her.* He sighed. *Too late now—deal with it.* It was a good thing that she had been sitting on a folded blanket, her bowels released when she expired.

He grabbed her silver pinkie ring for his trophy collection, then looked around the parking lot, and at the clock again. He couldn't clean her body there. He'd have to bag her and take her home with him. After pushing the body aside, he cleaned himself with hand sanitizer and napkins from the glove box.

He wrapped the blanket around her, dragged her over the seats like a rag doll and tucked her into the body bag in the back. He threw the used napkins into the bag and zipped it up. After taking another look around the parking lot to make sure that no one was there, he got out of the SUV, and tucked his shirt back into his pants. With the palms of his hands, he brushed his clothes, to remove any hair and smooth any wrinkles.

With his fresh kill neatly tucked away, he climbed back into his vehicle, and headed back into town for his last meeting of the day. He checked his cell phone to retrieve a message that he had ignored earlier, when he was busy. He adjusted his air freshener on the dash, to mask any foul odors that might be lingering.

The last rays of the evening sun beamed up and into the sorry sky, from behind the flat and low-lying clouds. He checked his cargo in the rear-view mirror, then sniffed the air like he was doing a line of coke. The exhalation almost hissed, escaping from his puckered lips. He noticed his cheeks were flushed—the same color as the setting sun.

14

The Cougar & The Fox

"A good head and a good heart are always a formidable combination."
—Nelson Mandela

Billy's Pub was a happening place, chalk full of a blue-collar crowd. Norm grabbed the last empty stool at the bar. It put his back to the wall, giving him a full view of the room; an old cop habit. The bar looked like so many other watering holes—a mix of sports memorabilia and fluorescent beer logos adorning the walls, and television screens strategically placed throughout.

The aboriginal man on the next stool was light-skinned and dark-haired, sporting a short pony tail that hung over his tattered denim vest. He wore a black tee shirt under the vest, the short sleeves revealing a tattoo on his upper right arm. He sipped from a mug of draft beer as he watched a lacrosse match on the television behind the bar.

Acknowledging Norm's presence, the man raised his right hand.

"How, Kemosabe."

He obviously had a sense of humor. Norm chuckled. "Lacrosse? Didn't your people invent that game?"

"Yeah, after your people took away our tomahawks."

Norm laughed out loud, and ordered a pint of Okanogan Springs from the bartender.

"So, Chief, I hear the wings are good here."
"I'm not a Chief—some might call me a medicine man, others, just a man. I heard the wings are good too, but I prefer buffalo tongue."
"They have buffalo tongue here?"
"No, that's why I eat the chicken wings."
"Is that what your tattoo is for, medicine? I've seen it somewhere before, on an ambulance or paramedic's patch maybe."
"You mean the caduceus—it's a staff with two snakes wrapped around it, and a set of wings on top."
"Yeah, but yours is different. That looks like a sword in the middle...the wings more like pistols."
"You're very observant. Are you a cop?"
Norm didn't answer. He waved over the bartender, and ordered Cajun dusted wings, with a side of ranch dressing. The other man's attention remained on the game.
"What makes you think I'm a cop?"
"The little things."
"Really. What kinda little things?"
"Like how you walked right by an empty table and picked your seat here, up against the wall. That was after you scanned the room, checking faces in the crowd. You carry yourself well and your confidence shows in your gait. You checked me out from head to toe—including my tattoo. You don't look gay, so I figured cop."
"Interesting. I thought medicine men conjured up visions or chased away demons...shit like that."
"The elders still do shit like that."
"Something tells me there's more to you than that."
"Really. Take your best shot, Kemosabe."
"Okay. Your adaptation of the tattoo says you were in the military, where you struggled with life and death every day—

maybe you were a medic in the corps. You're proud of your heritage, but joke about it to fit in with the white man. Things in your past still haunt you, probably a drunken father—maybe the reason you prefer beer over the hard stuff. You're divorced, your ex said she didn't understand you. And you eat buffalo, but you would never shoot one."

"Not bad for a cop, but I've been married twice and neither one understood me."

The bartender plopped a basket of golden-brown wings in front of Norm. In his famished state he grabbed one, but dropped it when it burned his fingers. "Ouch! Those are hot. How'd you cook them so fast?"

The server shook he head. We pre-cook them, then drop them again to crisp them up. Careful, they're hot."

"No shit." He turned back to the man with the tattoo. "I'm not a cop. I used to be, but I'm retired now."

"You might be retired, but you're still searching for something."

"Oh yeah, tell me more, my telepathic friend."

"You are the cougar in search of a mate, but she is lost in the wilderness. You have strayed far from familiar territory, so you have teamed up with the fox—he knows the terrain. The fox is clever and he can lead you to the den where the bear sleeps. It is there you will find what you are looking for. Beware of the fox; he is sly and has a hidden agenda."

Norm finished his beer and waved for two more—one for him and one for his new friend. "Wow, that's quite a story Chief."

"My friends call me Two Snakes." He offered his hand.

"Like your tat—I suppose there's another story behind that." He shook his hand. "I'm Norm Strom."

"I have a story for everything, maybe I'll tell it to you some time. What are you doing here in Prince George, Norm?"

"It's like you said, I'm looking for a girl, but not my mate. I met her in Jasper and she's gone missing on the Highway of Tears. Her best friend asked me for help. She said the cops here have a lousy track record, that they never find any of the women who have disappeared. I'm not sure how I can help, but I have nothing better to do with my time."

The bartender delivered the beers and Two Snakes reached into his pants pocket, but Norm waved him off. "I got this one."

"Thanks, Norm. That's a very noble undertaking, looking for the girl. I wish you luck."

"I'll need more than luck. That's why I offered my assistance to the Mounties. One named Jensen is on the case—that reminds me, I'm supposed to call him."

Two Snakes winced. "Mounties eh? Like I said, I wish you luck."

"Don't have much use for them?"

"Only when they had use for me. I did some tracking for them, they're too political for me—like the military."

"So I was right about that?"

"Yeah, I did two tours in Afghanistan. I left part of my right leg there."

Norm burped out loud. "Sorry—about your leg, and the burp...garlicky wings."

"I can smell it."

"Why fart and waste it, when you can burp and taste it?"

Two Snakes was just about to swallow a mouthful of beer, but he spewed it all over the bar. He laughed out loud, his shoulders bouncing up and down. "You're a funny guy, Kemosabe."

Norm chuckled at his own jocularity. He stared at the front door.

"Are you looking for your Mountie buddy?"

"He should have called by now, but no—I was looking at those posters of the missing girls. What do you think is happening to them all?"

"Wish I knew. I suspect some of them have just ran off; it's tough for them up here, small town with nothing to do. Some get bored and turn to drugs, then they have to work the streets to support their drug habits. There's rumors of truckers picking them up along the highway, then killing them after using and abusing them."

The conversation quieted down after Two Snakes said that he had a niece he worried about and that he knew some of the victims personally. Norm checked his cell and saw that he had missed Jensen's call; the phone was on vibrate and he didn't notice it. The alcohol's numbing effects, perhaps. Two Snakes ordered two more beers.

Norm turned and stared at the posters again while he listened to his phone message. Jensen apologized and said he got tied up with work. He asked Norm to meet him at his office in the morning.

Two Snakes spoke. "You really care about your missing friend and those other girls. I can see it in your eyes. Something personal maybe?"

"I have my reasons. I dealt with things like that when I worked Vice. A lot of it was domestic shit, but I was involved in a human trafficking case. They called Windsor the Tijuana of the north, back then, because of all the strip joints and rub'n-tugs. Americans came from hundreds of miles away to see our peelers take it all off.

Our bylaws actually allowed it. They only had to keep one piece of clothing on, like a scarf or necktie. Then came lap dancing. One of my informants worked at a peeler bar that featured Asian women. She told me what was going on behind the scenes. The owner kept their passports, forcing the women to dance, and sell themselves to pay for their trip to Canada."

Anyway…they owned a house where they kept all the women. The rooms were filled with mattresses—one half slept, while the other half danced or had sex for money. After we raided the house, health officials discovered that the girls carried every kind of communicable disease known to mankind.

They were too dirty to work in their own country, so they were shipped elsewhere. Right after the Asians left town, they brought in Croatian women. The traffickers move them from city to city, using them as sex slaves."

"That's pretty sad. It sounds like you had a pretty depressing job."

"Yeah, most of the time. Do you think it's possible that kind of shit is going on here?"

"I think anything's possible, Norm. The cops don't tell us much, and the white folks don't pay much attention when an aboriginal junkie or hooker goes missing. That's the way it is."

"That's fucked up, man. Hey, who's round is it? I'm empty."

"You drink too fast…I think it's your turn."

The bartender must have seen the empty mug in front of Norm, he grabbed it up. "Two more?"

Norm responded, "Sure, why not? And can you turn the heat down?"

"What? It's summer, we don't have the heat on."

"Well…my beers are disappearing faster than his…there must be a downdraft or something that's causing mine to evaporate quicker."

He ignored the comment and walked back over to the draft taps.

Two Snakes commented, "Okay, Norm. One more then I gotta go."

That phrase got repeated to the point that the bartender started saying it. When Norm checked the time on his phone, and noticed the numbers were blurry, it was time to quit. *Shit, I forgot to call the Mountie.* He counted out some money to cover his bill.

"You're an interesting guy, Two Snakes. I'd like to continue our conversation some time. How do I find you?"

"You're the cop. Look for smoke signals."

Norm left his cash on the bar.

"Thanks for the beer, Kemosabe."

"I'll catch ya later, Tonto."

15

A Ray of Hope

"The quality of life is more important than life itself."
—Alex Carrel

The beam of light shining through the square window in Hope's door hung on the dark wall, like a blank canvass waiting to be painted. She stared at it, picturing Charitee sitting in the middle of her bedroom floor, surrounded by her Barbie dolls and their accessories. She liked to dress them up, and tell a little story about each doll.

Hope got out of bed; it was harder as each day passed. She needed to refocus her energy if she wanted to survive. She peeped out the small window.

"Can I come out Bear?"

He appeared in front of the door naked from the waste up, with a towel around his neck. The look on his face was as blank as the light on the wall.

"Please, Bear?"

The door swung open and Hope was drenched in sunlight.

"I've been good to you, haven't I?"

He shrugged his shoulders and raised his eyebrows.

"You can trust me. It's such a nice day outside. I'd like to fill my lungs with fresh air and feel the warmth of the sun on my face—from the porch. Please, Bear?"

He scratched the top of his head, considered her request for a moment, and then walked over to unlock and open the front door. A cool breeze blew into the cabin; it tickled her face and bare arms. She squinted and stared into the sun. It's image burned into her retina like a flame. A lasting sign of life, and even hope.

Bear stepped into the opening, blocking the exit. His stare erased the sun's image. He said nothing, but she got the message. Her arm brushed his hip as he stepped aside and she moved through the doorway. The slight touch felt like an electric shock.

She was awestruck by the natural beauty outside the cabin. Standing at the edge of the top step, Hope closed her eyes and felt the warmth of the sun on her face. Mother nature sang to her; bird's chirped, leaves flapped in the breeze, and water splashed over rocks in the nearby stream.

"It's beautiful Bear, I can understand why you like living here."

He pointed to a chair on the porch, but she eased herself down onto the top step, like she was perched on a rock ledge overlooking the Grand Canyon. Bear grunted. Still shirtless, he walked over to the woodpile, threw down the towel, and picked up his axe. His thumb felt the honed edge for sharpness, his eyes watched her peripherally.

While he chopped wood, Hope escaped to another world. *She and Charitee were having a picnic; they sat on a pink and yellow blanket in a grassy meadow. Shasta daisies smiled all around them. The radiance of the sun encompassed her daughter's head like a halo. Charitee offered tea to her favorite Barbie, the one with the long black hair—like her mommy's.*

A tap on her shoulder brought her back. Bear towered over her with an empty water jug in his hand. He nodded toward the cabin. She went back inside to fill the jug. It was sad, but she had come to understand his sign language.

A thought came to her. *Maybe I can poison him.* She made a mental note to snoop in the cupboards, the first chance she got. Outside, at the bottom of the porch steps, he wiped his sweaty brow with the towel, and waited for his refill. His stare burned through the cabin wall, her flesh, and deep into her soul.

* * *

Norm ducked behind the motorcycle's windshield. He tried to avoid the pelting rain that was expelled from the bruised and swollen sky. The bitter cold bit through his rain suit. He stayed focused ahead on the Highway of Tears, looking for a place to pull off the road. The soggy pavement stretched for miles, offering nothing but drenched forest on both sides.

Headlights appeared in the rear-view mirrors. A dark form took shape behind the headlights, the front end of a logging truck loomed large behind him. The raging monster was right on his ass. He moved to the right side of his lane, offering more space for the truck to pass.

It was so close that he only saw the front grill in the mirror. There was plenty of room, but the truck inched closer. Norm tried speeding up, but the rig was on him like black on night. He saw a small bridge ahead, where the shoulder was paved. His glasses were soaked and fogged up; he had to get off the road.

Norm signaled and slowed down. The truck swerved over and pulled up along-side of him. He could see the driver. His face was covered in hair, like a werewolf. His eyes were burning red spheres.

The truck driver blasted the air horn. Norm opened his eyes and found himself staring at the glowing red numbers on the alarm clock. Happy that he was only dreaming, he patted the clock. It had been set for 7am so he could catch Jensen at the office, before he headed out for the day.

Something nagged at him before he fell asleep; the conversation with Two Snakes. The part about the cougar and the fox. *Did that mean something?* Maybe he knew more than he was letting on.

Norm threw on a tee shirt and fluffed up his matted hair with his fingers. It was quiet in the kitchen, when he walked in. Loretta had left him a note saying she went in to work early and caught a ride with Mark. She said there was rain in the forecast and he was welcome to use her car.

He really didn't mind riding his motorcycle in the rain, unless it was pouring and a lumber truck was bearing down on him. At home, rain was an excuse not to take the bike out for a ride. On road trips, when there was some place to be, rain was accepted as part of the journey. It's not something that bikers generally enjoy, but Norm was not one to whine about it.

He poured himself a glass of orange juice, and dropped a bagel into the toaster. Peering out the kitchen window, he considered the grey sky. It looked like the sun would show itself, eventually. He planned the day in his head. *Okay, first I have to call Jensen to see if I'm on the case...then I gotta touch base with Laurie...she must be wondering what's going on. Maybe she's heard something. I think Jasper should be my next stop. Hmm...I need to talk to Two Snakes.*

A thick gob of cream cheese on the bagel, topped with strawberry jam, roused his taste buds. Norm made a quick meal of it, then gulped down the rest of his juice. After wiping off the kitchen counter, he called Jensen. The call went straight to voice mail. *Shit! It's barely morning, where the hell it he?* Norm thought for a second, then hung up and called Inspector Nickerson.

"Hey Norm, I'm glad you called. Jensen left a message for you."

"What time does he start work? I got out of bed early just so I could talk to him."

"He's a busy guy, he called me from the road. We discussed it and neither of us have a problem with you helping out on the Lachance case. I have a copy of the file, if you want to stop in and pick it up."

"I wanted to talk to him about someone I met. Do you know a native guy by the name of Two Snakes? Says he's done some tracking for you guys."

"The name doesn't ring a bell, we do use trackers from time to time, especially in the remote areas. Why do you ask?"

"No particular reason. I just wondered if you guys have worked with him in the past."

"It's possible. This is Jensen's old stomping grounds so he's more familiar with the locals and this area than I am. Anyway, someone is standing in front of me so I have to let you go. The file will be on my desk if I'm not here when you stop in. I appreciate your offer to help, but please remember Norm, you're only a civilian now."

"I understand, Inspector."

Norm peeked out the window again; it seemed brighter outside. *Nah, it ain't gonna rain.* His next call was to Laurie, but she wasn't home. He left a message, telling her he'd call her back with an update.

Twenty minutes later, he mounted his shiny blue Road King and drove towards the Ramada. He decided to stop at Billy's Pub first. It was the only place he could think of to look for Two Snakes.

At the first red light, a lumber truck loaded with fresh-cut logs, rolled by on the intersecting road. He remembered building a cedar closet in his first house, and how he loved the smell of the wood. *What a weird dream.* He turned his head

Finding Hope

trying to see the driver, but the light changed to green. He chuckled to himself.

Billy's wasn't open for business yet, but there was a guy out back throwing garbage into the disposal bin. He took a step back when Norm rumbled up on his Harley.

The guy eyeballed Norm, then started walking to the back door. Norm shut off the engine and called out. "Mornin. Can I talk to you for a minute?"

The guy stopped in his tracks. Norm removed his helmet. "How ya doin? I'm looking for a guy who hangs out here, an Indian named Two Snakes?"

The skinny custodian was visibly shaky. He was probably a barfly or local crackhead, who was paid to clean up the place. Either way, he was nervous. Without uttering a word, he pointed back over Norm's right shoulder to a mobile home on the bluff across the street. There was a wooden sign on the side of the trailer facing the street. It read, Guide Services.

"Thanks man. You have a lovely day."

He put his helmet back on, fired up the bike, and headed over to the mobile home. Pulling into the driveway, Norm saw another sign by the front door that read, Hunting & Fishing Licenses. An old, tan-colored Chevy Tahoe was parked in the driveway. A pair of legs was visible by the front bumper; someone in faded jeans and worn cowboy boots was bent over, working under the hood. Norm stopped beside the Tahoe. He hit the kill switch, then swung the kickstand down with his left foot.

"So, Kemosabe rides an iron horse."

"And Tonto a heavy Chevy."

"Yeah, gas costs more than oats, but I don't have to shovel horse shit. Where's your Mountie buddy? I thought you two would be out looking for your girlfriend."

The Highway of Tears

"Apparently he's busy with more important cases. It looks like I'm on my own."

"Good luck with that."

Norm got off his bike and looked under the truck's hood. "You keep saying that; I guess that means you don't want to help me. I'm gonna start in Jasper and re-trace her last steps."

Two Snakes came out from under the hood. He laid his crescent wrench on top of the air filter, then stood up and pressed his palms into his lower back, massaging the muscles there.

"You're taking this serious. You should know that people aren't as easy to find here as they are in the big city."

"I found you didn't I?"

"Yeah, the Mountie probably gave you my address."

"You really don't like those guys, do you?"

"I told you. Mounties, military—they're all the same. They use people."

"So you said. What about Jensen, you know him?"

"Not personally, but he gives me the creeps. I have a bad feeling about him."

Two Snakes grabbed a ratchet from his tool box, and fumbled around in the top tray looking for a socket.

"A vision about the cougar and the fox?"

"No. I hear things—people talk."

Norm leaned on the fender, while Two Snakes went back under the hood.

"Talk is cheap. A wise man once told me that you can't believe anything you hear and only half of what you see."

"I do odd jobs at the women's shelter. The working girls talk about him—how he gives them the creeps. He lectures them about hitchhiking and working the streets, but undresses them with his eyes at the same time."

"Sounds like a concerned cop, doing his job. So what, if he's horny too."

"Can you grab me that torque wrench in the tool box? Seriously Norm, there's something evil about that guy. Have you looked into his eyes? They're like two dark caves. I for one, wonder what's lurking in there?"

"I dunno Two Snakes, I just met the guy. Anyway, I offered my help, and that's what I'm gonna do. If I need a tracker, can I give you a call?"

"My tribe has others—the Lheidli T'enneh, they've been doing it for years."

"The what?"

"Lheidli, it means, where the two rivers flow together. And T'enneh, is the people. At one time we owned all the land from the Rockies to the flatlands in Alberta."

"I could use someone who knows the lay of the land, and it's people. I don't think Jensen is going to be much help."

"I'm gonna be busy."

"Doing what?"

"Fishing."

"Okay, maybe I'll call you when you're done fishing."

"Sometimes I go for days."

"Sounds serious. Can I get your phone number—in case I need some fishing advice?"

"Like I said before, send smoke signals. Or you can grab a card from the mailbox, in case you don't have any matches to start a fire."

Norm climbed back on his bike and turned the key on.

"Thanks. I guess I'll be heading to Jasper."

"It's gonna rain."

"That's what they say. You can predict the weather too? You ever wonder how those weathermen keep their jobs—being wrong all the time?"

Two Snakes shrugged his shoulders. "It's gonna rain."
"Catch ya later, Tonto."

16

Leg Work

Norm called Laurie as soon as he got back to Loretta's house. "Thanks for calling me back, I wasn't sure if you got my message."

"Sorry, I didn't, I had my phone off. What's up?"

"I called the truck stop and talked to Betty. She said that Lonny had asked about Hope—how he hadn't seen her in a while. He's one of the truckers that she hitches with. She told him that Hope caught a ride with Dale."

"Anything about Dale?"

"Lonny told Betty that Dale is scum, something about drugs and making money from truckers who get blowjobs from young girls in his truck. I'm really concerned Norm."

"Do they know Dale's last name?"

"No, but I told her about you and she said you should talk to Lonny. He's in Jasper tonight, but Betty doesn't know where he's staying. She says he'll probably have breakfast at the truck stop in the morning, before he gets back on the road."

"That sounds like a good place to start. I'm still in Prince George, but I was planning on heading to Jasper today."

"Please stay in touch Norm, I'm worried sick. Should I call the Mounties and tell them what I told you?"

"Don't bother, they haven't touched Hope's file. I have a copy and they're letting me do some of the legwork for them. You take care of those girls. I'll call you from Jasper."

Norm travelled light, so it didn't take him long to pack up his things. Instead of calling Loretta at work he left her and Mark a note, thanking them for their hospitality. He told them that he would probably be back, but he didn't know when. Securing his travel bag to the backrest, he glanced up to the sky. *It's not gonna rain.*

Prince George to Jasper is about four and a half hours non-stop. Even with breaks for lunch and gas, he could still get there by dinnertime. Norm wasn't more than ten miles out of the city, when someone upstairs turned down the dimmer switch. Off to the east, where he was headed, the rolls of black clouds in the sky resembled a freshly tilled field.

Norm thought it was a pain in the ass to put his rain suit on, especially if it wasn't raining. And, it just didn't look cool. Besides, in the off chance that it did start to rain, he could just pull off the road, get under cover, and put it on.

When the sky opened up, it dumped the tons of gallons of wetness that it had gathered from the Coastal Mountains. Norm got caught in the middle of it. He was out in the open, with no visible shelter for miles, and no rain suit. Thankfully, there was no psychotic trucker bearing down on him, as in the nightmare.

He had choices: either get wet while searching for shelter, or stop and suit up before getting completely soaked. In reality he had no choice—there was no place to pull over and no shelter in sight. The heavy rain that fell from the sky felt as though someone up there was wringing out a giant sponge. Norm got soaked to the ass.

He figured there is an upside to a pouring rain, as opposed to a light rain—a downpour doesn't usually last long. Luckily, that was the case. By the time he stopped for a pee, Norm's shoulders and pant legs were wind-dried.

His weather-resistant travel bag faired well, so he was able to retrieve a dry tee shirt. The wet one had chilled his nipples to

Finding Hope

the point where he could have poked someone's eye out. Riding cold and wet was not fun. He eyed his wet crotch, it looked like he had pissed himself. After some consideration, he decided not to change his pants. The sun and wind would finish drying them.

Norm rumbled into Jasper carrying the setting sun on his back. He found the B & B that he and Louie had stayed at a week earlier, and the same room available. He looked at the tiny bed that he and Louie had shared and chuckled to himself. His stomach growled. He thought about Hope while he showered. *She's been missing a whole week already, what are her chances?*

It was too late in the day to look for Lonny or Betty at the diner and the post office was closed for the day, so he'd have to look for them in the morning. Norm walked over to the sports bar where he had met Hope. He watched the bar staff and looked for the perverted owner, Nick. Seeing that The Three Stooges were on the TV in front of him, he smiled and ordered a burger and a beer.

A man with swarthy Mediterranean features, but a bad comb-over, came out of the kitchen and asked Norm if he had been waited on. Norm nodded and pointed to the waitress who was busy pouring his draft. Her left arm was covered in tattoos. The man's dark eyes shifted from Norm, to the young girl's ass.

"I'm guessing you'd be Nick?"

"You guessed right. Do I know you?"

"No, but *you* know Hope Lachance. I'd like to ask you a few questions about her."

"She's not here. Hope only works part time."

"I know that, but no one has seen her since she left here last week. Do you know where she might be?"

"Why are you asking me? What are you—a cop?"

The Highway of Tears

Nick stiffened. Norm didn't like his change in attitude so he improvised. He pulled out his retired police badge and flashed it quickly.

"As a matter of fact I am. I'm a Special Constable, attached to the RCMP task force. We're trying to locate missing women in this area."

Nick took half a step back from the bar, still staring down to the spot where he had eyed the badge.

"I don't know what you want from me. She left here last week to go home. That's the last time I saw her."

"Relax Nick, I just want to ask you a few questions."

The tattooed waitress had been standing to the side listening, but she kept her distance from the conversation. Norm pointed to his beer, and waved her over. Nick sighed and dropped his shoulders. He flicked his eyes at the waitress, waving her away.

"I don't know anything. I'm a married man, and I don't keep tabs on my employees when they're not here."

Norm took a swig of his beer and watched Nick squirm in his shoes. If he hadn't banged the tattooed waitress, he surely had considered it.

"Nick, Nick, I don't know why you're getting so defensive—unless you know more than you're letting on?"

"What? I've never...I mean no, I have no idea what happened to Hope after she left here. I paid her, and she left at the end of her shift. She was standing right here watching the hockey game, and talking to a couple of bikers."

His eyes locked on to the front of Norm's Harley Davidson shirt.

"Hey, aren't you..."

"Nick, you were one of the last people to see her. Who else was here at the time?"

His eyes narrowed and he rolled his shoulders back.

"I told you, I don't know where she is. I have to get back to the kitchen to check on your food."

Norm cringed at the thought of what Nick might do to his food if he pushed him any further, even if it was for fun. It was one thing he missed about being a cop—mind fucking dirt bags. The tattooed waitress wore a big happy face. Norm winked and returned the smile.

He believed Nick, but doubted he would ever pass a polygraph if he was questioned about his infidelities. When Nick was out of sight, the young waitress said to Norm, "You should talk to Joyce. Hope crashed on her couch, when she was working here in town."

"Any idea where I can find her?"

"You just missed her. She works days, but sometimes she stops at the MI for a few beers on the way home. She can't stand Nick, and won't drink here."

"MI?"

"Sorry. The Mountain Inn. It's just up the street, on the left."

Norm asked the waitress to tab him out. After wolfing down his burger, he walked the two blocks, to the Mountain Motor Inn. The fieldstone façade looked like it had been constructed from glacial boulders that had been scattered throughout the valley ten thousand years earlier. The front of the building housed the motel office and a bar. An archway stood as the entrance to a horseshoe shaped courtyard where the rooms were accessible from the parking lot.

The bar was separated from the office by another stone archway. At the top of the arc, a massive set of moose antlers was mounted like a keystone. The smell of cigarette smoke and stale beer hung in the air. Four small tables lined the front windows, running parallel to the bar. Two men wearing matching shirts with a CP Railway crest, sat at one end of the

The Highway of Tears

bar. A slim, middle-aged woman, with salt and pepper hair, sat by herself at the other end.

Norm put his butt on the empty stool to her right. She tensed up, her personal space had just been invaded. She was reading the obituaries section in the local newspaper.

"Are you looking to see if your name is in there?"

She turned slightly towards Norm, offered a puzzled look, and laughed.

"No...not yet anyway."

"Sorry, I meant no offence. It's something my dad used to say all the time; he liked to look for his own name—to make sure he was still alive."

"Did he ever see his own name?"

"No, not yet. Are you Joyce, per chance?"

She still looked puzzled, but squared off, and stared directly at Norm.

"You found me. Have I done something wrong officer?"

"What makes you think I'm a cop?"

"Just a guess, honey, I've got a good sense about people."

Norm offered a friendly smile and ordered a beer.

"Don't worry Joyce, you've done nothing wrong that *I'm* aware of. I want to talk to you about Hope Lachance."

"Oh? She's a bit young for you, don't you think, mister...?"

"Strom, Norm Strom. It's not what you think. She's gone missing and I'm retracing her last steps here in town, in an attempt to find her."

Joyce looked like she just lost her best friend. She placed a hand on Norm's wrist. Her eyes instantly glazed over.

"What? Oh my god. I haven't seen her since she left last week, she stayed at my place the night before she left town. I thought she was home by now, with her little girl."

"Were you close to her? Any boyfriends or men in her life that you know about?"

Finding Hope

A good-looking guy with a block head slid on to a bar stool between Norm and the CP men. His head and square jaw reminded him of his Rock'em Sock'em Robots he had as a kid. He thought he'd seen the guy at the Sports bar. Norm looked back to Joyce.

She thought for a second, then leaned in closer to Norm. "As close as anyone gets to Hope, I guess. There are no men that I'm aware of; she was very private that way. There *was* one night we got really drunk and she told me about a friend of hers who was beaten and abused by her husband. She said it was her best friend, but I knew she was talking about herself. She said her friend lived in fear every day, and wondered if the husband would track her down. Do you think he's found her?"

"I have no idea. That's why I'm talking to you, and anyone else who might know her. I just came from the sports bar."

"Did you talk to the pervert?"

"Nick? Yeah. What's up with him?"

She straightened and folded her hands in front of her. "He came on to me a couple years ago, cornering me after work one night by my car, in the parking lot."

"How'd that turn out—if you don't mind me asking?"

"Not as well as Nick would have liked. Those railway workers at the other end of the bar saw what he was up to and put the fear of god into him. That's why none of us drink there anymore. I need the job, so I still work there. You don't think...?"

"I dunno. Something tells me he's afraid of Hope—or maybe his own wife."

"Probably both. I think someone spilled the beans to his missus, cause she watches him like a hawk. Shit! I Don't suppose he told you about the other waitress who disappeared about three years ago...sorry, I just remembered. "

"What? Did the cops ever find her?"

The Highway of Tears

"You're kidding right? They never find any of them."

Norm took a swig of his beer. "Maybe I should have the Mounties dig into Nick's life a little deeper. Is there anything else you can think of that might help me track Hope down?"

"Did you know she hitches rides home with truckers, guys she knows from the truck stop?"

"Yeah, I plan on visiting there in the morning."

Joyce put her hand over his. "I'm sorry Norm, that's all I know. I really hope she is okay, she's such a sweet thing."

Norm finished his beer, then stood and gave her a one-armed hug. "I know. Thanks, Joyce. You take care."

A tear broke free of her left eye, and rolled down her cheek. "Good luck, Norm."

17

Fishing

*"We do not inherit the land from out ancestors,
We borrow it from our children."*
—Indigenous Wisdom

Two Snakes loved fishing. His favorite lake was in the foothills of the Caribou Mountains. It was the morning after a hard rain. To him, the fresh scent of pine in the air was intoxicating. The trip was over an hour out of town, but well worth the drive. In the pre-dawn light, he almost missed the turn off at the devil's pitchfork.

He found the old logging road, by watching for the neatly planted rows of replacement trees. Like his father, and his father before him, he hunted and fished on the land of his people.

He stopped to unhook the chain blocking his path, and noticed fresh tire tracks in the mud. Anyone who was familiar with the laneway ignored the no trespassing sign that had hung there forever. It was unusual to see anyone else on the old logging road, but there were a few cabins in the area.

He stayed right at the fork. A second later, he saw taillights from the corner of his eye. It was a dark colored SUV. It came off the other fork, heading back towards the main road.

Two Snakes drove on, thinking that it was probably one of the log, bog, and fog guys—what he called the Forest Rangers. He thought it was odd, that they came off the old graveyard road. He quickly dismissed the idea, thinking that they were probably doing something like counting pine beetles in the dead trees.

The logging road dead-ended at a secluded mountain lake. Two Snakes backed in his truck by a circle of rocks that made a fire pit. He pulled his gear out of the truck and walked down to the water's edge. He unfolded his lawn chair, sat down, and opened his tackle box. Gazing across the lake, he saw the sun was pushing up the curtain of night, that was resting on the treetops. The mist that hung over the lake resembled a thin cloud, that had bedded down there for the night.

Two Snakes filled his lungs with the crisp morning air, thinking to himself, *It doesn't get any better than this.* He wanted to try for bass, or maybe even a northern pike; they liked to rest in the weeds. He picked out a lure that worked well in the past.

Attaching the lure to his line, he thought about the Ranger again. He remembered that they normally drove pickup trucks. *And now that I think of it, it looked like a Ford Explorer that I've seen in town. Strange. Oh well, I've got to catch me some lunch.* He stood up and cast the lure into the weeds.

* * *

Norm grumbled at the sound of birds chirping; it was time to get his retired ass out of bed. *They say the early bird gets the worm. Shit, I'd rather be a bat, and chase mosquitoes.* He sat on the edge of the bed, rubbing his eyes, trying to work them open. Long-faced, he gawked at the window—it was still dark outside.

After a shower to wakeup, he wondered where all the birds had gone. *Little bastards have probably gone back to bed.* It was too early for him, but he knew he had to get to the diner early to see Betty, and catch the truckers before they hit the road. The highways were too dangerous to drive at night.

Finding Hope

Drivers took advantage of every minute of daylight they could, for the long distances they had to travel.

The stink of diesel fumes from idling rigs, caught in the back of Norm's throat when he stopped in the diner's parking lot. His boot heel slipped when he put his kickstand down, so he had to roll the bike up a foot to avoid the gooey patch of oil. He made for the doors to escape the foul air, but a gauntlet of smokers blocked the entrance. *So much for country-fresh air,* he thought.

A waitress who looked like Betty White was easy to spot, the resemblance was uncanny. Norm saw an empty table in her section. He grabbed a menu from the deserted hostess station, and seated himself.

It didn't smell any better inside the diner. The stench of stale cigarettes and body odor almost ruined Norm's appetite. Almost. He didn't gross out easily—he'd seen too many things over his years on the job. Even a decaying body couldn't keep him from a meal. He remembered one in particular, a woman found in her apartment after two weeks. He thought his lunch—the Chinese food, smelled funny, but it was that putrid odor of rotting human flesh, that clung to the small hairs inside his nose. *That was a good meal...seafood fried rice, egg foo young and stir-fried veggies.*

Betty and one other waitress, were the only two women in the place—or so he thought. A couple tables over, he noticed a tough-looking trucker who wore too much jewellery, and not enough facial hair, to have a penis.

Betty spun around after pouring coffee at another table.

"Oh, I'm sorry—I didn't see you there. Coffee?"

"No thanks. Diet Pepsi or Coke, please."

"I see you already have a menu, I'll be right back with your pop."

Norm surveyed the room, trying to guess who Lonny or Dale might be. It was an impossible task without a description of them. Nobody was talking; their faces were buried in newspapers, or plates of food. The only noise in the room came from utensils scraping plates, and coffee cups clanking on saucers.

Betty reappeared at Norm's table with a giant glass of Diet Coke.

"Are you ready to order, or do you need a minute?"

He wanted to ask her about Hope, but Betty looked really busy. She glanced over at another table and signaled with her index finger that she'd be there in a minute. Any questions would have to wait.

"Can I have the hungry man's breakfast—eggs over hard, no toast or home fries, please?"

"Just the eggs and meat?"

"Yes, please. Some tomato slices if you have some, I'm doing a low carb thing."

Years prior, Norm had lost sixty pounds doing the Atkins Diet. It worked well for him. In Prince George the Dagostino women had fattened him up, so it was time to change things around and maybe lose a few of those pasta pounds.

Betty spun on her heals, and buzzed off to the kitchen before Norm could utter another word. He'd have to wait until things quieted down, but if Lonny was there, he needed to question him before he hit the road. He scanned the room again, then grabbed a newspaper from the empty table next to him.

He flipped through the paper while waiting for Betty. The local news didn't mean much to him. Even with all the open cases that the Mounties were investigating, there wasn't a single word written about any of the missing women. The big news story that day was about an old locomotive that had been converted into a tourist attraction.

Finding Hope

One trucker left the diner, and another settled up with the other waitress. If size mattered, neither of the two men seemed large enough to be Big Lonny. Randomly asking men in the diner if their name was Lonny wasn't the right way to go. Nobody likes prying questions from strangers. On cue, Betty charged out of the kitchen balancing a row of plates on each arm.

She dropped one in front of Norm, then sidestepped to the table behind him with the others. He turned to get Betty's attention.

"Excuse me, can I talk to you for a minute?"

After arranging four plates on the table behind Norm, she returned to his side.

"I'm sorry honey, did you need something else?"

"Yes, Betty, is it?"

"That's me. What do you need, sweetie?"

"I'm Norm. I can see you're busy, but I'd like to speak with you about Hope."

The woman stopped moving for the first time. Her perma-smile faded to a look of concern.

"Is there any news? I heard she's missing."

"I'm afraid not, but I'm trying to talk to anyone who might have seen her before she disappeared. I understand that she ate here, and may have gotten a ride with one of the truckers. I was told that I should talk to a guy named Lonny."

Betty smiled again and looked back to the table where she had just dropped off the four plates. She nodded her head in the direction of the man who sat behind Norm.

"Lonny's busy at the moment, but I'm sure he'd by happy to speak to you when he is free."

Norm was back to back with the man she had indicated so he had to turn around in his chair to see him. He resembled an oak wine barrel, with arms and legs. He wore a crew cut on top of a head that was way too small for his body. Norm leaned farther to the side and saw that Lonny's attention was consumed by what he was consuming. He had the big breakfast too, but his included all the fixings, along with a side of pancakes and bowl of oatmeal.

Knowing better than to disturb a serious eater like Lonny, Norm decided he should finish his own breakfast first, then wait for the other man to finish his. He savored the taste of his smoked bacon, while he thought of some questions. Norm loved bacon. Sometimes he'd order all bacon, instead of the sausages and ham that came with a big breakfast. Not that he would, but he could eat bacon at every meal.

He made sure he saved a strip of the crispy pork fat for his last bite. He had just swallowed the last remnants of it, when Betty returned and dropped off another giant glass of pop. He thought he should visit the men's room, before he attempted another half gallon, but Betty nodded toward Lonny again. Norm couldn't believe his eyes. The big man was done his breakfast. He mopped his chin with a wadded napkin.

Not wanting to miss his chance, Norm slid his chair sideways, to face Lonny at an angle.

"Excuse me big guy, do you mind if we chat for a bit?"

It was like Norm had awakened a sleeping giant. Lonny struggled to turn in his chair; having no neck made the chore more difficult. Norm moved his chair again to meet the man half way. Lonny had a flat face, the kind that you see when someone presses theirs against a window. When he spoke Norm had to lean closer to hear him. His voice had no pitch or tone, it sounded like an air gun, hissing words.

"Were you talking to me, sir?"

"Yes. Lonny, right?"

"Yeah, I'm Lonny. Can I help you with something?"

Finding Hope

"I hope so—do you mind if I join you, before we both strain our necks?"

"Please, do."

Norm took a seat in the chair across the table from Big Lonny. He looked down at all the empty plates, not a crumb was left on any of them.

"My name is Norm Strom. Your friend Hope has gone missing, and I'm trying to find her. I was hoping that you might be able to help me."

Lonny's face flushed red like a ripe tomato. His lips disappeared into his mouth, and his eyebrows rolled into a crease in his forehead. Norm was ready for the big man to burst, his words hissed like air escaping from the spout of a balloon.

"I'm mad at him."

"Mad at who Lonny?"

"Dirty old Dale. I just know he did something to her."

"What do you know, Lonny?"

"I was off sick, with my bad back. Hope got a ride with Dale. Betty says nobody's seen her since. He's a bad man."

"Do you know Dale's last name, or where he lives?"

"Dale Strickland. He has his own reefer truck—Strickland Transport. He hauls anything for anybody, and none of the other truckers like him. He tries to suck up by selling them weed or hookers. I don't know where he lives."

"When's the last time you saw him, Lonny?"

"Maybe a few days ago. He doesn't follow a regular schedule."

"Thanks, Lonny—one more thing. What makes you think that Dale has done something to Hope?"

"I dunno. Maybe the way he is with women. Like his wife—he treats her like a dog. I heard that one time when he was hurting for cash and needed gas money, that he pimped his wife out for the cost of a fill up. I'd be willing to bet that he's got something to do with Hope's disappearance."

Norm offered Lonny his hand. "Thanks big guy, you've been very helpful."

Lonny waved at Betty, got up, then walked over to the register, where she rang up his bill. Norm took a drink of his pop; a sharp pain in his gut reminded him it was time to empty his bladder. He went to the men's room to relieve himself. Standing there in front of the urinal he thought about his next move. *Time to call Jensen—I need an address and more info on Mr. Strickland. He sounds like a real piece of work.*

18

Getting Along

It didn't matter if the abuse was verbal, physical, or sexual, Hope found it was better to shut up and put up. Resistance was futile and only made matters worse; she had learned the hard way, from her abusive ex-husband.

It was amazing how much bullshit that she had endured. It was no wonder she fled in search of a better life. She ran clear across the country and thought she was finally safe. She always feared her psycho ex might find her, but she never imagined anything like the predicament she was in with Bear.

Other than the daily coitus ritual she had to perform, life in his cabin was tolerable. Sadly, sex had become just another chore for her. At least with Bear, it was over so quick she could almost pretend it never happened. There was no intimacy or attachment.

Hope took on other chores in the cabin too: cleaning, washing clothes, and even some cooking.

If she wasn't being held captive as a sex slave, life in the wilderness might have been enjoyable. The serenity and natural surroundings were peaceful and soothing. Hope was very independent and thought that life as a hermit might be okay. Charitee wouldn't have liked it; she enjoyed civilization and all the trappings that came with it. Was she going crazy—what was she thinking? She couldn't live anywhere without her little angel.

* * *

Norm settled up with Betty, and asked her if there was a phone he could use to make a long distance call. She showed him to the office, and said their plan covered all calls. He sat down at the desk, and scrolled through his contacts on his mobile phone. The gas from all the pop he'd drank exploded from his lips in the form of a loud belch. He glanced back over his shoulder hoping that no one in the restaurant had heard him.

Even without an audience, Norm chuckled to himself. It was memories of his mother that made him laugh. Although she was only average in size, she could belch loud enough to get a reading on the Richter scale. He recalled one time in a restaurant when she belched out loud and the whole place went silent. Then, nonchalantly, she said excuse me in a tiny little voice. The only better burper in the family was Norm's brother Al—he could burp his way through the whole alphabet. Mom was proud.

Laurie said she was working nights, so Norm thought he should check in with her while she was home.

"How's it going Norm? Any news of Hope?"

"Sounds like I woke you up, I'm sorry."

"It's okay, I'm glad you called."

"I'm at the truck stop in Jasper—I just talked to Betty and Lonny. It appears that she hitched a ride with a trucker named Dale Strickland. He's probably the Dan or Dave on your list."

"Shouldn't you tell the cops? Where's he at now?"

"Slow down, Laurie. I'm just bringing you up to speed. I don't know where the guy is—or even who he is. My next call will be to the cops to get his address and any background they might have on him."

"Can't they put out an APB and arrest him?"

"Arrest him for what?"

"For kidnapping Hope!"

Finding Hope

"Calm down, Laurie. I understand that you're upset, but we have to do this right. We don't know if Strickland still has Hope, or what he might have done with her if he doesn't. Arresting him doesn't guarantee that we'll find her. At this point I don't even have proof that she got in the truck with him. You have to be patient, this is going to take some time."

"Time is what I'm worried about, Norm. What's happening to Hope...is she even alive? And what about the phone calls?"

"I feel your pain, and I'm working on it. What phone calls?"

"I was watering the plants over at Hopes place and answered the phone when someone called, but they didn't say anything and hung up. I checked her machine and there was another hang-up."

"Okay, Laurie. We can't worry about hang-up phone calls right now. I'll call you back again tomorrow."

"Alright, Norm. I'm sorry for yelling at you."

He felt another gas bubble working it's way up the pipe so he answered quickly. "It's alright, I understand. We'll talk later."

Norm thought about what he told Laurie. Everyone assumed that Hope got in the truck with Dale Strickland, but a witness to that effect would go a long way when it came to questioning him. He saw Betty punching in an order in at the cash register, so he left the office and joined her there.

"All done with your phone calls?"

"Not quite yet, I still have to call the Mounties. Can I ask you a quick question?"

"Sure honey."

"Did anyone actually see Hope get in the truck with Dale Strickland?"

"Now that you ask, I don't know. I assumed she did—after she paid for his breakfast. That's what she did to chip in for the ride. You can check with Andy, he's the gas attendant, outside."

"Thanks, Betty. I will."

122

Norm walked out to the back of the parking lot where the gas pumps were. A frail man in his sixties, with a ponytail that hung out the back of his ball cap, was busy reading a newspaper in the tiny kiosk. He looked up when Norm blocked the natural light he was reading by.

"Can I help you sir?"

"I hope so. Betty says you're an honest man, and I can count on you."

"If she says so."

"She says you might know Dale Strickland?"

"Sure, I know him, but I ain't got no use for him. What'd he do now?"

"Well, I was wondering if you might have seen a young woman get in his truck about a week ago?"

Andy folded his newspaper and placed it on the desk. He stepped out of the booth and faced Norm. "You must mean Hope—beautiful young woman. She buys me coffee sometimes, while she waits around for a ride. None of my business, but I told her that Dale was no good. Come to think of it, that's the last time I saw Dale. Hope poked her head in here to say hello, then she used my squeegee to clean his windows and mirrors before the three of them left."

"Three of them—there was somebody else with them?"

"Some big burly guy...not fat like Dale—never seen him before. Looked like he climbed in the back bunk before Hope did the windows. She got in the truck when Dale did. They left here heading north."

"Any idea where Dale lives?"

He glanced over at a truck that pulled into the parking lot and gave the driver a cursory wave.

"Nope. I mind my own business—get along better that way."

"Thanks for your help, Andy."

"Have we met before, sir? My memory ain't as good as it used to be."

"No, Andy. Here's my card though. Can you call me when you see Dale again?'

He read part of Norm's old business card out loud.

"Police Detective. I knew Dale was no good—I tried to tell her that."

"She's missing, Andy, and it sounds like you're the last one to see her when she left here with Dale."

"Holy mackerel, that don't sound good. She's such a sweetheart."

Andy looked down at the card again, reading the rest of it to himself.

"Damn shame! Hope missing. Don't you worry sir, I'll call ya when that no good son-of-a..."

"Thanks again, Andy."

Norm walked across the parking lot and went back into the diner. He found Betty sitting in the office with her shoes off. She had her left foot up on her right knee, massaging the insole with her hands.

"Can't run around all day on my feet like I used to."

Norm nodded and smiled. "Do you think I can use the phone again, Betty?"

"Help yourself. Did Andy know anything useful?"

"Maybe. Did you see another man with Dale or Hope that morning?"

"No, sorry."

Betty moved to the smaller chair beside the desk so Norm could have access to the phone. "Do you need some privacy?"

"Not at all, Betty. Give your feet some more rest."

"Thanks anyway, but I'm back on in five."

Norm called Jensen and was surprised when he answered his office phone on the first ring.

"Detective Strom, how was your breakfast?"

"Call display huh? We couldn't afford that luxury at the PD back home."

"Canada's finest—what can I say?"

"I'm glad you're in the office, Jensen. I want to run a couple names by you."

"Shoot. I'll run them through CPIC and check them locally."

"First is Dale Strickland—ever heard of him?"

"Nope, should I?"

"If you're familiar with the dirt bags in Jasper. The locals here say he's a mutt for hire; he transports anything for anyone. Runs a reefer truck under the name of Strickland Transportation."

"I'm typing him in as we speak. What's his connection to the case?"

"It looks like Lachance hitched a ride home with him, on her way to Stewart. They knew each other, but I've been told another man was in the truck with them, name unknown."

"Strickland's coming up on the computer now—looks like a winner: convictions for assault, possession of narcotics, possession of stolen property, another theft charge..."

"Any current address for him?"

"Up near Fraser Lake on...just a minute Norm, from what you're telling me we have enough to bring him in for questioning."

"I know, that's what I'm afraid of."

Betty had her shoes back on. She had a look of concern on her face. She gave Norm a little wave and left the office.

"What do you mean by that?"

Norm was doodling on a note pad beside the phone and he wrote down a single word. "Strickland's been through the system before, he's not going to tell you anything."

"And you have a better idea?"

"Yes. Leverage."

"You mean that you want to catch him dirty, then use that against him. You do remember that you're not a cop anymore, don't you?"

Norm started to draw a picture of a truck. "Exactly."

"I'm not following you."

"I'm not a cop anymore so I don't have to follow cop rules. I don't need probable cause or search warrants or any of that bullshit. I'll catch him dirty, then call in the cavalry. That would be you guys."

"I'm not sure I agree, but I do see your point. Just don't forget to call me before you act. No cowboy stunts. This isn't the wild west anymore."

"Funny, that's what they used to call Windsor."

"I don't share your sense of humor, Norm."

"Okay, boss. Now can I have his address please?"

"I have to bring that screen back up. You said you had another name?"

"Yeah, it's in the file—Nick, the owner of the Pro Sports Bar in Jasper. Last name of Popodoplous, I'm not sure of the spelling. He should be listed as owner of the business."

"And what's his story?"

"According to his female staff, he's a major pervert. One of them said a young girl who worked there went missing about three years ago. I thought it might be something to check out."

"Okay, I'll look into it. Anything else?"

"Nope. Just that address."

Jensen gave Norm the address for Strickland, then finished the conversation in an official voice.

"Stay in touch every step of the way Mister Strom—we're putting a lot of trust in you on this."

"I will, boss. Talk to you later."

19

Dakota

"The two most important days in your life are the day you are born and the day you find out why."
—Mark Twain

Two Snakes recognized the scowl on his sister's face when he pulled into the driveway, back from his fishing trip. She sat on his front steps. Her black hair was matted and a grey stripe at the roots reminded him of a skunk. Her skin was darker than his. She wore a red Addidas tracksuit and white sneakers. The woman was at the driver's door before he could get out of his truck. He ignored her ranting and nudged the door open, pushing her back so he could step out.

"Where have you been? You don't answer your phone. How is anyone supposed to get a hold of you? Do you care about anyone, but yourself."

"Nice to see you too, sis."

"Don't sis me—you never visit anymore."

"Gee, Glory, I wonder why."

"If you bothered to come around or answer your phone, you'd know that your niece is missing."

"Dakota? I just saw her the other day."

"She hasn't been home since then. She's just like you—only thinks of herself. Who's going to buy my smokes or baby-sit your nephew? I don't even have time to get my hair done."

Finding Hope

"You seem to have time for bingo all day and boozing all night. Your daughter is missing and you're worried about your cigarettes and your hair?"

"At least when she's home I know she's not doing drugs."

"Yes, Glory, you're such a good influence on her. Did you call the police to report her missing?"

"Yeah, right. Like they're gonna do anything. Can you drive me back home? Jeremy's with the woman next door, and I told her I wouldn't be long."

Glory walked around the front of the truck and climbed into the passenger side before Two Snakes could answer her. He turned and got back into his truck.

"Maybe we can stop for smokes. Dakota usually picks them up for me. And while we're out that way we might as well hit the liquor store too. I'm expecting company tonight."

"You're so concerned about your daughter that you're gonna get shit-faced with that loser, Malcolm?"

"No, he's long gone. I've been seeing Charlie; he treats me like a Princess."

"Well, maybe Prince Charles can help you find your daughter."

"That's what my big soldier-boy brother, David, is for. You're friends with the girls over at the Help Center, maybe they can *help* you."

Two Snakes knew better than to argue with his sister, he just shut up and drove. He let her babble on about all her ailments, and how the whole world was trying to keep her down. He'd heard it all before.

He thought about Dakota. She was no angel, but she never went missing for more than a night at a time. It was usually when Glory was on a binge, and she needed to escape for awhile. The Help Center had been her latest refuge. Two Snakes had taken her into his own home in the past, when his sister was out of control, but he never heard the end of it. She accused him of being a bad influence on her daughter. Go figure.

Considering the history of missing women in the area, he thought the worst. If she had taken off on her own, he couldn't think of where she might go. He knew Dakota had experimented with drugs, but maybe she was more into it than he was aware of. Awful thoughts whirled around in his head.

***

According to Jensen, Dale Strickland lived near Fraser Lake, almost two hours north of Prince George. Since there was nothing else for Norm to do in Jasper, he got the bike ready for the trip back up to PG. He chatted with Andy about the weather, while he filled up his tank with gas. When he handed the nozzle back to the old gas attendant, his phone rang. It was Laurie.

"Hi, Norm. Did you find that Dale guy yet?"

"No—I'm still at the truck stop and he's not here. According to a witness there was another man in the truck with Dale and Hope."

"Do you think it could be her crazy ex-husband?"

"What—why would you think that?"

"I forgot to tell you. The school needed copies of the girls' birth certificates for a field trip that they are planning so I had to search through some drawers at Hope's place. I found Charitee's birth certificate, but with her real name....apparently Hope changed both their names when she moved here."

"Take a breath Laurie. I doubt that the other man is her ex—that wouldn't make any sense. What did you find?"

"Charitee's birth certificate says her real name is Charlene Chambers. Her parents are listed as Robert and Faith Chambers, of Truro, Nova Scotia."

Norm thought about it for a few seconds. "It makes sense— she changed their names, but there are similarities. It's not unusual when people try to come up with new names. From Faith to Hope, Charlene to Charitee, and Chambers to Lachance. I can see the connections. I'm on my way back to Prince George. I'll run Robert Chambers' name by my police connections, just for shits and giggles. Thanks, Laurie. I'll call you later."

"Okay. Ride safe, Norm."

Norm got back to Prince George late in the afternoon. It was a lovely day for the ride, but seeing the same scenery was like watching a repeat of your favorite TV show—it's nice to see the familiar characters, but you already know how the story ends.

Although he was tempted to stop for a beer, Norm headed directly to the Ramada. An older man stood behind the front desk, he wasn't nearly as pretty as Melanie. Norm nodded and waved at the man, as though he knew where he was going.

Inspector Nickerson and three other investigators were busy working at their desks. The youngest cop in the room looked up, eyeballing the guy in the black Harley shirt and jeans like he was on their top ten, most wanted list. He stopped beside the Inspector's desk. "Good afternoon, sir. I'm Norm Strom."

"Good afternoon, Detective, it's nice to finally meet you. I hear you may have a lead in the Lachance case. Jensen briefed me this morning."

"I hope so, Inspector. The witnesses sound reliable."

"Have a seat, Norm. Jensen told me we have enough grounds to bring your suspect in for questioning, but you want to handle him in a different way."

His white hair and the deep wrinkles on Nickerson's forehead were clues to his many years on the job. His jade-colored eyes and large cranium told Norm the man was intelligent and knowledgeable. He had just a touch of a British accent. Perhaps he'd gone to school or spent some time overseas. He looked a bit miffed.

Norm knew he had to tread lightly with the man in charge. Jensen could plead ignorance if Norm got into trouble, but the Inspector would ultimately be the man responsible for anything that went wrong. Things like political correctness, rights to privacy, and constitutional rights, were thorns that had collected in Norm's ass throughout his career. They were the reasons why he didn't miss the job. Cops had to play by rules, but the bad guys didn't.

"Yes, Inspector. I've thought a lot about it. With all due respect to you and your task force, this case was as stale as week-old bread when I got involved. In my humble opinion, I feel that bringing the suspect in for questioning at this point would prove to be futile."

Nickerson took his reading glasses off and placed them on the desk. He folded his hands in front of him and leaned back in his chair. Norm's polite and politically correct bullshit had caught his attention. "How so, Norm?"

"Well, sir, Dale Strickland is a repeat offender, with multiple criminal convictions. He knows how the game is played. The witnesses are solid, but their story doesn't give us enough grounds for an arrest. He has nothing to gain if he talks to us, and if he lawyers up, the game is over. I was also told there was another man in the truck with Strickland and Lachance. We need the name of that man, and Strickland is the only person who can give it to us.

"So you're saying we should try to identify the other man before we question Strickland?"

"I don't know if that's possible at this point, but if we were to catch Strickland in the act—committing some type of crime, we'd have leverage on him. He seems like the kind of guy who'd give up his own mother, if it was to his benefit."

Finding Hope

"Turn him into an informant—I understand you were pretty successful back home with that sort of thing." Nickerson leaned forward and smiled. He fiddled with his glasses on the desk.

"Yes, sir. When I retired they told me that I had more informants than any other cop on the job. They were the secret weapon that helped me bring many of my cases to a successful conclusion."

"I see, but you'd be walking a fine line here, Norm. Technically, if you are acting on our behalf, you are a police agent."

"I know, sir, I have no problem testifying in court as long as you pay my airfare back here, if and when the time comes. And if I'm technically your agent, a little gas or expense money would really come in handy. I'm retired and on a fixed income."

Nickerson chuckled. "I was old school once, but I had to change with the times. I understand what you want to do, Norm. I'll give you some rope—just don't hang me with it. Oh, before I forget...Jensen left a package for you. It's on his desk."

"Thanks Inspector, I'll go check it out."

Norm walked over to Jensen's cubicle and sat down in his chair. The top of his desk looked like it was set up for a store display. Hope's file was placed perfectly in the middle. Had he measured the space on both sides, equally? *Wow, is this guy OCD or what? I should re-arrange it just for fun.* He saw that Jensen had done some follow-up work on the file. *It's about time.* He had the CPIC and record card printouts for Strickland, and to his surprise, Robert Chambers.

There was a personal note to Norm. It read: *I had our computer do a nationwide check for missing persons with names similar to Hope Lachance, figuring she may have changed it before she moved here. Faith Chambers and her daughter Charlene were reported missing in Nova Scotia by her husband, Robert. He has assault and drunk driving convictions.*

The cops there suspected domestic abuse and possibly foul play when she went missing, but they couldn't prove anything.

I made sure to tell my counterpart out there not to say anything to the ex-husband. I also spoke with a patrol cop from the Fraser Lake detachment. He says that Strickland parks his reefer truck right out front of his trailer when he's home. If he's using it for work, then there is usually a green pickup truck parked there. He leaves it for his wife, who lives there with him. The plate registration is in with the CPIC printouts.

Norm looked for a pen and paper to write the plate number down. In the top right desk drawer he found both. When he removed the pad of paper a small piece of jewellery fell to the floor. It was a silver earring, a feather. Inspector Nickerson appeared beside him as he picked it up.

"I see you found the file. What's that you found on the floor?"

"Someone's earring. It fell from this pad, something else Jensen's working on, I guess."

Nickerson handed Norm a wad of cash. "Here's three hundred dollars for your expenses. Get me receipts whenever you can." He cleared his throat. "And by the way, that's not beer money."

"Cool. Thanks, Inspector."

Norm put the earring back in Jensen's drawer, and left him a note thanking him for the information in the file.

20

Tag Team

"In three words I can sum up everything I've learned about life: it goes on."

—Robert Frost

After a day on the road, and his chat with the Mounties, Norm needed a beer. Thinking he might need a shower first, he lifted his left arm and performed the smell test. It failed, so headed to Mark and Loretta's place. He let himself in the front door, hollering as not to scare anyone. The pungent aroma of frying onions hung heavy in the air. Norm pried off his boots, and left them by the front door with his travel bag.

He walked into the kitchen where Loretta was bent over in front of the stove, removing a pan from the lower drawer. She hadn't heard him come in.

"Wow, that looks great."

Loretta jumped, straightened up, and spun around all at the same time. Her face flushed red. Norm flashed a big smile; she knew what he was thinking.

"What...I didn't hear..."

He chuckled, raised his eyebrows, and nodded his head towards the stovetop. "Dinner smells awesome."

She was embarrassed and he was busted. In his opinion it was okay to look, but he would never touch another man's wife. Not that he hadn't considered it, Loretta was cute and petite and had bumps and curves in all the right places. She only had two faults as far as he was concerned: she smoked and she was married.

"Thanks, Norm. I'm fixing some toppings for the burgers I have on the barbeque. I made extra, if you're hungry."

"Sure. Is Mark working late again?"

"He practically lives there. I usually make a plate for him so he can eat whenever he gets home."

"I'd love a burger, but I need to hit the shower first. Do you think I can have..."

Loretta knew exactly what he was thinking and intercepted him on his way to the fridge. She retrieved a can of beer and handed it to him.

"Ah, you're the best—the perfect wife."

"Yeah, if only I had a husband who was here to appreciate me."

Norm decided not to answer. He popped open the beer, took a couple of big gulps, then went back into the living room to retrieve his travel bag.

"I'll see you in a bit, I have to go and wash the road off of me."

She shouted back from the kitchen, "Dinner will be ready when you're done, I'll be outside at the picnic table!"

When Norm met Loretta outside, she already had a plate fixed for him. He gawked at her, smiled and shook his head.

"What?"

"Nothing. I guess I'd forgotten how nice it is to have someone wait on me."

"Don't worry, Norm, I'm sure you'll find someone and fall in love again. Hey, what's going on with the missing woman. Can I assume she's still missing?"

He took a swig of beer, and gazed across the manicured lawn and tidy perennial borders surrounding the back yard. On the other side of the back fence, the General was outside,

Finding Hope

watering her flowers. She caught him looking in her direction and waved.

"I'm afraid so. I don't even know if she's still alive. I do have a lead though—witnesses saw her get into a truck with two men. I know who the driver is so I'm going to track him down and do surveillance on him."

"Can't the cops arrest him?"

"No. They could question him, but there's no grounds to arrest him at this point. They're giving me a chance to see what I can dig up."

"It sounds like they trust you. Aren't you scared, doing something like that all by yourself?"

"Not really. Besides, I'm going to enlist the help of a local guy that I met at Billy's Pub. He has military and tracking experience— I'm going to visit him after dinner. You're welcome to tag along and meet him, he's quite the character."

"No, thanks. Mark likes me to be here when he gets home, even though he just eats and then watches TV. He's always too tired, even for sex."

"Really? I could never be that tired. Men are usually pretty simple—just feed us and fuck us."

Loretta laughed out loud. "Oh, Norm. You're funny."

"I'm serious, Loretta. Serve his dinner naked when he comes home; he'll want desert."

She reached over the table and squeezed Norm's hand. "You're such a hoot. Maybe I'll try that, when you're not around."

* * *

The driveway was empty when Norm pulled in at Two Snakes' house. He looked back over his shoulder, and spotted his pickup down the hill, in Billy's parking lot. Two Snakes was sitting in the same seat at the bar when he walked in. It was like déja vu when Norm took the seat beside him, but this time a cute brunette was behind the bar. Two Snakes raised his glass. "Well, if it ain't the Lone Ranger. Do you want a napkin?"

"What...why?"

"You're drooling on the bar."

"Hope I didn't get any on you." Norm nodded towards the bartender. "Friend of yours?"

"No. She's too young for you...I doubt if you could keep up."

"Maybe not, but I'd die happy, trying."

Two Snakes took a sip of beer. "Aren't you busy enough looking for your missing girlfriend, I take it you haven't found her yet?"

Norm waved at the hot bartender and pointed to the Okanogan draft beer tap. "No, but I'm glad you're so concerned. I was thinking you might like to help."

"I've got enough of my own problems."

"Like what—fish weren't biting at your favorite hole?"

"Fishing was good. It's family stuff."

"I hear ya, driving you to drink, eh? Seriously. I got a good lead on a suspect and the cops have agreed to let me work him. I might need some backup though, and a different set of wheels."

"How the hell did you get the Mounties to let you work the guy on your own?"

"I'd like to think it has something to do with my good looks, charming personality and vast police experience, but honestly, I think they're just too busy to give a shit."

The hottie put Norm's beer in front of him, and asked if he wanted anything else. He could only wish...and he smiled.

Two Snakes interrupted his wishful thinking. "You have a plan?"

"Have you heard of a trucker by the name of Dale Strickland?"

"Nope."

"I've got witnesses who put Hope in his truck with another guy, leaving Jasper. I don't know who the guy is yet...a friend of Strickland's, I would guess. That's the last time anyone saw her. The cops gave me Strickland's address, up the road, near Fraser Lake. According to them and the witnesses, he's a real piece of work. He runs drugs, stolen property—even hookers."

"Sounds like a bad man. What are you gonna do about him?"

"I want to sit on him, spin him, track him, whatever it takes." Norm talked with his hands and almost knocked over his beer. "If I catch him dirty it will give me some leverage to squeeze him, and maybe find out what happened to Hope."

"Sounds like you've done that sorta thing before."

"Once or twice, but I had a gun and badge and backup then. That's where I hoped you would come in. If you're too busy with the family thing, maybe we can swap vehicles for a couple days. Can you ride a bike?"

Norm's eyes followed the bartender's moves as if he was a linebacker waiting to make a tackle.

"Same as a horse, ain't it?"

"Almost, but it has more gears and goes a lot faster. Maybe you could rent me your truck, the Mounties gave me some expense money."

"You're shitting me."

"I shit you not."

"Wow, you really did charm them. It's okay, I have a car in my garage."

"Cool, I'll take that."

"No you won't—it's a 1970 GTO, in mint condition."

"Now you're shitting me."

Two Snakes shook his head and laughed. He finished his beer then waved at the hot brunette for another. Norm nodded when she pointed to his nearly empty mug.

"This one's on your tab, Kemosabe, since the Mounties are covering your expenses."

"They already warned me that my beer ain't covered. Hey, do you think the barmaid likes retired cops?"

"You sound hornier than a ten-peckered owl. You've got socks older than her."

"I know, I know. I just need to get laid."

Two Snakes nodded in acknowledgement.

21

Searchers

"Life is the sum of all your choices."
—Albert Camus

Norm was awoken by the most obscene noise in the world—the buzzing sound of his alarm clock. He knew people who said they woke up on their own, before their alarm went off. Not him. He could easily sleep till noon, no matter what time he went to bed. Anxious to set up surveillance on Dale Strickland and find Hope, he whipped the sheet back. *If only the rest of me moved that fast.* Norm sat on the edge of the bed and rubbed his eyes, trying to get them focused.

Strickland was his only lead. As a courtesy, Norm called Jensen before going to bed and gave him the description of the truck he borrowed from Two Snakes, in case someone called it in as a suspicious vehicle. It had happened to Norm in the past, while doing stake-outs.

Jensen told him to check the transport terminal before heading up to Fraser Lake. Cargo was transferred between trucks and trains there. It made sense—Strickland had to pick up his load somewhere.

When he got to the terminal Norm realized he'd made a wise choice, taking the pickup truck. Amongst all the commercial vehicles, his bike would have stood out like a nun in a strip bar. Blending in is what surveillance is all about.

The terminal was a long rectangular building with loading docks on one side, and train tracks running along the other. There was lots of activity, but he didn't see Strickland's rig. It was early though, and other trucks were still arriving, so Norm pulled into the employee parking lot. It offered him a clear view of all the trucks coming and going.

His stomach growled. He didn't have time for breakfast, but sweet Loretta had packed him a lunch. *Damn, that Mark is a lucky guy.* He thought about his dream that the brunette bar tender was in. He was admiring her ass, but when she turned around it was Loretta. That's all he could remember. Norm pulled an apple from the lunch bag and noticed the big bottle of Diet Pepsi. He chuckled to himself, knowing he'd be cracking that baby open soon, for the caffeine jolt.

For some reason, Norm found it difficult to stay awake in the morning. Maybe his body clock said that he should still be in bed. There were times he'd nod off while driving home after a day shift. Oddly enough, it was different for him at night. He could stay up until sunrise without getting tired. Working midnights was never a problem, until the morning sun and the sandman did their thing.

Norm learned and worked two types of surveillance: static and mobile. Static means stationary, where he sometimes sat for hours on end, watching and waiting. It is easier with a team—everyone takes turns in different positions, with one person on the eye. That's the one watching the target. The others stay in the area, but out of sight. Mobile surveillance is more fun. He got to drive like a madman, while trying to keep the target in sight and not get burned at the same time. It was more of a challenge.

It had been an hour and Norm couldn't wait any longer, he cracked open the pop. Eyeing the top of the bottle, he remembered being stuck in the back of a surveillance van for

Finding Hope

eight hours, relieving himself in a juice bottle and stopping before it overflowed. It seemed odd that more came out than went in.

Only three trucks remained in the loading docks. If Strickland didn't show up Norm planned to check his home near Fraser Lake.

The truck at the first bay started to pull out, but a reefer truck cut it off. Norm recognized it from the hotel in Hyder—it was Dale Strickland's truck. The letters t and r were still missing from stenciling on the door.

The other truck driver blew the air horn. Strickland casually glanced over and flipped him the bird, then backed into one of the empty docks. Norm had a clear view of the front of his truck and the driver's door, but not the back loading area.

The man who got out of the truck had to be Strickland. Clumps of greasy brown hair stuck out from the sides of his ball cap. The BC Lions jersey that he wore wasn't long enough to cover his big belly. His gut hung over the waistband of his jeans like the top of a giant muffin. He yelled something to one of the guys on the loading dock then waddled over to meet him. His left index finger was buried so far up his nose, he could have scratched his brain.

Norm couldn't see what was loaded into Strickland's truck, but it only took ten minutes to get it done. The fat man stood and smoked beside his truck until the dockhand waved him over. The dockhand passed Strickland a clipboard, and he signed for the load. Before climbing back into his truck he took a long pull off his cigarette and flicked the butt into the next ramp.

Norm waited until Strickland exited the parking lot before he moved. He felt solo surveillance was risky, but it could be done if Strickland wasn't the suspicious or paranoid type. He doubted that he was; the tub of lard rarely looked in his mirrors.

Norm kept his distance anyway. He let the other traffic fill in between him and the truck—it was an easy vehicle to keep an eye on.

Norm felt a tightness in his stomach that wasn't from hunger. It was something he hadn't experienced since his days on the job. It was the thrill of the hunt, and the excitement of the chase. He was not one who got excited easily, but he did enjoy catching bad guys.

* * *

Two Snakes felt giddy when he pulled the cover off of his Pontiac GTO. Looking at his prized possession was one of the few things in life that still delighted him. He got in and fired up the engine. The sound of the four hundred—four barrel motor, growling through Hush mufflers gave him goose bumps. He revved the engine twice, just for fun. The sound drove the old woman next door crazy, but he couldn't resist.

Two Snakes backed his baby out of the garage, then stood beside it, and marveled at how the metallic blue paint and polished chrome sparkled in the sunlight. He ran his hand over the fender as though he was petting a puppy dog. It appeared there was a fresh scratch on the driver's door, but he was happy to see it was only the remnants of a cobweb.

Unsure of how long he'd be gone, Two Snakes rolled Norm's Harley into the garage for safe keeping. *I wonder what the old lady would think if I fired this thing up every morning.* He locked the garage and climbed back into the Blue Bomber; it was one of the fastest muscle cars in town.

When he backed out of his driveway, the old lady was peeking out her window, so he grinned and waved. She ducked back behind the curtains. Revving the engine, he dropped it in gear, squealed the tires, and drove off.

His smile turned upside down when he thought about his niece. Two Snakes tried to be a father-figure for Dakota—her own father never made it back from Afghanistan. Roger died from the same IED that took part of Two Snakes' right leg. He assumed his sister would act more responsibly after her husband's demise, but he was wrong.

Dakota had a wild side, just like her mother. She got in trouble soon after her father and uncle went off to war. To pass the time her mother replaced her husband with pills and booze. Both women spiraled further downhill when Two Snakes returned home with his best friend in a closed coffin.

His sister blamed him for her husband's death. Although it wasn't his fault, he sometimes wished it had been him who died from the blast. It seemed that everyone, including his own ex-wife, would have been happier with that outcome.

Two Snakes fiddled with the car radio trying to find an upbeat tune—Lynyrd Skynyrd's Simple Man, came on. He loved southern rock. Heading to the Women's Help Center, he thought about the last time he saw Dakota. It was the same day that he met Norm Strom. *Was the disappearance of Dakota and his friend, Hope, a coincidence? Probably, there were so many missing women.*

Two Snakes drove by the Ramada, noticing two Ford Explorers—one blue and one white, parked side by side in the front lot. The blue one looked like the SUV that he saw on the graveyard road when he was fishing. The thought quickly slipped his mind when he turned the corner, and pulled into the Help Center.

It was his hope that one of the girls there would know more about Dakota. Marjorie, the lead counselor, met him at the front door. She was a sweet little thing, with a squeaky voice. Two Snakes knew she had a crush on him, but he feared that her voice would drive him crazy, and she'd become his next ex.

The Highway of Tears

"Hello, David. It's always nice to see you. I suppose you're here about Dakota, her mother's already called several times. The way she talks it sounds like she's more concerned about who's going to fetch her smokes."

"Yeah, that's a big concern for her. When's the last time you saw Dakota?"

"Gee, it's been a few days now. She spent the night like usual— said her mother was drunk and mad at her for something. She was fine until she found out that Dee wasn't here."

"Dee?"

"Dee Reynolds, one of the other girls. Her and Dakota hung out whenever they were both here. She left for Calgary that same day to visit some friends there. Dakota got all pissy and said something about Dee ripping her off."

"Any idea what that was all about?"

"Not at the time, she wouldn't elaborate. One of the other girls filled me in the next morning, after Dakota left. She said the two of them were doing tricks and pooling their money to run away together. She didn't want her mother to find the money, so she left it with Dee. After learning that Dee took off without her, Dakota left here the next morning. That's the last time I saw her."

Two Snakes stood there, dumbfounded. He shook his head in disbelief.

"I just saw her. I can't believe she was selling herself on the street. Except for the usual bullshit with her mother, I thought she was okay. She's come to me for money in the past. What the hell was she thinking?"

"I honestly don't know, David. These young girls just don't comprehend the danger out there. For them, it's easy money. They come here with such low self esteem; it's one of the things we try to work on."

"Do you think she tried to catch up with her friend?"

"I doubt it. I don't think she knew where Dee was going."

"Do *you* know?" Two Snakes put a hand on her shoulder. "It might help if I can talk to her."

"Sorry. Maybe she'll be back when she runs out of money. Dee's a regular here."

"Do you have a picture of her?"

"We keep a picture of every girl in our files, but I can't give it to you because of privacy issues. Wait, the girls have a bulletin board in the back where they post pictures and notes to each other. I think I saw something there—I'll be right back."

Marjorie returned a minute later and handed Two Snakes a photograph of Dakota and Dee. He recognized the silver feather earrings, he had bought her for her birthday.

"I don't see why you can't have this. One of them left it on the board."

"Thanks, Marjorie. Please call me if you hear anything else."

"You bet. So how are *you* doing, David?"

"Not so good, now. I'll talk to you later, I gotta go."

* * *

After he pulled out of the loading dock, Strickland lit up a cigarette and cranked up an old Merle Haggard song on the radio. He blew a stream of smoke through his nose, the grey cloud escaped out the open window. He thought about the deliveries he had to make, on the way north. Although he'd just demolished a giant bear claw with his morning coffee, he contemplated lunch. *I hope the fat cow has something good to eat, when I get home.*

It wasn't just lunch that waited at home for Dale. He had to pick up twenty pounds of weed that was stashed in his chest freezer. He took a long haul off the fag, the ash fell into his lap with the pastry crumbs. As he headed north, out of Prince George, he squirmed in his seat. Finally, he bent forward, and forced out a big fart.

22

Natural Order

"May the stars carry your sadness away,
May the flowers fill your heart with beauty,
May hope forever wipe away your tears,
And, above all, may silence make you strong."
—Chief Dan George

After his usual grunt and quick climax, Bear rolled over. The satisfied grin on his face quickly twisted, and distorted into a look of horror. He jumped out of the bed as if it was on fire. There was blood on the sheets and all over his genitals. He thought he'd injured his little bear and he carefully examined it. He stared at Hope wide-eyed—his expression showed more fear than concern.

She had tried to warn him, when she casually mentioned that mom was coming to town. That went right over his head so she tried to explain how Mother Nature was responsible for her moodiness and stomach cramps—it was that time of the month. She thought he understood after he offered her chamomile tea. He said his mother used to drink it whenever she had a tummy ache.

Bear never talked about his mother, although he did mention once how she hated living in the wilderness. Hope assumed that his mother had left him and his father for the comforts of civilization. Judging by his cluelessness, it was obvious that Bear was never taught the female side of the birds and bees story. He staggered out of the bedroom in shock.

Hope had washed herself and was removing the soiled bed sheets when he reappeared in her doorway. His eyes drooped and his lower lip hung loose, like a little boy who knew he did something bad.

"It's okay, Bear, you didn't hurt me. This happens to women once every month. You've never heard women talk about their period?"

He sucked his lower lip in and raised his eyebrows. Puzzled, he shook his head.

"It's a natural thing, Bear, I tried to warn you it was coming. I need some feminine products, did your mother leave any tampons or napkins behind?"

He looked as though she'd just asked him if he'd seen any aliens lately.

"I know it's a lot to ask, Bear, but I need some things to help me with the bleeding. You'll have to take me into town so I can buy some tampons."

It was wishful thinking on her part. He had been letting her stay outside the cabin longer each day, strolling as far away as the stream, so it was worth a try. Once, she tried peeking through the trees to see down the road, but the cabin was at a dead end. No traffic ever came their way. If he took her to town, maybe she could drop a note, asking for help.

Bear disappeared from the doorway for a few seconds, then returned with a pencil and paper. He held them out to Hope.

"Write it down. I'll go."

She had to try. She'd hoped that he was freaked out just enough to take her into town with him. Most men hate the thought of having to buy feminine products. Obviously, his ignorance made it easier for him. *Damn it! What's it gonna take to get out of here?*

* * *

Jensen stood with his arms folded across his chest, facing a bulletin board with the photos of six different women posted on it. He ignored the sound of the ringing phones, voices, and tapping on keyboards, that came from behind him. He focused on the photograph of a man, the only one that was pinned up. His picture was connected to the women's by different colored lines. Each color represented a reason for contact: known associates, co-workers, or acquaintances.

John Alan Lewis was a person of interest in more than one of the missing women's files. Jensen finally put together a connection. Hard work and luck helped to solve cases; in this instance he felt it was both. He spent countless hours trying to figure out how the women and the suspect were connected.

It wasn't until he dug deeper into Lewis' work history that he saw it. According to his file, Lewis was a part-time taxi driver. Jensen thought it was possible Lewis' job gave him opportunity in some cases, but for others in out of town locations, it was a stretch.

Investigating further, he found that Lewis was licensed to drive truck and school bus. He had quietly left his school bus driving job after complaints of inappropriate behavior. A non-disclosure agreement between Lewis and the School Board stopped Jensen from digging any deeper.

He also discovered that Lewis worked for an expediting company that operated out of Prince Rupert. The owner there told Jensen that he let Lewis go because of a difference of opinion. When pressed for further details, the owner would only say that Lewis broke company rules in regards to having passengers in his vehicle. They were bonded and that was not allowed.

Jensen followed up by stopping one of their drivers for a minor traffic violation. Fearing he might lose his license, the driver told him that he heard Lewis was picking up female hitchhikers in the company truck on his highway runs. After subpoenaing records from the cab and expediting companies, pieces of the puzzle started to fit into place.

Dates when Lewis was on the road coincided with the dates of disappearance for three of the six women. Trip records with the cab company put him at locations where two of the other women had been picked up or dropped off before they went missing. Jensen heard from two other cab drivers that the last victim was a prostitute with whom they had traded rides for sex, but he had no physical proof that she was connected to Lewis.

Inspector Nickerson joined Jensen in front of the bulletin board.

"Do you think you're on to a serial?"

"I believe so, sir."

"Didn't we have him in for questioning, once before?"

Jensen folded his arms, still staring at the board. "No, it was a cursory interview at the cab company. Like the other drivers, he was only questioned about any connection he might have had with the prostitute and he denied knowing her."

Nickerson's eyes flipped back and forth, between Lewis and the victims. "Are you going to bring him in?"

"That's what I've been standing here thinking about. If there are six, you know there's a good chance there are more."

"You're thinking we should watch the guy for a while and maybe catch him in the act?"

"I know it's a long shot, and we're stretched pretty thin here, but I think it's worth the effort. We're chasing our tails just sitting in the office, and following up on all our cases after the fact. I think we need to be more proactive, sir."

Nickerson put both his palms in the small of his back and massaged himself. "I agree. Let me see who I can free up to help you with surveillance—you don't mind putting in some overtime?"

"Not if it means catching a killer."

"I'll get back to you by day's end. Hey, any word from that retired cop—has he been of any help to you?"

"He's doing surveillance on a trucker who was last seen with the Lachance woman. I pointed him in the right direction to get him started. He seems capable, for a city cop. Why, do you think I should reel him in, or be more hands on?"

"No, I agree, he seems capable. I checked, he had a good reputation back home. It's too bad he's only a civilian now. Let's see how he makes out on his own. I know you've got your hands full, but don't let him too far out of your sight."

Jensen nodded. "Will do, Inspector."

23

Follow the Leader

"Life isn't about finding yourself. Life is about creating yourself."
—George Bernard Shaw

Norm was ecstatic when Dale stopped for lunch at home, near Fort Fraser. His bladder was about to burst. He was eyeing up an empty pop bottle, wondering if he could use it without pissing all over himself and the front seat. He assumed the ramshackle trailer was Strickland's, because of the ugly green pickup truck that was parked out front. The color reminded him of the homemade pea soup that his mother used to make. It tasted better than it looked.

There was no inconspicuous place to stop after Dale pulled into his driveway, so Norm drove past the place, and caught part of the license plate number on the pickup. It matched the one that Jensen had given him.

By the time he found somewhere to get off the highway, his target had gone into his trailer. Norm turned down a gravel road, pulled over, and relieved himself. The relief felt almost as good as sex. Almost. There was no way to keep an eye on Strickland's place from the road, so Norm took the two cookies that were left in his lunch bag, and headed into the forest.

He perched himself on a fallen tree stump a few hundred feet from the road. Dale's place was a half kilometer away, but Norm had a clear view of the driver's side of the reefer truck.

Finding Hope

He shook his head while he surveyed the Strickland estate. The beat up mobile home looked like it fell off a truck, and landed where it sat. There was a rusty steel shed, once the box on a reefer truck, sitting near the residence.

The top of a John Deere riding lawn mower was barely visible, sitting in the weeds that surrounded the home. Outdoor furniture consisted of a worn old couch, and an empty vegetable crate sitting on pallets, near the front door. Satellite dishes on top, at opposite ends, looked like wheels—like the trailer really did fall off a truck, and landed upside down.

Norm started to get comfortable, and then a bit drowsy, as he sat listening to the birds chirping and mosquitoes buzzing in his ears. The nasty little blood-suckers and the odd passing truck kept him awake. He had just killed number thirty-seven, when Dale exited the front door carrying a large black duffle bag—the kind used for hockey equipment. A person who could have been his twin, stood in the doorway. As far as Norm could tell, the only different features were longer hair and bigger boobs. He assumed it was Mrs. Strickland.

Dale dropped the bag at the back of the truck, then fiddled in the front cab for a few seconds, before returning to the back, where he loaded the bag into the cargo hold. About two minutes later, he came out with an arm full of produce and handed it to his wife. She had another black duffle bag at her feet. Dale took the second bag and stowed it in the back. He climbed into the cab, and waved goodbye to his wife. Norm was heading back to his pickup when Dale drove past, a cigarette dangling from his lower lip.

Giving him a big lead, Norm got back on his trail, and followed Dale north on Highway #16.

After a while, having passed through Burns Lake, Norm noticed he was getting closer to Dale. The pervert slowed down, pulled onto the right shoulder, and picked up a female

The Highway of Tears

hitchhiker. Not to look suspicious, Norm drove past and took the lead. It wasn't a problem being ahead of Strickland; it was a valuable surveillance technique—taking him by the nose. Norm had used it many times on the job. Unsuspecting criminals usually only looked behind to see if they were being followed.

Barely twenty minutes had passed when Dale pulled over again, and left his passenger off. Norm knew better than to touch the brake pedal and activate his taillights, so he let up on the accelerator and coasted. He could see the young girl was animated; she flailed her arms like she was yelling at Dale. He drove off and left her in the middle of nowhere.

Norm had Dale by the nose the rest of the way to Smithers, where he stopped and made a delivery at a grocery store. The lull in the action allowed him a pee break. He grabbed a Diet Pepsi, and a half dozen cookies—peanut butter and chocolate chunk at Tim Horton's. The Aspartame in the pop might have killed him, but the sugar and caffeine was the perfect blend to keep him awake on the highway. He had no idea how far north Dale was going.

Strickland made another delivery in New Hazelton, then made the turn on to Highway #37. Norm knew they were headed up to Hyder. He was a happy camper when Dale pulled over for a pee, their bladders must have been in sync. He took the opportunity to call Laurie, and tell her he was heading her way. He got her answering machine and left a message.

As the bloodied sky swallowed the sun, the deep rumble in Norm's stomach made him check his watch for the twentieth time that day. He figured it would be after nine by the time they got to Hyder. Hopefully, there was some place for him to stay. Even though Two Snakes told him there was a bedroll behind the seat, he didn't want to sleep in the truck.

"Hey stranger, what brings you to the Sealaska?" Laurie's lips formed a warm smile, but the dark circles under her eyes said that she was tired, and had not given up hope on her friend. She set a cold beer on the bar in front of Norm before he could ask for it. He downed most of it before answering the question.

"Ahhh, that hit the spot. I left you a message—you didn't get it?"

"No. I spent some time with the girls in the park and I just got here. Why, what's going on?"

"I followed Dale Strickland here in his delivery truck. I gave him some time to check in and settle into his room. He took some beer in with him, so I figured it was safe for me to come in here. I'm starving, what's for dinner?"

Laurie was quiet. It was like she was thinking, but didn't know what to say. She acknowledged the grey-haired guy at the other end of the bar, then poured him a draught and brought it over to him. There were only three other men there, one was playing a video game mounted on bar top. She returned with a menu for Norm.

"Did you get a look at Dale when he checked in?" He asked.

"No. The owner is handling the rooms and the kitchen. She was taking delivery of some produce when I came in."

"Dale made the delivery."

"I don't even know what he looks like. Should I be worried, Norm?"

"No, I think he's tucked in for the night. From what I saw on the way up here, I think he's delivering more than just produce."

"Like what—you mean drugs? The owner is a reformed alcoholic and born again Christian. She wouldn't have anything to do with that."

Norm took out his phone and showed Laurie a picture of Dale, that he had taken at the loading dock in Prince George. "I don't know—maybe he's meeting someone here. I saw him load two duffle bags from his home onto his truck, but I don't know if he still has them. He may have dropped them off with one of his produce deliveries. I need to take a look in his truck."

Laurie grabbed her cheaters from behind the bar and put them on. Her eyebrows popped up and her mouth dropped open. "That's Kenny—that's what we call him, because he drinks Kokanee. And you're right, Norm, he always takes his beer back to his room. A cheap bastard, he doesn't have to tip us that way. So he's the asshole who took Hope?"

"Yep. I don't want him to see my face in here. Can you pack me up a couple pounds of wings to go?"

"Sure thing. If he's here, where are you going to stay tonight?"

"I don't know, I have to be ready to get back on him first thing in the morning."

"Why don't you crash at my place—or if you're more comfortable, at Hope's place? It's empty and only five minutes from here. I can get off early if I want, the owner said she'd close up tonight."

"That would be great, Laurie. It's best if Dale doesn't see me or my truck."

"Truck? Where's your bike?"

Norm chuckled and took a drink of beer.

"I traded with a friend. Ninety-nine percent of the vehicles up here are trucks. It blends in."

He downed the rest of his beer, grabbed his keys from the bar, and left some cash to cover his tab. "Can you deliver my wings to me in the parking lot? I'll be in the grey truck—it's the only clean one out there."

"I thought you wanted to blend in?" She tried to force a smile and headed to the kitchen.

Norm walked out into the parking lot and grabbed his mini-Maglite from his truck. He crept through the shadows along the front of the hotel to Strickland's reefer truck. It was parked near room numbers 10 and 12. The rooms were dark with the exception of the televisions being on in both.

At the back of Strickland's truck, Norm checked the handle on the sliding door. It was unlocked. He quietly flipped the latch back and only raised the door high enough to look inside. It was empty. Norm thought about it for a few seconds. He'd seen plenty of hidden compartments during his time in the Drug Squad. He pushed the door up a few more inches, until he was able to crawl into the back.

After closing the door, he turned on his flashlight and climbed to his feet. There was nothing, just some rotting vegetable leaves on the floor and empty space. He walked the inside perimeter checking the walls for lose panels. Nothing. He stood near the front of the empty cargo hold and turned three hundred and sixty degrees, using his flashlight, looking for anything out of the ordinary. Nothing.

He leaned up against the front wall, and thought about the various stops that Strickland had made along the way. The loading docks weren't always in Norm's line of sight. He must have missed the drop.

When he pushed himself off the front wall his right foot slipped. He looked down at a rotten cabbage leaf on the floor. *That's strange.* He used the toe of his boot to claw at the leaf— only half of it was visible. The other half appeared to be stuck in the bottom of the wall. He laid down on the floor and rolled his flashlight along the wall with the beam pointing toward it. The cabbage was definitely stuck under the wall. *Hidden compartment.*

Norm stood up and felt the wall section for movement, but there was none. There were three separate panels that made up the wall. Looking more closely, he found light scratches on the floor that suggested the middle panel somehow slid open, to the right. He played with the panel some more, but it wouldn't budge. There was obviously a button or latch secreted somewhere else in the truck.

He had come across hidden compartments in vehicles before. Acting on a tip from one of his informants, he'd arrested the driver of a brand new Lincoln Continental, who was supposed to be in possession of a large quantity of cocaine. After towing the car to the police garage and tearing it apart, nothing was found. The informant later called Norm back and told him how to disengage the latch for the secret compartment that was built into the bottom of the car.

A sequential activation of three electrical components was needed to unlock the compartment: the radio had to be on and the heater control set to high, and finally the brake pedal needed to be depressed. When that was done an audible *click* sound was heard. It took the garage mechanic another twenty minutes to find the loose piece of metal at the bottom of one of the rocker panels. The cocaine was concealed inside.

There was a chance that Strickland still had the dope hidden in his truck. Norm had to head back south anyway, so maybe he'd get lucky on the way, and see the delivery. He left Strickland's truck the way he found it.

24

Wings & Whoopee

Ten minutes later, Laurie entered the shadows in the parking lot and handed Norm a big brown paper bag.

"The owner says Dale's in room number 12 and he asked for an eight o'clock wakeup call. I'm done for the night, so you can follow me home if you want to."

Norm circled around the parking lot before Laurie got to her car. The window in Dale's room glowed blue, from the television that was on inside. Through the gap in the curtains he could see the man's hefty mid section—a huge lump of fat that resembled a sperm whale, laying belly-up on the beach.

He followed Laurie down the main drag to the border crossing. The customs officer must have recognized her, because he just waved her and Norm's vehicles through.

Dinner smelled really good. He peeked inside the bag and salivated. A whole flock of chickens must have sacrificed their appendages. Laurie also threw in a pile of fries, a tub of coleslaw, and a six-pack of beer. He couldn't resist and started into the wings. The third set of bones flew out the window, when she turned into her driveway.

Norm stopped behind her. The lights were on inside the unit on the right, Laurie's half of the semi-detached bungalow. The unit on the left was in darkness. She got to his door as he was trying to suck the meat off another wing bone.

"C'mon in and eat your dinner—if there's any left."

The Highway of Tears

He looked like a big kid, grease dripped down his chin and crumbs were scattered across his chest. He grabbed the food and his travel bag, and followed her into the house.

"You've been on the road since Prince George. What's that, ten hours?"

"Yeah, maybe a couple more with the stops Dale made for deliveries."

"That's a long day, Norm. Sit down and eat your wings before they get cold."

"That's quite the dinner you packed me, I especially like the dessert in the blue cans."

"Buying you a few beers is the least I can do. I really appreciate what you're doing, Norm. I haven't heard a thing from the cops."

"I don't think you will—I'm pretty well doing this on my own. Shit! I forgot to check in with the Mounties."

"Eat first, they can wait. Do you mind if I go get the girls? The sitter is only a few doors down. I'd like you to meet Charitee."

Norm's mouth was stuffed full of fries so he couldn't answer. He waved her towards the door. Laurie smiled, patted him on the shoulder, then left to go pick up the girls. Not to lose his rhythm, he swallowed, and dug into the coleslaw. It was the creamy kind—his favorite. He laid off the fries so he could work on the wings.

After a loud belch that echoed through the empty house, he finished his last wing and cracked his third beer. Satisfied, he glanced down and gave his belly a little rub. *So much for the diet.* As he stuffed the leftover fries and heap of chicken bones back into the paper bag, he heard giggles and voices coming up the side of the house. Laurie opened the kitchen door, and a little girl bounced into the kitchen.

"Hi, I'm Hanna. I'm six. What's your name?"

She could have passed for Shirley Temple with her pug nose, curly hair, and freckles. A slightly taller, black-haired Barbie doll, stood shyly behind her.

"Hi, Hanna, I'm Norm. Who's your friend, hiding behind you?"

"That's Charitee, she's older than me. Our teacher lets her lead the class out for fire drills."

"Hi Charitee, I'm your mom and Aunt Laurie's friend."

Her big brown eyes got wide for a second, then she grabbed Laurie's hand and snuggled up to her leg. Laurie patted her on the head, gazed at Norm, and sighed. It probably wasn't a good idea for him to mention her mother.

"C'mon girls, lets get ready for bed. Why don't you go relax on the sofa, Norm. The TV remote's on the coffee table."

He wondered into the living room, and plopped down onto the couch. To him, Laurie's color scheme felt depressing: a dark grey sofa and chair, with black and white tables. The walls were a lighter shade of grey than the furniture. There were a few aboriginal prints done in black and white, on the walls. A silver picture frame on the end table caught Norm's eye. It was a photo of Laurie in one of those glamour shots.

He picked up the frame and looked closer. The photo appeared to be recent. Her shoulder-hair length was the same, makeup accented her high cheek bones and amber-brown eyes. He hadn't noticed their unique color before. The picture was obviously taken at a happier time in her life; her open smile and relaxed composure said so.

Laurie was standing in front of him when he looked up. She blushed.

"Great picture, girl."

"Yeah, it's amazing what some make-up and a professional photographer can do."

"No, really, you..."

The Highway of Tears

"You must be tired, Norm. Grab your beer and I'll let you into Hope's place."

She grabbed the baby monitor from the coffee table, and slipped it into her back pocket.

"I like to listen in on the girls, Charitee has wicked nightmares."

Norm grabbed his overnight bag on the way out. When she reached in and turned on the kitchen light next door, he immediately saw the difference in the two women. Hope liked color. Her furnishings were sparse, but accents like the drawings of flowers posted by Charitee, made the house feel alive.

Like his mother had taught him to, Norm removed his boots, and left them by the door. Laurie gave him the nickel tour. Hope's place was laid out exactly as hers, but opposite. He dropped his bag on the floor inside the bedroom door, when she pointed it out to him. He followed her back into the kitchen, where she took a wine glass from the cupboard and filled it from a box of Pinot Grigio that was in the fridge.

"How's your beer, Norm?"

"I'm good."

"Can we sit for a bit? I want to ask you about Hope."

"Sure."

He sat at one end of the couch and she sat at the other—she folded her legs beneath her, and turned towards him. She let out a long sigh that sounded like that last bit of air escaping from a deflated air mattress. Her eyes welled up. He felt her pain and took a swig of beer to cool his throat—he didn't want to get choked up.

She asked, "Do you think I'll ever see her again?"

"I don't know. I won't lie to you, Laurie, the more time that goes by, the less chance there is of a happy ending."

Finding Hope

The floodgates opened. Flowing tears came with a whimper at first, then she sobbed. Norm grabbed some tissue from the box on the table beside him. He turned toward Laurie and put one hand on her shoulder, while he blotted her tears with the other. She cupped his hand in hers then pulled herself closer, and nuzzled her face into his chest. His arms fell around her torso and he hugged her tightly.

It felt like he had dust in both his eyes; he sniffed and blinked hard a few times, effectively holding back the reflex to cry with her. They embraced in silence for at least a minute. Laurie's sobs slowly subsided and became sniffles. Norm handed her more tissue. She gazed up at him like a puppy on death row. Instead of taking the tissue, she craned her neck and kissed him. It was a soft kiss that neither of them backed away from.

Norm stopped first. "Laurie, I..."

"You don't have to say anything, Norm."

He kissed her back. Her lips had the texture of marshmallows and tasted like pears. A sauvignon blanc, he guessed. Laurie broke contact for a split second to catch her breath, but Norm pulled her back to him and kissed her harder. He gently parted and traced her lips with the tip of his tongue then took her lower lip into his mouth like it was a juicy wedge of a tangerine. They fell backwards on the couch, with Laurie on top, melding her body into his.

He felt his own heart beating in his chest, or was it hers? Her breasts tried to push their way out of her low-cut blouse. He set them free and pressed his face into her cleavage. She smelled like baby powder. They ripped at each other's clothes. The excitement and awkwardness of it all made him feel like he was back in high school. His loins were on fire—it was great to be so alive.

They found themselves writhing and naked on the sofa, their eyes locked in a trance. He marveled at her soft skin and she admired his muscled arms. Their heat and passion brought a happy ending for both of them.

They remained glued together like two dogs in heat. Their pleasure lingered, and a glimmer of hope shone in both their eyes. It was as though they had known each other for a lifetime. Gratification produced smiles that would become lifelong memories. It would be their special bond.

The phone rang and the machine answered it. Someone could be heard breathing on the other end, but the caller said nothing and hung up.

25

Secreted

Norm wanted to set up surveillance on Strickland before he hit the road, so he got up early and headed for the Alaskan border by seven-thirty. Crossing into Hyder, he drove into the Sealaska parking lot to make sure the reefer truck was still there.

It was, so he headed back to the edge of town, and pulled into a driveway, just north of the border crossing. There was only one way out of town. Strickland would have to drive right by him on his way back to Canada.

While waiting for the great white whale to swim by, Norm dug into the goodie bag that Laurie had handed him on the way out the door. She was sweet—not really his type, but a good woman just the same. *I need to get me one of those, some day.* There was an insulated cup in the bag that felt warm. Sure enough, Laurie had filled it with coffee—too bad he didn't drink the stuff. How could she know?

There were two sandwiches, some cookies, and an apple in the bag. He made breakfast of the apple while he waited. And waited. At about ten minutes after nine, just as Norm eyed up the cookies, he saw the reefer truck heading his way. He slouched down in the seat as Strickland passed by. To Norm's surprise, Dale turned off the main road before the border, towards the harbor.

By the time Norm caught up at the marina, Strickland was backed up to a boat that was moored at the main slip. The place

The Highway of Tears

was deserted with only a handful of other boats in the water. *Shit!* Norm stood out like a uniformed cop at a crack house. *Think fast and blend in.* He drove past the truck and went further down the dock. A man stood near a light blue boat, waiting for Strickland. Norm casually waved, like any other local would do. The man hesitated for a second then waved back.

Norm parked in front of a fishing trawler, three berths down from them. He got out of the truck, grabbed a tool box from the back and boarded the empty boat. Out of the corner of his eye, he saw Strickland and the other man talking to each other and looking in his direction. Norm pretended to ignore them and fiddled around in the tool box. They continued to watch him so he sat on the back seat, pretending he was working on something.

The two men stared at him for what seemed like an eternity, but it was probably only a few minutes. He watched them with his peripheral vision. Strickland was animated and talked with his hands. He acted like he was in a hurry. The other man seemed to be in charge, and he was very calm. Grey hair bushed out from under his black captain's hat and he sported a big Colonel Mustard type moustache. Norm couldn't hear what they talked about.

Finally, Colonel Mustard nodded, and Strickland climbed into the back of his truck. One at a time, he removed and handed the two black duffle bags to the Colonel. He carried them onto his boat.

Big fat Dale sat and waited on the back end of his truck, while the colonel disappeared below deck. He returned a couple minutes later with three plastic crates, each about the size of a big cooler. They looked heavy when he handled them up to Dale, one at a time. He also gave Strickland a plastic shopping bag.

He stuck his chubby face inside it, like he was bobbing for apples, then nodded to the colonel, and disappeared into the back of his truck.

Norm had his back to the men, with his head cocked just enough to watch them from the corner of his eye. It was time to call the cavalry. He checked the clock on his phone and dialed Jensen's number. It rang through to voice mail. *Shit, that figures.* He tried Inspector Nickerson's number next. He answered on the second ring.

"Good morning, Inspector. It's Norm Strom, how are you today?"

"I'm fine, Norm, but I haven't read the overnight summary yet. How are you doing? Any luck with that trucker...Strickland, is it?"

"Dale Strickland—that's who I'm calling you about. I spun him from the loading docks on your end like Jensen suggested, all the way up to Hyder."

"That's a fair haul, Norm, did he do anything suspicious?"

Norm learned during his years as a cop just how to play with a deck that was stacked in favor of the bad guys. He knew exactly what he had to tell the Inspector to get what he needed to get the job done.

"As a matter of fact, Inspector, Strickland stopped home along the way, and picked up two duffle bags full of marihuana. He just delivered them to a guy on a boat, here in Hyder."

"How do you know it's marihuana?"

Norm shook his head. "Call it cop's intuition, during the exchange the guy with the boat gave Strickland a shopping bag and...holy shit! Hang on a minute Inspector."

Norm's chin fell to his chest and he almost dropped the phone. "You're not gonna believe this—the boat guy just took a woman with a black hood over her head, from his boat to the truck."

"What? That sounds like kidnapping...not a drug deal. What does she look like?"

Norm looked through the binoculars, but couldn't offer any more detail. "I can't tell, because of the hood. Her hands are tied in front of her. This isn't good—I've gotta do something."

"Stay put, Norm. You don't know who the other man is or if he's armed. I'll make a call and send some uniformed cops your way. Are you at the harbor in Hyder?"

"Wait, Inspector, it looks like they're packing up. Your guys will never get here in time. Do they have jurisdiction on this side of the border?"

"Technically no, but..."

"I'm not worried about technicalities, but I worked in a border town, and I have an idea. We have to work fast because the boat is casting off. Can you call the border guard and have him stop Strickland on his way back into Canada—make it look like a routine inspection? Maybe they can look for the secret compartment."

"What secret compartment? Hang on, Norm, let me call Canada Customs first. I'll have to put you on hold."

As the boat drifted away from the dock, Strickland slid off the back deck of his truck like a walrus slipping into the sea. He pulled the back door shut, flipped the latch, and waddled towards the driver's door. Norm rifled through the tool box looking for something to write with so he could copy down the serial number of the boat, but his pen and notepad were in the truck. Strickland drove off.

Colonel Mustard's boat passed in front of Norm's, heading out of the harbor. He recited the serial number on the way to his truck, but it was too long to remember. Reaching in the open driver's window, he grabbed the pen and pad off the dash. *For shit's sake!* Now the other boats obscured the Colonel's. The name of the boat was painted on the stern. It was the Seven Shees. The capital S's were curvy mermaids.

"Hello...hello!" The Inspector shouted on the Norm's phone—it was still on the seat in the boat. He jumped back in the boat and picked it up.

"Sorry, Inspector. I tried to get the serial number off the boat, but could only catch the name of it—the Seven Shees. It's an older, faded blue fishing boat, with down riggers on both sides. The captain is..."

"Slow down, Norm, I don't take shorthand. Let me tell you first off, that a patrol car is on the way to the border—the customs officer requested backup because he's alone there. Are you going to talk to them?"

"I was hoping to stay out of sight, and be an anonymous informant...for the time being. I'm not sure what they'll make of a civilian telling them how to do their jobs. The Customs Officer has the authority to search the truck—with or without my input. I'll be nearby, watching. What can you do about the boat? Is it in international waters once it leaves the harbor?"

"That's a good question Norm, I'm not up on maritime law. I'll look into it and pass on the information."

"They might want to watch where the Seven Shees goes and who takes delivery of the weed. Besides the drugs, it looks like the captain is into human trafficking."

"I hear you, Norm, but that decision is beyond my control."

Beyond my control. Norm had gotten used to hearing that phrase way too often during his career in policing. It was basically an excuse to pass the buck, or avoid responsibility. It was a common theme among those in the top brass who were not decision makers.

By the time the Inspector hung up the phone, Norm had parked within eyeshot of the Canada Customs booth. The Customs Officer was questioning Strickland about the paperwork that he produced. An RCMP cruiser pulled up near the booth, but the uniformed cop remained in his car. Strickland became agitated. He swiveled his big melon back and forth between the two officials as though he was watching them play ping pong.

The Customs Officer wasn't satisfied with Strickland's paperwork, and he motioned for him to open up the back. Norm strained to listen, and was able to catch a few loud words that were uttered by Strickland—something about perishable goods that would spoil. The Customs Officer moved to the back of the truck, and demanded that it be opened. The Cop got out of his car and joined them.

From where Norm was parked, he could see the driver's side of the truck and about half way inside the cargo hold when Strickland opened the door. The Customs Officer had Strickland move the plastic crates closer to the door where there was more light. The Cop joined in the search. He slipped past the other two men and started snooping around inside the back of the truck.

Dale was told to open the crates. From Norm's vantage point, it looked like some kind of fish, packed on ice. Strickland waved his hands, and stammered a hundred miles an hour. He kept watching the Cop while he talked to the Customs Officer. Norm couldn't see the Cop until he got closer to the door—he was examining the wall and floor panels. Some of Dale's ranting was aimed in his direction, but the Cop never said a word.

Obviously not happy with the paperwork for his load, the Customs Officer waved Strickland over to the office. The Cop stood in the back door of the truck watching the fat man, who looked back over his shoulder at him. To Norm, it was a sure sign of a guilty mind. The Cop took another quick look inside the cargo bay, then hopped down from the truck and pulled out his mobile phone.

Norm's phone rang; It was Inspector Nickerson. "Norm, the patrol cop is on the phone and says there's nothing in the back of the truck except for some salmon on ice. He doesn't see any trap doors or secret compartments...or women."

"That's the whole idea, there's probably a switch or release in the cab somewhere. They didn't even search the front of the truck."

"Hang on, Norm, he's on another line."

He could see the Cop was listening—he nodded his head and looked around, as though he was looking to see where the information was coming from. Norm sat there in the truck, on the edge of his seat. Did he have to go and show these guys how to do their job? He had no authority to search that truck. Part of him wanted to grab the tire iron and charge over there and rip the back wall panel off.

"He says he doesn't have any grounds to search the front of the truck, according to the information he's been provided."

"You gotta be kidding me. Whatever happened to the ways and means act? Aren't you the one giving the orders?"

"Easy, Norm. He's a rookie, a new breed that goes by the book. They're all paranoid that they'll get their asses sued and lose their jobs. And he doesn't work for me...different detachment, different boss. His has probably gone fishing for the day, and the rookie doesn't want to disturb him. I'm sorry, we're not perfect. Listen, Norm, I am thinking that..."

"I'm way ahead of you, sir. What goes in, must come out. I'm going to follow the tub of shit and see where he takes the girl. It might just prove to be a lead in helping me find Hope Lachance."

"You took the words right out of my mouth, Norm. It sounds like a good plan. If the girl is in that truck, I hope she's okay. We'll look like a bunch of idiots if something happens to her before we can find her."

Norm mumbled under his breath. "Too late for that."

Strickland left the customs office with more paperwork than he went in with. He closed the truck's back door, and flipped the latch. When he got to the driver's door, he crumpled the papers into a ball and threw them into the open window. The Cop just shook his head, and started to walk to his cruiser, but he heard a noise that stopped him dead in his tracks.

26

PTSD

"Death smiles at all of us; all a man can do is smile back."
— Maximus Meridius, Gladiator

Two Snakes had never seen so many cops in one place. The task force's operations room at the Ramada was abuzz. A local farmer had discovered a body on his farm. Nobody paid attention to the aboriginal man who stood inside the doorway, in awe of the chaos around him. Cops in uniform and plain clothes were busy on their phones, interviewing people at their desks, and hurriedly bee-bopping around the room.

Two Snakes walked un-noticed across the room to a large bulletin board full of photographs. He saw pictures of a young girl—in life and in death. There were other pictures: a high school yearbook photo, a naked girl in a shallow grave, and the surrounding farm where the body was discovered. The body was posed, with her hands crossed over her genitals.

The girl looked familiar. Two Snakes reached into his pocket and removed the picture of Dakota and Dee. The hairs on the back of his neck came to attention when he held his picture up to the one on the board, for comparison. A voice, over his right shoulder, caused him to turn about. It was Jensen.

"Can I help you, sir?"

"I'm looking for my niece—she's missing."

Jensen pointed to the end of the room. "You'll have to go over to that desk, and make a report with the officer."

The Highway of Tears

"This girl in the photo up here on the board—I think it's Dee Reynolds. She is...was a friend of my niece."

Jensen looked at the picture Two Snakes was holding in his hand, but didn't let on that he recognized the other girl—the one with the earrings.

"Yes, we believe it's Miss Reynolds. We're waiting for her family to arrive from Calgary to identify her. Who's the dark-haired girl in your photo?"

"That's my niece, Dakota. Did you find any more graves on the farm?"

"I'm not at liberty to discuss anything about this case with you, sir. Please, go see the intake officer, she'll take a missing person's report from you. You'll have to excuse me, I have a lot of work to do."

Two Snakes walked over to the desk he'd been referred to. A young female Constable, in uniform, asked how she could help him. He sat down and slid the picture of Dakota and Dee across the desk to her, with his index finger pointing to his niece. She asked for his name, and who he was reporting missing. He saw her mouth forming the words, but it was like he was looking at her through a glass of water. He answered the questions, but his words sounded muffled in his ears.

He stared at the Constable. He could see her talking, but it wasn't her—It was Dakota. Then he couldn't hear the words anymore. *Her face was pale, like Dee's in the picture of her dead body. He saw Dakota in the bottom of the grave. Then the corpse was her father, Roger—his best friend. His body was mutilated from the IED that killed him. He was covered in blood...there was so much blood.*

Two Snakes reached out to Roger and saw his own hands were bloody. It was his own—from the gaping wound on his right leg. He felt the searing pain and broke out in a cold sweat.

Someone yelled at him but he couldn't hear the words over the ringing in his ears. "Trooper...are you okay?"

He stared at the face, but it wasn't the medic. It was the female Constable, she was talking to him. He read her lips and tried to focus on her voice.

"Mr. Greene...are you okay?"

He noticed he was gripping his injured leg with both hands. "I'm sorry—I'm not feeling well. I have to get out of here. Maybe I'll come back later."

"But sir, I didn't get all your information..."

"Sorry. I'll call you..."

Two Snakes struggled to get up from his chair. He was unsteady on his feet. He stumbled out the door, and didn't look back until he got outside the building. He leaned on one of the cement pillars under the carport outside the lobby. He wiped his brow with his trembling hand. He took three long and deep breaths, trying to regain his composure. The ringing in his ears subsided. It wasn't the first time he'd lost it. He suffered from PTSD.

27

Well Laid Plans

Once again Hope found herself locked in her room with nothing but her own thoughts—of each and every moment that she missed being with her little angel. Hurtful and hateful thoughts of the men in her life continued to torture her mind, body and soul. What did she ever do to deserve such a life? Would it ever end?

After her request for feminine products, Bear said he would go into town to buy her some. He didn't look happy so she promised to make him a special dinner when he got back. Pushing the envelope, she asked if she could get started in the kitchen while he was gone, but he only pointed to her room.

The notches on the wall that signified her days in captivity resembled a picket fence, the third section was in progress. She contemplated escape since day one. Her first plan was to use a knife, or even a fork to gouge his eyes out, but he was twice her size and watched her every move.

She searched the cabin whenever she had an extra second, looking for some kind of poison that she could put into his food or drink. There was nothing that he wouldn't taste or discover.

Sitting on the front porch one day, while Bear was cutting wood, she thought of making a run for the road. She went so far as to count how many steps he was away from her, trying to guess at how fast he could run and if he would be able to catch her. She had to be faster than him, but where would she run to?

Where did the road go? He had the truck, and could just run her down with it.

He kept the truck keys somewhere in his room. Even the guns were locked up and that key ring never left Bear's pants pocket. It was the same ring that held the key to her room. He guarded that key ring as though it was his third testicle.

She thought of ways to kill him when he was grunting and groaning on top of her. What else was there to think of? But how do you kill a man who's twice your size when he's on top of you. If only she could get a message to someone...anyone, somehow. Was trying to escape worth the risk of him physically hurting her or even killing her? She really had no idea what he was capable of.

Bear wandered around inside the trading post, picking up some of the items that were on Hope's list and a few things that he needed. He scratched his head while he stood in the aisle, looking at the note. The store clerk approached him.

"Can I help you find something, sir?"

He was instantly relieved and handed the note to the older woman. She held up the note and smiled when she read it.

"Don't worry, young man. We have exactly what your woman needs."

Bear was horrified. He stared at the back of the note that the woman was holding up in front of her. There was writing on that side.

It read: *"Help me! I've been kidnapped by this man."*

* * *

Jensen pounded away at his keyboard. He was almost done the search warrant for the residence of John Alan Lewis. His suspicions had proven right about Lewis. Now he just had to build a case to prove it. The farmer finding the body was a good piece of luck. Some investigative work on his part was making the picture on the puzzle more recognizable.

It was the farmer's hunting dog that found the body. After the dog scratched away some dirt and exposed a piece of clothing, the farmer saw a human hand. While the body was being exhumed, Jensen questioned the farmer. There was no evidence to suggest that he had anything to do with the crime. He would never have reported finding the body if he was involved.

According to the owner, the cattle farm was a busy place, with different people coming and going, but one man's name caught Jensen's attention. The farmer said that a man named Johnny, did odd jobs for him. He was an unemployed truck driver who sometimes drove cab. Johnny picked up and delivered a load of straw to the farm and stacked it in and around the back of the barn, where the body was found. He said that Johnny worked into night, unsupervised.

Jensen had a photo array of suspects that included John Alan Lewis. The farmer identified Lewis' picture as being the same Johnny, who worked for him. He said he didn't know where the man resided.

After a little more legwork Jensen located Lewis' residence. A trucking company confirmed the address in their records, and a neighbor near the residence identified his photograph.

The house was a duplex in the older part of town, where the suspect rented the back half and garage. Jensen was reluctant to talk to the landlord before he obtained the warrant in case the man tipped off his tenant.

With the suspect having access to the scene of the burial, Jensen had plenty of reason to question him if and when he was located. His grounds for a search warrant at Lewis's residence were thin, but he had to try. Forensic evidence from the grave site and the autopsy would take days or even weeks to process and he could always re-apply for the warrant later if it was denied.

If Lewis was home when the warrant was executed, he could be arrested on suspicion of murder. Once arrested, anything in plain sight around him was fair game to the police. It is one of those loopholes in the law that works in favor of the police, if the suspect is stupid enough to leave any evidence lying about.

It was almost noon by the time Jensen finished preparing the search warrant. He wished the process was as quick and efficient as you see on TV, where the cops make a phone call and the warrant is issued on the spot. In his world, it took hours to complete. He checked on the status of the surveillance team before he got the warrant endorsed. All was quiet, with no signs of movement at the suspect's residence. Jensen went to see the Judge.

When he walked back into the task force office, Inspector Nickerson shouted to get everyone's attention. Jensen looked around the room and thought it was excessive, but after all, they were dealing with a suspected killer. There was a six man ERT, along with four investigators, two forensics specialists and four uniformed officers.

The plan, with everyone's assignment, was already laid out on one of the bulletin boards. The uniformed officers were to block the street off to any traffic, while the ERT stealthily approached the house and made a quick entry, forcibly if necessary. The investigators and forensics people would go in after the house was secured. Jensen stood proud as a peacock, feeling superior to everyone else in the room, as they went over the plan one last time.

That afternoon the landlord found out just how terrifying it is to be physically taken down at gunpoint by a heavily armed assault team. The man literally shit himself. The ERT thought

The Highway of Tears

he was Lewis when they found him in the garage. The target was not home.

After the landlord cleaned himself up Jensen interviewed him. He was still visibly shaken, but told Jensen that he didn't know where his tenant was. He said he hadn't seen him in a couple days and that was quite normal since he came and went at different times of the day and night. The landlord said that Lewis was a good tenant, who usually paid his rent on time, although he'd asked for extensions a couple times when he was short on cash.

Jensen asked about the old taxi cab that was in the garage. The man said it belonged to Lewis—he was always tinkering with it. He said he'd seen him take it out on the road on more than one occasion. One of the forensic technicians examined the car while the interview was taking place. The other, along with investigators, tore Lewis' unit apart.

After the interview Jensen checked on how the search of the house was going. He walked from room to room, disgusted at how dirty and unkempt the place was. There were empty takeout food containers on the counters, dirty dishes in the sink, and dust bunnies the size of slippers, on the floors. Jensen went into the bedroom where another cop was going through the closet.

Without turning around, the cop suggested, "You might want to check that jewellery box on the dresser...souvenirs maybe?"

Jensen opened the jewellery box with a gloved hand. There was an assortment of medallions, chains and trinkets—some men's and some women's. He looked in the mirror, seeing the other cop still had his back to him. Jensen quickly slipped his hand in and out of his pocket and dropped a silver feather earring into the jewellery box.

He answered the cop. "Yeah, maybe—mostly costume stuff, can you bag and tag it before you finish up in here?"

"Sure, no problem. There's nothing in the closet."

Jensen cracked a smile as he left the house, and went to check out the garage, the forensic technician had towed the taxi outside.

"We're taking it to our indoor facility, Sir, so we can have a closer look at it. It's pretty dirty inside so I'm sure we'll have hundreds of samples to examine."

Jensen barked, "Do what you have to do, but put DNA comparison at the top of your list. We need evidence to link Lewis to the body found at the farm."

"Understood, sir."

One of the investigators searching the garage, called Jensen inside. "What do you make of this?" He indicated a newer patch of cement in the centre of the floor, where the taxi had been parked.

Jensen stared down at the floor. "I don't know. Go fetch the owner and we'll ask him."

A few minutes later the landlord stepped into the garage, his eyes were drawn to the new cement where Jensen was standing. No question was necessary.

"Strange. That's not the original floor, officer. His taxi is always parked there. I don't know why he would fix the cement, there was nothing wrong with it."

"The search warrant authorizes us to rip up that floor."

"But I thought you were only looking for evidence of a crime...oh, my..."

"Yes, sir. If we find what I believe is under that floor, it will be evidence of a crime."

"You think something is buried under there, don't you?"

"Someone. We won't know until we get down there. You'll have to wait outside, sir. We'll never get a backhoe in here. Someone get a sledgehammer and pick."

28

On the Road Again

Dale Strickland also heard the thumping noise, but he purposely ignored it, climbed into the truck's cab and shut the driver's door. Before he could drive away from the customs booth, the Police Officer was at his door.

"Hey, what was that thumping noise I just heard?"

"Oh, that was the refrigerator's compressor kicking in."

The Cop wasn't convinced. "Can you shut the engine off, Sir, so we don't hear the compressor?"

Strickland became animated again. Norm could see him talking with his hands in the window. The Cop held his ground.

"It's not good to shut the engine down, Officer—I have perishables in the back that have to stay cold, or they will spoil. I have hundreds of miles to go and if the delivery is rotten I don't get paid."

"You only have to shut it down for a minute."

"You don't understand. It takes time for the diesel to fire back up and more time for the generator and compressor to kick in. The fish could thaw by then."

"Okay, Sir. You can keep the engine running, but I need you to step out of the vehicle, please."

"What for? This is police harassment—I already cleared customs and now I have to pay some bullshit fine for my paperwork."

"Step out from your vehicle now, Sir. I need to search the cab."

"This is fucking bullshit, I'm an American and I have rights!"

"And you're trying to enter Canada, Sir. I have reason to believe you are carrying contraband in your vehicle, and I'm going to search it."

The Customs Officer returned to the Cop's side before Strickland climbed out of his truck. They weren't releasing him. Norm wanted to cheer out loud. Maybe the Policeman was smarter than he'd let on. He pointed into the cab, and said something to the Customs Officer.

Strickland reluctantly got out of the truck, continuing his tirade. The Customs Officer climbed up into the cab to search it while the loud chubby man verbally assaulted the Cop. He flailed his hands in the air, like he was fending off a wasp attack. Norm shook his head, remembering the hundreds of times that he'd been in that situation—where he wanted to punch someone in the mouth, just to shut them up.

After what seemed like an hour, but was probably only ten minutes, the Customs Officer stepped down from the truck waving a women's brassiere, with cups that could have held basketballs, and a hair brush.

"What are you doing with these things in your truck, sir?"

"Those are my wife's, I didn't know they were in there. She rides with me sometimes and sleeps in the back bunk. What's the big deal?"

The officers stepped away from Strickland to converse in private. Norm could tell that they had suspicions, but they had not found the secret compartment or any way into it from the cab.

The Cop waved Strickland on. He stopped yammering and turned towards his truck. The officials walked away from the reefer, looking to the ground, and shaking their heads back and forth—the battle was lost.

Norm was pissed. As he pulled out to follow Strickland, his phone rang. It was Inspector Nickerson, he ignored the call. Driving by the Cop, Norm saw that he was on the phone—probably with Nickerson. *Canada's Finest...yeah right, whatever happened to Dudley Do Right and always getting their man?*

The Customs Officer waved Norm on before he could even pull over. *Good move, Buddy, I would have just said something stupid anyway.* While Strickland headed back south, Norm stuffed a sandwich in his mouth to stop himself from clenching his teeth in anger. Food always had a soothing effect on him.

While he drove, he wondered about Hope. *Is she even still alive or is this all a waste of time? Time, now I have a girl stuffed into the back of a fat pervert's truck to worry about.* He looked at the gas gage, and was glad he'd filled up earlier in the morning. There was a lot of nothing on the road ahead of him. *Hmm...where is that place with the homemade pies I stopped at with Louie? I wonder what he's up to?*

It was almost noon when Norm saw Trans-Canada Hwy #16 in the distance. Being that Strickland had fish on board, Norm assumed he'd be heading back south to Smithers or Prince George. It didn't look like much of a load, but perhaps he had more pick-ups to make. Time would tell.

He assumed right. The big blimp stopped to visit the crazy Indians in New Hazleton. He made a cash deal there for three more containers of fish. They were done fishing for the day, and about half way through a bottle of whiskey, probably not their first. Strickland shared a couple of belts with them before he got back on the road.

The down time was much appreciated. Norm managed lunch—fresh smoked salmon with cream cheese on an onion bagel. It was awesome, considering the sandwich was from a ramshackle roadside hut in the boonies. If he had a cooler he would have taken more salmon to go. He was looking in the mirror, wiping a glob of cream cheese off his moustache, when Strickland threw him a curve. He drove north, towards Kispoix.

Norm scrambled to grab the map. *Where the hell is Humpty Dumpty going now? Maybe he's dropping the girl off...but where? To some mountain man in the middle of nowhere? That makes no sense at all. Guess I'll have to play follow the leader for a while.*

Somewhere before Kispoix, Strickland turned off the highway on to a side road. Norm was so far back, trying to keep out of sight, that it took him a couple minutes to reach the road. It was not signed and not on the map. The loose, rocky road turned and disappeared into the bush. He was euchred, Norm had no idea where the road went and if he tried to follow down the laneway he could run right into the truck.

He sat at the intersection for a moment in thought. There was a good chance that Strickland was dropping off the woman or the weed somewhere down the road. Norm had to see what was going on, so he drove a bit further up the highway, and parked. Before leaving the truck, he used an old surveillance trick and opened the hood to make it look like he was broken down. He grabbed his binoculars and trotted into the bush, trying to stay parallel to the road.

Norm walked and jogged through the bush for at least two kilometers, dodging trees and stumps, and occasionally getting his feet caught in tangles of vines. It was brutal and slow going. Then he came to a stream, which was too deep to cross. He followed the stream a couple hundred meters and was able to scramble over it by traversing a fallen tree. He froze in his tracks when he heard voices.

Hiding behind a tree, Norm peered through the binoculars in the direction of the voices. He saw the back of Strickland's truck, and a log cabin behind it. He heard the truck's door close and the engine start. *Fuck!* Strickland was on the move again. He ran back to where he crossed the stream, and saw that there was a path that led back to the cabin.

Dodging fallen trees, Norm worked his way back towards the highway. When he heard the truck getting further and further away, he took to running on the laneway to make better time. He was not as young or as in shape as he once was; his legs ached and his lungs burned. Sweat poured down his forehead, and into his eyes.

When he finally made it back to the highway Strickland was nowhere in sight. He stopped on the shoulder of the highway and bent over with his hands on his knees, trying to catch his breath. A silver minivan drove by, going south. The driver looked right at him as he drove by. The man looked familiar, but Norm was too tuckered out to think about it. He staggered back to his truck, and closed the hood.

Thinking there was nothing further north up the highway to interest Strickland, Norm headed back south, the way that they had come. He wiped the sweat from his eyes with the bottom of his tee shirt, then put the pedal to the metal. Downing the half-bottle of water that was beside him, Norm wondered what Strickland was doing back in the bush at that cabin. He made a mental note of landmarks near the private road, then raced after big fat fucker.

* * *

Two Snakes sat in his blue bomber, shell-shocked. He performed some relaxation exercises to pull out of his episode. He inhaled and exhaled deeply through his nose three times, then stretched and relaxed his muscles starting with his neck. He rolled his shoulders and stretched his back. Just when he thought he had regained his composure, he looked in the mirror and saw Dakota's face. He slumped forward, tears flowed and he sobbed.

He snapped out of his funk when he heard a car door close, and an engine start. A dark blue SUV with government plates drove by him in the parking lot. It was Jensen. *Asshole! There's sure a lot of those SUV's around here. He should wash that thing—looks like he's been driving through the bush. Damn Cops—what are they good for? I wonder what that retired bastard is up to? Maybe we can help each other now, I should call him.*

Norm sounded out of breath when he answered the phone.

"I didn't think you'd answer—beings you're on a fixed income and can't afford the long distance. Why are you out of breath, Kemosabe?"

"I wouldn't have answered if I knew it was you. I thought you were Jensen—I've been tailing that trucker named Strickland, I asked you about. I lost him in the bush, and had to run back to my truck...I mean your truck."

"Jensen. I just saw that asshole."

"Really? Him and his boss aren't answering their phones."

"Yeah, things are a bit crazy—they found a body on a farm, just outside town. I kinda know the girl."

"Kinda? That sucks."

"Where're you at? I'd like to meet up and talk about some of the shit that's going down around here."

"I'm up in the boonies, heading south towards New Hazelton."

"Shit, that's almost a full day from here. Good country for bear hunting."

"Yeah...I'm trying to catch a big fat one, but your truck doesn't go fast enough."

"Don't worry, Norm. There ain't many roads up that way. You'll run into him, eventually. Don't take that literally— unless you want to sign over your hawg to me."

"Yeah, yeah. Hey, I think I see my guy up the road. I'll call you back later."

"Be safe, Kemosabe."

29

Booty Calls

Hope agreed, it resembled an elephant. Charitee pointed to it while they lay on their backs, studying the ever-changing collection of puffy clouds in the big sky. Hope loved picnicking with her little Angel. They had just finished their blueberry pie and were trying to see how many animal shapes they could find floating effortlessly above them.

Charitee's voice faded. Hope felt the warmth of the sun on her eyelids. Startled, she opened them, and recognized the wooden surroundings of the room she was being held captive in. Sunlight was beaming through the window in her locked door. She heard footsteps on the porch, and then in the kitchen.

"Hi, Bear. Can I come out for a while?"

He stomped across the kitchen, directly to her door. If looks could kill, she was in big trouble. He peered in the window. His face was red and his eyes looked like they were about to pop out of his head. *Crap, he saw the note.*

"Is something wrong, Bear?"

He removed the note from his pocket, then crumpled it in his fist and threw it at her face. The note bounced off the top of her head when she ducked. She stepped back from the door, afraid that he would reach through the window and strangle her. The gig was up. She sat down on her bed and peered at the wall across the room. Bear's cold stare chilled her to the bone.

A million different thoughts ran through her mind...did anyone else see the note? Did Bear say anything? What would he do to her now? She closed her eyes tight, trying not to think about the possible consequences. Hope felt flush. A burning sensation in her eyes, then tears that soaked her eyelashes. They pooled there for a moment, then spilled gently down her cheeks. She was left with only one thought. Despair.

While she lay there crying, she heard the sound of gravel crunching under tires, in the driveway. Odd. She had not seen anyone but Bear since she'd been abducted. She looked at the door. He had slammed the window shut when he walked away, but it was ajar and unlocked. She heard a metal door close, then voices. They had company.

* * *

Dale Strickland felt proud, he giggled to himself. Life was great. He made good money transporting drugs and women. Fish and produce covered his truck expenses, so the other cargo was gravy. Of course, he kept most of it from his wife. He wondered why he even kept her around. She didn't work, but had no time to clean the house. The only thing she knew how to cook was chicken nuggets and fish sticks.

Then there was the sex, or the lack of it. Blowjobs stopped the day after they were married, and banging her was like trying to do the Pillsbury dough girl—he had to look though her rolls to find the wet spot. At least she kept his dogs fed.

He thought about the girl in the back of the truck. *Maybe I should pull off the road somewhere and take a round out of her. Someone has to test the merchandise.* It wouldn't be the first time he'd done it, but the last one got a little rough and he left some marks. The buyer wasn't happy and paid him less than the agreed price for the spoiled merchandise. He got excited just thinking about getting his nuts off.

Up ahead, on the highway, Dale saw the private road that led to Bear's cabin. Maybe he would pay him to have some fun with the girl and he could watch. That way he could honestly say he didn't touch the merchandise. Bear usually bought his fish so either way, he'd make some money by stopping in. As he turned onto the side road, he wondered what Bear had done with Hope. He regretted not taking a piece of that action.

Dale pulled up behind Bear's pickup, and saw him splitting wood with an axe. He stared for a minute, reminding himself to never make the man angry. Bear was as solid as an oak tree. He turned towards the truck, and slung the axe over his shoulder. He looked angry, but Dale couldn't recall ever seeing the man looking any other way.

"I come in peace, bearing gifts."

Bear leaned the axe against the chopping block then pulled the front of his tee shirt up and wiped the sweat from his face. The two men met half way between the truck and wood pile, where Dale waved Bear towards the back of the truck.

"I've got some fresh fish...and maybe a little something else for dessert."

He eyed Bear, who scrunched his face, then raised one eyebrow. A bead of sweat rolled into his eye. He raised his arm, and wiped it with his shoulder.

"Hey man, I really gotta take a dump—can I use your shitter while you check out the fish?"

Bear hesitated a second, looked toward the cabin, then shrugged. Dale popped one of the coolers open. "Here, take a look. I'm crowning man—the turtle's poking its head out." He started toward the cabin.

Hope's shoes were on the porch next to the front door. Dale was on the first step when he noticed them, but he never broke stride. He was too busy doing the poop-walk, with his ass cheeks clenched tight. Bear dug into the ice in the cooler, and pulled some fish out for a closer look. He was rooting through the second cooler when he heard screaming and shouting in the cabin. Bear dropped the fish and ran inside.

Hope looked like she was trying to climb through the window in her door, but it wasn't even large enough to get her head through. Her face looked resembled kneaded dough being pushed through a cookie cutter. She called Dale every four letter word imaginable.

The bathroom door was closed, but Bear could smell Dale. It was like something crawled in there and died. He looked at Hope. She was hysterical. Not sure what to do, he turned around, and went back outside.

Hope's tirade continued until Dale left the cabin—twice as fast as he went in.

"Jesus Christ...can't a guy shit in peace around here? What the hell is she still doing here? I thought you would have gotten rid of her by now."

Bear didn't answer, he was still looking at the fish.

"I always wanted to bang that half-breed, but she'd probably rip my dick off and shove it up my ass, just for fun. Hey, I got something else in the truck you might be interested in—if that bitch ain't playing nice."

The remark was met with a cold stare.

"Lookie here...I'll show you what I got." Dale grunted out loud as he hefted himself up into the back of the truck. He had released the latch for the secret door before he shut the engine off. He waddled up to the front of the cargo bay and waved for Bear to follow.

Bear was shocked when he saw the secret wall panel open. He was astonished when he saw what was behind the wall. A young girl lay on the wood floor, gagged and bound. She looked lifeless.

"How'd you like a taste of that, Buddy?"

Bear reached down and poked her arm with his thumb, as if he was testing his steak to see if it was done cooking. He backed away from her as though she had the plague, and stared at Dale.

"I had to knock her out with some pills. She was making so much noise I almost got caught at the border."

Bear looked back at the girl, his drooping eyes and pouting lower lip, showed the sadness he felt for her.

"Well, whadda ya you think, Buddy? She's gonna get banged like a screen door in a hurricane where she's going. I'll let ya go a round with her for a C note and throw the fish in for free."

Bear just shook his head, and pointed to the fish.

"Okay, okay, I guess you're happy with the half-breed screamer in there. Sooo...yer keeping her around like yer wife or somethin?"

Bear gave Dale the squinty-eyed Clint Eastwood look.

"Hey, you don't have to worry about me—what happens in the bush, stays in the bush...right?"

Bear handed Dale twenty bucks, grabbed four nice salmon that he had picked out, then turned and walked back to the cabin.

"Alright, Buddy. I gotta get this stuff down the highway; I'll see you later."

Dale headed back out the laneway. When he got to the highway and looked both ways for traffic, he saw a pickup truck broken down on the shoulder of the road. Shortly after he turned left, a silver minivan passed him in the opposite direction. It was the most traffic he'd ever seen in the area. He turned up the radio and lit up a smoke.

* * *

Jensen was elated when another body was discovered, this one under the garage floor at Lewis' residence. It was a young female, found naked and posed with her hands crossed over her genitals, just like the one on the farm. Both women had a single puncture wound below their left breast. He stared down into the makeshift grave.

He got word that Lewis had been apprehended, and brought in for questioning. *This should make me a local hero...maybe I'll get a promotion.* He expected accolades and pats on the back from his peers, but he received neither.

Thoughts of how the two young girls met their demise intrigued and excited him. *Damn, I need to get laid.* He thought about the girl from the farm, then looked at the one under the garage floor. So far Lewis' victims were of the same race. Both were Aboriginal.

30

Hijacked

Strickland's reefer truck was about a kilometer ahead of Norm on the highway. Two Snakes was right about the lack of roads in the boonies. The porky pervert pulled into a gas station in New Hazelton. Norm looked at his fuel gage. He had a little more than a quarter tank, but service stations were few and far between. He pulled off the road where he could keep and eye on Dale, from a distance.

He was still pissed with the Mounties and Customs, and considered his own plan of attack. He knew all too well that Cops have to play by the rules, but as the Mounties pointed out to him on more than one occasion, he wasn't a Cop anymore. The rules no longer applied. It was time for some street justice—time for Norm to take action. No more watching and waiting and wondering. Strickland had to go down—one way or another.

Mister lot-a-fat paid for his gas inside the station, and came out drinking a Coke. He stopped near the front of his truck and lit up a smoke. A woman who was pumping gas waved frantically at him—probably for smoking so close to the fuel pumps. Being the true gentleman he was, Strickland grabbed his crotch, blew a puff of smoke in her direction, then got back in his truck and drove off.

Norm raced to the gas station, while the bumbling blimp continued south on the Highway of Tears. He filled up Two Snakes' pickup truck, cursing under his breath at how expensive it was to fill the beast. It was only a fraction of the cost for his motorcycle. With the truck full, Norm paid inside then grabbed some junk food and drinks for the road.

By the time he caught back up to his heftiness, Norm saw Strickland stopped off the road, near the salmon ladders, in Moricetown. Norm got close enough to see that blubber boy was meeting with an Indian and buying more fish. He put the new purchase in the back of the truck with his other cargo. It looked like Strickland padlocked the bay door when he closed the latch.

Norm's stomach growled like an angry Grizzly bear. It had been hours since he'd eaten, so he shoved half a Chunky Kit Kat bar in his mouth and washed it down with a diet Coke. Dale continued south on The Highway of Tears.

Smithers was on the horizon. Norm thought about Louie's uncle Sal and his wife Carol. It would be nice to see them again before heading back home—if and when that ever happened. It would be even nicer to eat a home cooked meal. The junk food was killing him.

Norm saw the Tim Horton's sign in the distance, the one where he first met uncle Sal. The fat bastard turned in and drove through their lot into the adjacent parking area. He backed his truck in at the rear of the empty lot.

By the time Norm got there, Strickland was inside the coffee shop shaking hands with another man. They sat near the front window; Dale had his back to his vehicle.

It was a perfect set up. Norm pulled up on the far side of the reefer, where he was completely out of view from anyone in the coffee shop. Wasting no time, he grabbed the tire iron from the back of the pickup and a hammer from the tool box. He giggled to himself, thinking about the mischief he was about to cause. Finally, a little payback for all those years of having to follow the rules, while the bad guys laughed in his face.

Nobody seemed to notice when he casually strolled over to the bay door at the back of Strickland's truck. The pad lock was a cheap one. Norm stuck the tire iron in the top loop of the lock and whacked it hard with the hammer. It broke. He peeked around the corner of the truck at the coffee shop, but nobody was watching.

He went straight to the back wall, and examined the center panel. From the looks of the smushed and rotten cabbage leaves on the floor, it appeared that the door swung out or slid to the right. He tried to force the tip of the tire iron into the edge of the panel, about halfway between the floor and ceiling. There was no play, he couldn't wedge the tip in. A couple of whacks with the hammer on the tire iron, loosened it a bit. Something thumped against the other side of the wall.

The sound caused Norm's heart to beat faster. He knocked on the wall in response. Adrenaline started pulsing through his veins. The girl was still alive. Prying on the tire iron allowed enough room to get the claws of the hammer in behind the panel. Reefing on the hammer made more room to slip the tire iron in farther, but it was blocked by a piece of metal. He hoped it was the latch.

Norm whacked the tire iron as hard as he could with the hammer and the metal snapped. The left side of the panel came loose, but the right side was still rigid. *Must be the hinge side.* He put all of his two hundred and sixty pounds on the end of the tire iron and pulled as hard as he could. The right side of the panel creaked and groaned and gave way with a loud crack. The wood around the hinges split wide open.

The tire iron flew from Norm's grasp, bounced off the side wall then came back and hit him on the outside of his left knee. He almost buckled from the impact and sharp pain, but what he saw behind the wall gave him the strength to remain standing. A young girl lay on the floor, bound and gagged, in the hidden compartment. The air inside was rank, it smelled like she had soiled herself. Her eyes went as wide as saucers.

He moved the panel aside, then reached down to the girl and gently loosened the gag that was in her mouth. She tried to talk, but only coughed. She was parched. Norm put his finger to his lips, motioning for her to remain quiet. Her wide-eyes relaxed for a second, then she closed them tightly. Tears appeared. He removed the rope around her hands first. While she rubbed them together to bring back her circulation, Norm untied her feet and helped her to stand. She was unsteady when she stood.

There was a plastic shopping bag on the floor in the corner of the hidden compartment. Norm looked inside and smiled. There were two large vacuum-sealed bags of marihuana inside. He scooped up the plastic bag and looped the girl's right arm over his shoulder to help her walk. Before helping her from the truck, he took a look outside to see if the coast was clear. Strickland still had his back to the windows, but appeared to be murdering a large donut.

Norm tucked the girl into the passenger side of the pickup truck and handed her a bottle of water. He grabbed a pen from the center console and returned to the doughboy's truck. Before picking up his tire iron and hammer, he scribbled his cell phone number on the wall beside the broken wall panel. No name, just his number. He left the bay door open, and drove off with the girl and Strickland's weed.

As soon as they got on the road the girl started talking. She sobbed and spewed her words. Norm couldn't understand what she was saying. She spoke in a foreign language that sounded Eastern European or maybe Russian. He nodded and put a hand on her shoulder to re-assure her, but she tensed up and moved back a few inches in her seat. Norm held his hand up, showing her he meant no harm.

"My name is Norm—I'm a friend."

The girl relaxed a bit. She used the backs of her hands to wipe away her tears. The mascara that had once lined her eyes was streaked down her face like a watercolor painting that got wet.

"I Bozena—from Romania. I stealed from dare."

"Do you speak English?"

"No, only few word."

Norm held his hand up again, signaling that he meant her no harm. He offered her a Kit Kat bar. She gobbled it like a starved animal.

"It's okay, you're safe now."

Uncle Sal. That's the first person who popped into Norm's mind. It should have been the cops or the Mounties in Prince George, but he needed some time to think the rest of his plan through. He had to get the girl away from Strickland before he passed her on, but he needed to figure out his next step. The other guy in the coffee shop could have been the buyer, for all he knew. If that was the case, Strickland had some explaining to do.

Bozena finished the bottle of water and looked at the other one on the seat. Norm nodded to her. "Go ahead, drink it."

She opened the bottle and guzzled it. He bit down on his lower lip, and shook his head, wondering when she last ate or drank or bathed.

Norm headed for Sal and Carol's place. Sal was cutting the lawn, but he shut off the mower when he saw the strange pickup truck pull into his driveway.

"Hey, Norm. I didn't recognize the truck. Where's your bike?" He noticed Bozena. "Oh my God! What happened to your friend?"

"It's a long story Sal...she was kidnapped and I'm helping her. Can we come in for a while?"

Finding Hope

"Yeah...sure. Carol's inside, she'll be happy to see you. C'mon in, we were just about to eat lunch—you know you're always welcome here, Norm."

The three of them walked to the house. Bozena's eyes were glued to the majestic alpine view. She looked like a kid seeing Disneyland for the first time.

"Carol, we've got company. You'll never guess who's here?"

"Norm, how are...oh my, you poor girl. What happened to you?"

Norm explained. "This is Bozena, Carol. She was kidnapped and doesn't speak English—says she's from Romania. It's a long story. I could really use a beer...then I can fill you guys in."

Sal was one step ahead, as usual, he handed Norm a beer. Bozena's gaze was fixed on a plate full of wraps and sliced veggies that were on the kitchen table.

"She looks starved, Norm. We were just about to eat—come and sit down, you two. Join us." Carol put an arm around Bozena's shoulder, guided her to a chair at the table and put a fresh plate in front of her. "Don't be shy...eat, please."

She looked at Carol, then Sal and Norm. They all motioned for her to eat. She took celery and carrot sticks with her left hand and two turkey wraps with her right.

Carol looked at Norm. "I guess I better make a few more wraps. She's filthy, Norm...and she doesn't smell very nice either." Carol patted Bozena on her shoulder. "Poor thing. I'm gonna go upstairs to run a bath for her and find some fresh clothes she can wear."

Sal asked, "What the hell is going on, Norm? I thought you'd be halfway across Canada by now. Louie already called us to say he made it home."

The Highway of Tears

"Yeah, I haven't talked to him since he left Prince George. I got involved with the Mounties there—I'm helping them find a missing woman that we met."

"Louie mentioned you might...is this her? Do the Mounties know you have her?"

"No...and no. It's complicated Sal."

He twisted his face as if he was trying to solve a Rubik's Cube. Norm gave him the Cole's notes version of what had happened since he left Prince George. Sal waited until the story was finished. "Hey, I got it. My neighbor is Romanian...or maybe Serbian. We go moose hunting together. You two finish your lunch, and I'll go see if he's home from work yet."

"That would help a lot—just don't tell him the kidnapping part, you don't want to freak him out."

He went to fetch his neighbor. Norm finished the beer in hand, then reached for the fresh one on the table. Sal was a good man. Bozena finished her glass of milk. She held her stomach like it was about to burst. Carol took her empty plate, then waved for Bozena to follow her upstairs.

Norm wondered about Strickland, and if he would receive a phone call from him. He bet he would, figuring the two pounds of weed was worth about five grand. Who knew what porky would get for the girl, and he had no idea what the fish were worth. Norm laughed out loud, thinking about the surprise he left for Strickland. It was a little taste of street justice.

Norm had his mouth full of a turkey wrap when Sal returned with his neighbor, Joseph. The man explained that he was Croatian, but that the dialects in what was formerly the country of Yugoslavia, were similar. Sal asked Norm where Bozena was.

"Carol took her upstairs for a bath and some clean clothes."

"Yeah, she was pretty ripe, poor girl."

Joseph squinted and rubbed his chin, trying to fully comprehend what was going on. Norm sensed his confusion, and filled him in while they waited for Bozena to return. The more Norm revealed, the further Joseph unconsciously slid his chair back from the table. It looked like he was going to bolt at any moment. Norm forgot to tell the man that he was a retired cop, Sal mentioned it and he seemed more at ease.

A young woman walked into the kitchen with Carol. Her long dark hair was wet and combed back. She was slender, but any curves she had were hidden under the baggy track suit she wore. When she sat down at the table, her chestnut eyes sparkled in the sunlight that was pouring in through the patio doors. She turned to Norm. Her expressionless face relaxed, and she offered a flat smile. It melted his heart.

He introduced Bozena to Joseph. He spoke to her in his native tongue. She perked up, leaned forward and blurted out what sounded like her life story.

31

Nagging Thoughts

Two Snakes drove to the women's shelter. He thought he'd check with Marjorie to see if she'd heard anything else about Dakota, and deliver the bad news about Dee at the same time. She was sitting on the front porch when he walked up. Her eyes were red and watery, she'd been crying.

"I take it you've already heard."

"Yes, David. The girls have their own communication network. We're all pretty upset here. Have you heard anything from Dakota?"

"No...I was hoping that maybe you had."

"Sorry, no, but there's another girl that I think you should talk to. If you wait here, I'll go in and get her."

Marjorie returned a few minutes later with a young girl who looked no older than twelve. She was petite, with pale white skin that was covered in acne and she had short black hair, streaked with pink.

"David, this is Kimberly. Kimberly, this is Mr. Greene— He's Dakota's uncle. Please tell him what you told me after we heard about Dee."

If Kimberley was upset about Dee's death, she didn't show it. She stared hard at Two Snakes for a second, then turned back to Marjorie.

"It's okay honey, Mr. Greene is trying to find Dakota, before something happens to her...like Dee."

"Do you know something that might help me find my niece, Kimberly?"

"Maybe...like, I was out hitchhiking with her after Dee took off from here. Dakota was mad at her—she like stole the money they'd been saving together. She asked me if I wanted to help her make some quick cash. I know what they did to make the money, I don't do that. Like once, I asked for the money up front, then jumped out of the car and ran."

Two Snakes was dumfounded. Kimberly resembled a Cabbage Patch Kid, but she talked like the Happy Hooker.

"Did you see Dakota get into a car with someone?"

"Yeah, like...I told her not to cause I didn't think two of us would be able to get away fast enough. So like...we tried to talk the guy into a threesome for more cash, but he like...was only into Dakota. He like never took his eyes off her. It was like I wasn't even there."

"Did you get a look at him?"

"Like...not really—they all look the same, old white guy."

"What about the car?"

"One of those big truck things."

"You mean a monster truck, with big tires?"

"No, like a boxy truck—with a door on the back."

"You mean a four by four or SUV?"

"Ya, I guess."

"What color?"

"Like...dark." Kimberly's eyes wandered. She was losing interest in the conversation. She played with her hair, wrapping some of it around her forefinger.

Two Snakes didn't relent. "Did you happen to look at the licence plate number?"

"No. I was like...mad at Dakota—she dumped me, with no money."

"Did you ever see the guy or the SUV before."

"I dunno—don't think so. Can I go now?"

"Sure. Thanks for your help, Kimberly."

He looked at Marjorie after Kimberly went back inside. "Kind of young to be working the streets, ain't she?"

"Not around here. She's fourteen—they can't do anything to her on the street that hasn't already been done to her at home."

"She could get killed, like Dee."

"Sorry. I know, David. You're so right—I was just saying. Was she any help to you?"

"Maybe. The SUV…I need to look into that, it's something I'd forgotten about. Thanks for your help, Marjorie, I have to go. I'm sorry for your loss."

"Anytime, David. I hope you find Dakota safe and sound. Take care."

Two Snakes sat in his car, frazzled. It had nagged him ever since his fishing trip: that blue Ford Explorer he'd seen there. The one that he thought belonged to the park rangers. Then the ones he'd seen at the Mountie office and the one he'd seen Jensen driving. He knew there were a lot similar vehicles in the area. It was time to go back to where it all started, on that road by the lake.

There was no way he was going to drive his pride and joy into the bush on those rocky roads. He drove to his mechanic's garage and asked if he could borrow his pickup for a few hours. Without asking why, George threw him the keys.

"Can you change the oil and do a tire rotation while you've got her, George?"

"Sure, Two Snakes. It'll be done by the time you get back. Check the gas in the truck, I think it's on empty."

"Good trade. Thanks, George."

Two Snakes stopped at home to get some gear. He waved at the old lady next door. She was peeking out her curtains, as usual. He grabbed his binoculars, hiking boots, and a six pack of beer. *Gotta keep hydrated.*

Outside the city and down the highway, he watched for the burnt sign of the devil. He turned towards the Caribou Mountains, and found the logging road. After removing the chain, he headed towards his favorite fishing hole. At the fork he veered left, where he had seen the SUV.

The road narrowed and then forked again. Two Snakes stayed to the right, and crested a hill where the road ended, at what looked like an old orchard and graveyard. It was odd that he never ran across it in all the years he hunted and fished in the area. He saw a huge boulder and large tombstone, inside a wooden picket fence. It had seen better days.

As Two Snakes walked closer he saw that some of the grass was trampled, someone had been there recently. He dropped to one knee and let his eyes follow the direction of the bent grass. It lead to a slight rise in the ground. There, he found what appeared to be a fresh grave. There was no marker. *What the hell? Why would anyone bury someone here and not leave a marker.* He pulled back a loose piece of sod and took a handful of the soil. It was loose and damp.

He walked over to the tombstone. It looked homemade—from a huge chunk of granite, taken from the surrounding mountains. There were two names chiseled on the stone. According to the dates they had died a couple of years apart; the man first. His name was Heinrich Johansen and hers Emily Johansen, nee Salmon, of the First Nations people. Two Snakes knew of the aboriginal family name, but not of anyone in the area. The name Johansen was a mystery to him.

He looked at the trampled grass again. There were faint signs of an old path, which led down the hill, and into the bush. It headed in the direction of where the other fork in the road would have taken him. He followed the path and came upon a log cabin. He froze in his tracks, and listened for a couple minutes. There was only the sound of leaves flapping in the breeze, and birds chirping the distance.

The path continued alongside of the cabin near a wood pile and the chimney. There was freshly chopped wood in the pile, but the chimney felt cold to his touch. He quietly worked his way around to the front of the cabin. Curtains were closed in the windows and it looked dark inside. There was a vehicle under a tarp at the far end of the front porch, in the driveway.

The curtains were slightly apart in the window to the left of the front door. Two Snakes peeked inside and saw part of the living area, but there were no signs of life. After checking around the other side, he returned to the vehicle and looked under the tarp. It was a dark blue Ford Explorer, just like the one he had seen when he was fishing. He felt a knot in his stomach.

Two Snakes worked his way around and checked all the doors. They were locked and it was difficult to see inside because of the heavily tinted windows. It had no plates on it and the hood was cold to the touch. By looking at the dirt on the tires and fresh tracks behind them, it appeared that it had been driven recently. He saw a footprint and took a knee to examine it. The impression looked like a man's dress shoe—size eleven or twelve.

Two Snakes stayed crouched there, in thought, scratching the top of his head. He went back up on the front porch, and knocked on the door. He wasn't sure what he'd say if anyone answered, but he was pretty sure no one was there. After waiting a few seconds and not hearing anything, he quietly opened the screen door and reached for the door knob. His telephone rang, and he yanked his hand back so fast his elbow smashed into the door jamb. His heart almost leapt from his chest before he realized what happened.

He fumbled to answer his phone before it rang again—the sound was deafening in the surrounding silence. The number on the screen was familiar.

"Jesus Christ, Norm—you scared the shit out of me."

"How's that? I said I'd call you back."

"Hang on—I bashed my funny bone, I gotta change hands."

"What were you doing, whacking off?"

"I'm up near my fishing hole—I think I found the Ford Explorer that abducted my niece."

"Explorer...what niece?"

"My sister's daughter, Dakota. She went missing a few days ago. One of the girls at the shelter says she last saw her getting into in a dark colored SUV. I think it was a dark blue Ford Explorer, like the one here at the cabin, where I'm at. Your friend Jensen drives one too."

"What? Slow down, Tonto. Do the plates match? Wait a minute—why would Jensen abduct your niece? That's crazy!"

Two Snakes shook his sore arm, and sat down on the porch step. "I don't know what to think, but I have a bad feeling about this."

"Oh-oh, you been smoking that funny stuff again and having visions?"

"I'm telling you, Norm, there's something sinister about that guy. He gave off evil vibes when he stood beside me at the cop shop. And how would you explain a fresh, unmarked grave in the family plot here?"

"I dunno, maybe the family dog. What makes you think Jensen has anything to do with the place?"

Two Snakes turned his head from side to side, like he was checking to see if anyone was watching. "The family name on the tombstone is Johansen...pretty close to Jensen, don't you think?"

Norm chuckled. "I think you need rehab, your visions are starting to look real."

"It's not funny, Norm."

"Is to me...did you get a plate number or VIN from the Explorer?"

"No plates. Never thought of the VIN. I'll look for it, and when I get back to civilization, I'm gonna try and find out who owns this place. When are you coming back this way? Maybe we can team up and look for both our girls."

Two Snakes got up off the porch, and started walking the path back to the graveyard. The phone reception got spotty when he walked into the bush.

"That's why I'm calling you...hey, are you there...I'm getting static. Okay, that's better—I rescued a young girl from the back of Strickland's truck..."

"You found your girlfriend?"

"No, no—she's a Romanian girl. Strickland got her from a guy on a boat, up in Hyder. They're involved in some kind of human trafficking thing."

"Strickland was hiding where? Hang on till I get to the top of this hill, I'm losing you. Are you there? What do the Mounties say? Can you hear me now?" Two Snakes picked up his pace to clear the forest and crest the hill for better reception.

"I hear you...I haven't told them yet."

"You're not the Lone Ranger, you know. What are you going to do with the girl?"

"I haven't figured that out yet. For now, we're staying with some friends in Smithers. I grabbed the girl and some dope from Strickland when he wasn't looking, and then left him my phone number to see if he's willing to trade for Hope."

"Dope? Trading women? You better not call the Mounties, they'll arrest you."

Norm expelled an evil laugh. "I never said I would actually go through with the trade, but I know that someone is expecting Strickland to deliver them a girl. The weed is worth at least five grand. He's a lowlife piece of shit—he'll jump at the chance of getting his meal ticket back. That's where you come in—I could use some backup."

"That's pretty heavy, aren't you supposed to be a cop...or at least working for them?"

"They pissed me off. I told them about the dope and the girl hidden in the back of Strickland's truck, but they let the fat prick go."

"Figures. And you wonder why my people hate the cops?"

"I know, I know—they have rules, but I don't. Not anymore. They keep reminding me that I'm just a civilian now, all the more reason to do it my way. We can call for the cavalry if and when we need them. Besides, Strickland's been around the block, he won't deal with the cops if they have nothing to offer him. They can have him after I'm done with him."

"Wow! That's a lot to chew on, Kemosabe. Maybe we need to discuss your plan over a few beers. Where do you want to meet?"

"Can you come up to Smithers? I thought I'd stay here until I hear from Strickland."

"I can be there in less than three hours."

"Great, Tonto. I'll see you soon."

32

Body Count

"They treated her like garbage, wrapping her up in a bag and throwing her into the river," she says. *"She wasn't garbage. She was my baby."*
—Thelma Gavel, Tina Fontaine's Aunt
Maclean's Magazine

Jensen was vibrating with excitement when Inspector Nickerson stopped and stood by his side, in the garage.

"I don't think I've ever seen you smile, Jensen. It would seem you're enjoying this."

"Sorry, Inspector. I'm just happy how the case has come together—that I was right about Lewis being a serial. The m.o. is the same here as at the farm. I know there's only two so far, but race, age, body disposal and posing are all the same. We have the killer. I was just about to head in to interview him."

"You might want to hold off on that, the cadaver dogs just found another body at the farm. I'm sure you'll want to see the victim before you interview your suspect. And just to let you know...the media has caught wind of it and is all over us. They've clogged the front gate at the farm and are whining to get closer, because they can't see the action. Our guys caught one of them right at the gravesite. She was dressed in rubber boots and coveralls, using her phone to take pictures."

Jensen tingled all over, and felt like he was eight feet tall. It was his time to shine. "Yes, Lewis can wait. I'll get back over to the farm right away, Sir."

"This has gotten to be more than we can handle—I've called in some help from the neighboring detachments. It's all hands on deck. Oh, in case I forget to tell you in all the confusion...good work, Jensen. This will probably earn you another stripe to sew on your red serge."

"Thank you, Sir. I'll touch base with you later."

* * *

Two Snakes emerged from the bush at the graveyard where his truck was parked. He glanced over at the tombstone again, thinking about the names on it and a possible connection to Jensen. An anomaly in the long grass caught his attention. He walked back to where he found the fresh grave. When he crouched down, he noticed how the rise in the earth there caused the greenery on top of it to be taller than the area that surrounded it.

Squatting, with his eyes at the same level as the grass, he discovered what had caught his eye. There were other places within the fenced plot that looked the same. He walked to one of them and kicked at the turf. It was higher and softer than the ground around it. *Shit. Another grave.*

He walked back and forth, from fence to fence, discovering three more gravesites, none of them marked. A chill ran down the back of his neck and spine. He stood there for a moment, in silence, taking in the macabre scene—the stillness of the branches on the dead fruit trees, and the pale grey boulder that looked like it had rolled there from a distant mountain. Heavy clouds in the mackerel sky cast dark shadows across the ground and left a chill in the air. Goose bumps raced down his arms.

Not even a flutter from a butterfly's wings disturbed the still air. His eyes were drawn to the tombstone—the coldness of the rock nipped at his skin from twenty feet away. Beads of cold sweat broke out on his forehead, and a wave of nausea came over him. *The scenery blurred as if there were waves of heat rising from the ground.*

Suddenly, the boulder burst into flames—the heat was intense. He threw his hands up in front of his face and dropped to his knees. Sweat soaked his palms and burned his eyes. He tried wiping them with the back of his hands. The flaming grey bolder transformed into the bombed house in Afghanistan.

His best friend lay on the ground in front of it; his uniform burnt and smoldering. His eyes danced in his head, searching for an explanation. He screamed in pain. Two Snakes tried crawling to him, but his right leg wouldn't move. The smell of cordite and burnt flesh filled his nostrils. He reached for his friend, but someone grabbed his arm and pulled him away from the fire.

What was left of Roger lay beside him. Two Snakes couldn't hear the medic shouting, but he understood what it meant when he shook his head. He reached out to his friend and screamed, "No!" Startled, he opened his eyes and saw that he was kneeling in front of the tombstone, soaked in cold sweat. *I gotta get out of this place.*

* * *

Bear had been giving her the silent treatment, more than usual, ever since he found the note for help. The fact that he hadn't touched her in any way was a welcome relief. What bothered Hope was the solitude. She missed humanity. She missed gabbing with Laurie and Charitee. Oh, how she missed Charitee.

Finding Hope

A giant paw reached through the window in her door. It was holding a plate with a sandwich and potato chips on it. She grabbed the plate with one hand and Bear's wrist with the other.

"I said I'm sorry, Bear. I had to try. Can I come outside—you know I can't go anywhere. It's lonely in here...maybe I can make you a nice dinner."

There was no answer. Hope peeked through the window and saw Bear standing in the front door, looking out into the forest, as though he had seen something. It wasn't unusual for wildlife to wander into the yard or forage for food around the cabin. He turned around, walked back to her door, and unlocked it.

"Thanks, Bear. Do you mind if I go outside for some air? I won't go off the porch."

Hope took her lunch with her, out to the front porch. The air was a bit more damp than usual. An overcast sky kept the sun at bay. Bear followed her from the house, and assumed his position at the chopping block. He always chopped wood when he was frustrated or upset. Unconsciously, she admired his muscular back and arms, almost forgetting that he was the man who held her captive. Almost.

She nibbled on her chips and ate her sandwich, and tried to imagine what it would be like to be treated as a lady. What it would be like to be in love—to have a man who doted on her for the woman she really was, and not the sex slave she had become. Was such a man out there? She remembered the retired cop in Jasper—he was cute, maybe someone like him. *Men...who needs them?*

A sound in the trees, near the stream, caught Hope's attention. She didn't see anything, and thought it sounded like a squirrel hopping branches. Bear didn't seem to hear it over the cracking noise of the splitting logs under his axe. She watched him; he worked like a machine.

Hope turned to put her sandwich plate on the bench beside her, then heard another sound near Bear and looked back that way. It was a blur—she couldn't quite comprehend exactly what she was seeing. It was a man, charging at Bear. He attacked Bear's blindside and whacked him on the side of his head with a length of a tree branch, the size of a baseball bat. The sound was like a watermelon hitting the pavement; it made her cringe.

The scene unfolded in slow motion. Bear's head barely moved from the impact, but his legs wobbled and his knees started to buckle. He staggered backwards, managing to stay on his feet. The man swung the club again, but Bear ducked at the last second and the blow glanced off his shoulder. When the next blow came, he blocked it with his axe then wheeled it around and swung it at the man's head.

The stranger deflected the axe with the branch, then brought it back and hit Bear hard in the ribs. Hope thought they snapped—it sounded like cracking wood. He doubled over in pain, the axe hung loosely in his right hand. Blood streamed down the left side of his face from a gash above his ear. The stranger raised his club in the air with both hands, like he was going to bash Bear over the head.

Hope saw his face. Her mind froze, like someone hit the pause button. Her jaw fell slack and she gasped. It was Robbie—her ex-husband. She didn't see the blow that landed and knocked Bear to the ground, she was awestruck.

Robbie looked over at her, grinning from ear to ear."Hi Honey, I've missed you."

He stood there with open arms, the club still in his right hand. Her mouth was agape, she couldn't speak.

"So this is your new man...big guy. Well, not so big now."

She glanced down at Bear and then back up to Robbie. The axe lay near the porch, closer to her than Robbie. He saw her looking at it.

"C'mon Sweetie, you could never hurt me. Don't you love me anymore? I still love you. And our daughter...I saw her, she's beautiful—just like her mother."

"You bastard! If you touched her, I'll kill you! There's a gun in the house—I'll shoot you and bury you in the woods and nobody will ever know."

Hope's mind raced. *Can I get to the axe...or get past Robbie...get the keys from Bear's pocket...then the gun...and load it in time? Maybe if I lock myself in the cabin. What's the use, there's no phone or any way to call for help.* She looked at Bear again. He was sprawled facedown on the ground and not moving. The side of his face was covered in blood; he appeared to be dead.

Robbie winked at her and inched his way forward, smiling. She hated every man that ever winked, because of him. And that cocky smile of his...funny, it had been the first thing she found attractive when they met. *Does he have Charitee? What will he do to her...or me? I can't let that happen, I need to rescue Charitee, I need to survive.* Hope tried to move toward the axe, but it felt as though she was wearing lead boots. Robbie came closer.

A big hand grasped his right leg. He tried to turn and club Bear, but lost his balance and fell to the ground. Bear pinned Robbie's right arm with his left, rendering the club useless. Bear reached for the axe, but Robbie punched his injured rib cage and jumped on top of him. He grabbed Bear in a head-lock and tried to choke him, but then Bear head-butted Robbie, smashing his nose.

Rolling on the ground, they punched and kicked, and grunted and groaned, and bled all over each other.

Hope looked at the axe and then the club. The men were fighting to the death and were oblivious of her. She took a step towards the axe, but then stopped. *What the hell am I thinking? Run!*

33

Sad Stories

Dale Strickland parted company with the other man at the Tim Horton's. He lit up a cigarette outside the front doors, took a long drag, then left it hanging from the corner of his mouth as he walked to his vehicle. He squinted to keep the smoke from his eyes. His jaw dropped and the cigarette fell from his lip, rolling off his fat belly like a ski jumper. His fish were scattered all over the back of his truck and in the gravel parking lot.

He found the back door wide open and saw the broken panel to the secret compartment. He climbed up into the cargo hold and in his haste, slipped on a fish carcass. The side wall helped to break his fall, but he landed in a belly flop onto more fish. He cursed out loud and crawled to the back wall on his hands and knees. Using the door frame for support, he pulled himself up and looked inside.

Strickland yelled out in agony and disbelief. "No!" The girl and his dope were both gone. He continued cursing and he pounded on the wall with both fists, like a little boy who just had his video game taken away. The pounding stopped when he noticed something scrawled on the wall in pen—it was a phone number. *What the fuck?* He reached under a fat roll then pulled his phone off his belt and dialed the number. He hung up. *Shit— I better think about this.*

Coated in smelly slime, he paced around in the back of the truck, thinking. *Fuck. Who the hell would do something like this? It doesn't make any sense—nobody knew what was in here.*

Damn, that stinks. Even though the truck's refrigeration unit was still running, the warm air from the open door spoiled the fish. Completely pissed off, Strickland kicked the rotting fish out the door and mumbled to himself. *Nothin but fucking cat food now.*

* * *

Norm sat with a long face as Joseph translated Bozena's tale of her kidnapping and abuse. He'd heard stories like hers before, but was never personally involved in one. She and her best friend were taken from Bucharest, where a man they met at a dance club invited them to a private party. Once there, they unwillingly became the entertainment. After being raped repeatedly by four men, they were taken to a warehouse where other women were being held.

The girls tried to comfort each other; some were in shock and one, catatonic. After days of competing for bad food and water, all the young women were loaded onto a truck and taken to a boat. While in transport, the sailors took turns abusing them. Bozena said it was hard to sleep at night because of all the screaming and crying. After many more days, another truck took them to an abandoned hotel, where they were cleaned up and given fresh clothes.

All the girls were lined up in the old ballroom, where they were forced to dance for a group of men in suits. Each man took a turn selecting one or more of the girls, then took them to their rooms. There, they were told to take their clothes off for a closer, more intimate inspection.

Bozena's best friend was separated from her at that point, and she never saw her, or the other girls again. There were three girls in her new group, and they were all forced to have sex together with the man who bought them.

After having his way with them, he took them by truck to another boat, and then another truck, and so on. The girls were sexually abused all along the way. Only one other girl remained with her for the last boat ride. Norm found her in Strickland's truck after that. She said the fat and smelly truck driver groped and fondled her when he gave her food and water. He threatened to, but never went beyond that.

Joseph was teary-eyed the whole time he translated Bozena's story. He hung his head in sorrow and anger when he finished. Everyone remained silent for at least a minute. Norm looked at Sal and Carol. They were both in tears. He picked up his phone off the table and checked the time. The display showed a missed call earlier, from an unknown number. The phone rang again, while in his hand.

It was Inspector Nickerson. "Norm, I've got some good news—the coast guard stopped the Seven Shees and arrested the captain. They found two duffle bags, each containing twenty pounds of marihuana."

"That is good news, Inspector. Congratulations. I have..."

"And that's not all, Norm. They found a young girl being held captive on board. They think she's Middle Eastern, but there's a language barrier."

"She speaks Romanian, sir."

"What? How would you know that?"

"She's probably from Bucharest, Romania—one of several girls that were abducted by a human trafficking ring."

"What's going on, Norm. How do you know all this?"

"Because I have the girl that was hidden in Dale Strickland's truck. She just filled me in on the whole story."

Carol saw that Bozena was upset and she took her outside for some air.

"You have a kidnapped girl with you—why didn't you call us?"

"I tried, but you and Jensen didn't answer your phones."

"I'm sorry, Norm. Jensen's on to a serial killer and we're still digging up bodies as I speak. It's chaos here...and to make it worse, the media is all over us."

"Wow, it sounds like you have your hands full, Inspector. Don't worry about me and the girl, we're fine."

"What's that mean—where are you at?"

"In Smithers, with friends."

Sal nodded to Joseph and motioned for him to join him outside so Norm could have some privacy.

"How did you get the girl? Never mind, it's probably better if I don't know. What about Strickland?"

"I left him my phone number so we can make a deal for Hope Lachance."

"What kind of deal...or do I want to know?"

"If you don't know, you'll have deniability. And it's not like he's gonna call the cops to report that someone stole his kidnapped girl and his dope. Don't worry, sir. I'll call in the cavalry when the time is right. Do you remember that leverage I talked about? Well, I have it now. Strickland is low-life—I dealt with his kind for thirty-one years."

"I hope you know what you're doing, Norm. I really don't have the time to worry about you right now. What are you going to do with the girl? She'll have to be debriefed about the human trafficking operation."

Norm glanced at the others out on the deck, taking in the alpine view. It was hard for him to believe how something so ugly could be happening in a place so beautiful.

"For now she's safe and she needs to know that. I'll try to connect her with her parents by phone or email; they need to know that she's alive. Once I deliver Strickland to you, she'll be next. Your people can sort it all out then."

"I hope you're planning on delivering Strickland in one piece."

"That's the plan, but ultimately, it will be up to him."

"Are you sure I can't send you some backup?"

"No, I'm good, I've got my own backup. Strickland is my last chance at finding Hope...if she is still alive."

"All right, Norm. I'm going way out on a limb here. Oh yes, before I forget, Jensen left a message for you...something about Robbie Chambers—the cops in Nova Scotia lost track of him. He has a silver minivan that's registered to him. I emailed you the registration and plate number."

"That's interesting—he's Hope's ex-husband, but I'm not worried about him right now. Thanks, Inspector. I'll stay in touch."

34

Trading Company

*"Never argue with stupid people, they will drag you down to
their level and then beat you with experience."*
— Mark Twain

Bozena was emotionally drained and physically beat, Carol took her upstairs to the bedroom to get some rest. Joseph, Sal and Norm sipped their beers out on the deck. After hearing Bozena's story, they sat there in silence, staring off into the mountains. The other two men lost their appetite, but Norm worked on finishing the sandwich he had started earlier. He wondered why all the bad things he'd seen during his career never affected his appetite.

Norm remembered how young and naïve he was when he started the job at eighteen. He was mature for his age, but he had no idea how badly people could treat each other. His parents separated when he was eleven, but neither of them used him or his siblings as pawns, while trying to settle their differences.

One of the worst domestic calls he responded to involved the custody of a child. When he arrived at the scene, each of the hysterical parents had an arm of their young child, pulling him in separate directions. You can only imagine how the child was emotionally affected by that move.

Sal and Joseph looked like they were counting trees in the landscape. Norm figured they had their own memories from the

Finding Hope

past. If not, they would surely never forget Bozena's story. Sal and Carol had two children who were grown up and had moved out. When Sal wiped a corner of his eye with the back of his hand, Norm was sure he was thinking of them.

Watching the twin falls in the distance was mesmerizing. Norm's eyelids grew heavy in the silence. The picture was burned into his retinas and he could still see the spectacle with his eyes closed. He heard his own breathing and his thoughts faded, but he worried about Hope. His head fell back and his loud snort woke him. The other two men laughed.

Norm's phone rang. He didn't recognize the number, but answered it.

"Who the hell are ya—an where's my cargo?"

"This must be the fat man—the piece of shit who treats dead fish better than live women."

"You cost me allot-a money—you had no right..."

"What about the girl's rights?"

"I want my cargo back."

Norm picked up his beer, but it was nearly empty. He dumped the backwash over the railing. "I would imagine so. Do you wanna trade?"

"Trade what? Whadda ya talkin about?"

"I want Hope Lachance back—you wanna swap?"

"I don't know who you're talkin about."

"Guess you're not interested then." Norm hung up the phone.

Sal and Joseph stared, wide-eyed.

"Don't worry, he'll call back. He just needs a minute to think about it."

Norm's phone rang again. "I was just looking up the number for the Mounties so I can turn the girl over to them. I don't know if I should give them the weed or sell it myself..."

"Wait...wait! Don't do that—I know where Hope is."

"Is she alive?"

"Yeah, I just saw her...she's fine. She's staying with a guy. I don't think he'll give her up though."

"That's bad for you, Dale. Give me five minutes to talk to Bozena."

"Who?"

"The girl you kidnapped."

"I didn't kidnap..."

"I'll call you back in five minutes."

Norm hung up again and turned to Sal. "Kispoix. Do you know the area?"

"Vaguely. Why do you ask?"

"I followed the lard ass there—he disappeared down a side road for a while, like he was visiting someone."

"That could be, Norm. I told you before, there's mountain men up there who live like hermits. Was the road marked?"

"No, it looked like an old logging road, but it had some gravel scattered along it."

"It could lead anywhere. A lot of those laneways end in the bush or at inland lakes where they used them to float timber out. Someone could be living up there."

"Strickland had a reason to be up there and it looked like he knew exactly where he was going. He just admitted that Hope is alive and staying with a guy near there. I think it's on the road I followed him to."

"Shouldn't you call the cops, Norm?"

"They wrote off Hope before I got involved, but I did tell them about Bozena."

"Are they coming to get her?"

"Not yet. I didn't say where she was and I may need her as a bargaining chip."

Joseph remained silent. Sal winced, showing his concern.

"Geez, Norm. Are you sure you know what you're doing? You know I'd like to help, but this is way beyond my comfort zone."

"It's okay, Sal, my backup is on the way."

As if on cue, a pickup truck pulled into the driveway. Two Snakes parked it, waved at the men on the deck, and headed there.

"You made good time, Tonto. Joseph, Sal, this is my friend, Two Snakes. It's good to see you—I was just talking to Strickland on the phone."

The men all shook hands.

Two Snakes pointed to Norm's beer. "I could use one of those."

Carol was already on it. She came out of the house with more beer and leftover sandwiches. "I heard someone pull up and figured we had more company. There's still food left you guys—eat up."

She extended a hand to Two Snakes, introduced herself then handed him a beer and held out the plate of sandwiches.

"That looks great...don't mind if I do. Thank you, Carol. So Norm, what's going on?"

"I was just about to find out. Strickland says that Hope is still alive and that she is with some guy up near Kispoix. I think I know where—he pulled off onto a logging road when I was following him. He might be the guy who was in the fat bastard's truck when Hope went missing."

Two Snakes stuffed a turkey wrap into his mouth, while Norm called Strickland back.

He answered on the first ring. "So when do I get my stuff back?"

"Are you willing to swap Hope for your stuff?"

"Yeah, but I can't just go and take her away from the guy. He acts like they're married or somethin—he's weird with

The Highway of Tears

women that way. We usually trade for fish or meat, Hope was a last minute thing—it really wasn't planned."

"Why don't you call him, and say you have a new girl for him?"

"I tried that when I was there—I didn't know he was playing house with the broad. He don't have a phone, and I can't just show up there again. He's private and don't like surprises...what about my weed?"

"Let me tell you what you're going to do, Dale. You're going to tell me exactly where Hope is and draw me a map of the area. You can give it to me tomorrow morning, when we meet. In return, I'll give you the weed."

"What about Bojangles and all the fish you ruined?"

"Consider the fish thing a lesson for your stupidity. You get the weed for Hope's location. When she is safe then you can have Bozena. I cleaned her up and she looks pretty good...I might just take a round out of her myself."

Everyone stared at Norm, wide-eyed. Carol covered her mouth, restraining a gasp. Norm shook his head, and waved off their concerns.

"What the hell is Hope to you, anyway?"

"She's my wife, Dale. I've searched the whole fucking country, trying to find her. She belongs to me and I want her back."

"Holy shit—I heard about her psycho ex...I mean you, sorry. Okay, okay—I'll do it, but I get Bozo back in the end, right?"

Norm walked away from the others, to the opposite end of the deck. "That's the deal, Dale. She means nothing to me. You can do what you want with her once I have my wife back. Are you still in Smithers?"

"No, I'm headed back home. I didn't know where else to go—I'm gonna be in big trouble if I don't deliver the Russian girl by tomorrow night."

"That's perfect. Meet me at nine in the morning at the abandoned lumber yard south of town. You know where it is?"

"Yeah, I know—you better have my weed."

"Don't worry, Dale. You'll get everything you have coming. I promise."

When Norm hung up the phone all eyes were on him.

Two Snakes nodded slowly. "You wove a pretty tall tale there, Kemosabe. Did he buy it?"

"The fat piece of shit is as dumb as a stump. I had to make him think that I'm more of an asshole than he is. He's supposed to deliver Bozena somewhere tomorrow night so he doesn't have much of a choice."

Sal joined in the conversation. "You're not going to give Bozena back to him, are you?"

"After I get Hope back, the only thing I'm going to give Dale Strickland is a pair of handcuffs that will be slapped on him by a couple of Canada's finest."

Carol let out a sigh of relief. Sal and Two Snakes chuckled, but Joseph looked pale. He excused himself and said he had to get back home. Norm thanked him for all his help. He said he'd return to check on Bozena in the morning and he wished Norm luck. Two Snakes finished his beer and turned to Norm. "You're pretty crazy for a white man, Kemosabe. I'm starting to like you."

35

Trapped

Hope didn't care who would win the fight, she just ran. If Bear managed to get the best of Robbie, things would go on the same forever. She couldn't even imagine what Robbie would do to her if he won. A good beating would be imminent, no doubt. She didn't even think about which direction she ran, but found herself on the path that led to the stream and then a small bridge.

"Come back here...you bitch!"

It was Robbie, yelling at her. She glanced back over her shoulder, he limped in her direction. Bear was face down on the ground, near the porch. He wasn't moving. She lost her footing near the end of the bridge, and fell to her hands and knees on the rocky creek embankment. Scrambling to get up, her feet slipped on the wet moss—she was barefoot and just then realized it. Pain shot through her left knee when she stood up. It was scraped and bleeding.

Hope ran from the stream and into the bush, away from Robbie. She stopped for a few seconds to catch her breath and listen. She heard his heavy steps on the bridge, but then something snapped, and there was a primeval scream. It roared through the trees, scaring birds into flight. It was Robbie, he was in terrible pain.

She froze. *Did Bear catch up and axe him?* She thought he was dead when she last saw him on the ground. The sound of Robbie's screaming made her feel sorry for him. *You can't be serious—he deserves the pain.* It was like the forest was eerily alive, his guttural sounds vibrated each leaf and needle on every tree. Hope didn't hear Bear, or anything else, for that matter. She wanted to run, but mixed emotions of sorrow, curiosity, and hate held her fast. *Why isn't he coming after me and what's causing him so much pain?*

She looked toward the road and then back to the path, which led to the cabin—she just had to know. She crept back towards the noise, peeking around every tree on the way, looking for Robbie. He was lying near the foot of the bridge, on her side of the stream. She stopped dead in her tracks when he screamed at her.

"Faith! You bitch...I'm gonna kill you!"

She'd heard those words attached to her real name many times, but it still sent a chill down her spine. Robbie was squirming and tugging at his right leg. He looked up and saw her hiding behind a tree. "Help me, please...help me, Faith."

His leg was caught in one of Bear's traps; he laid them out around the cabin to snare any dangerous animals. Not quite sure why, she moved in closer. Part of Robbie's shin bone was sticking out of the skin below his knee. He was bleeding. The trap was clamped onto his leg, and a chain attached to it was tied to a tree.

"Faith, please...help me get out of this thing."

Even though he was trapped, she was still terrified seeing him face to face. All the bad memories washed through her mind like a tidal wave. Even so, she couldn't help feeling sorry for him, lying there in pain. *What's the matter with me?*

"No. It took me years to build up the courage to run away from you, and I'm not going to stop running from you now. You're on your own—you can die here for all I care. What have you done with Charlene?"

He whimpered and spoke softly, letting his tears flow freely down his cheeks. "Help me, honey, and I'll take you to her. She's really grown—it's so nice to see my family again. Don't you want to be a family again?"

"We're not your family. You never cared for her when she was born, and I was just your punching bag and cum dumpster. That big man back there cared more for me than you ever did."

"Ahhh! Look at my leg, baby, it's busted. Help me, please?"

"I hope it hurts like hell. If you live through this, don't ever come looking for me again. Do you understand, Robbie? I hate you, and want nothing to do with you...ever."

"Don't leave me here. You know I love you...I can change...it'll be better."

His words faded to whimpers after Hope turned away and headed towards the road. Strangely, she felt some concern for Bear, but more importantly, she was free. It was time to leave the two worst men in her life behind, and go home. Charitee was waiting for her...or so she hoped. There was no reason for Robbie to take her. He never had any use for her.

She reached the logging road and headed away from the cabin. Her way home lay somewhere ahead of her...the highway. She started to jog. Rocks and stones jabbed and poked at her feet, she wished she'd grabbed her shoes from the porch. The feel of the cool air on her face was liberating, she was almost two weeks in captivity. She heard the sound of a truck on the highway, off in the distance. It was the sound of freedom. Hope ran faster.

36

Thunder & Enlightening

*"Oh great spirit whose voice I hear in the winds,
I come to you as one of your many children,
I need your strength and your wisdom.
Make me strong not to be superior to my brother,
But to be able to fight my greatest enemy: Myself."*
—Chief Dan George

Jensen drove through the media gauntlet, impressed by their numbers, for the small population of Prince George. Hungry journalists toting cameras and microphones swarmed him, when he stopped at the front gate to the farm. Either someone tipped them off that he was the lead investigator, or they pounced on everyone who looked official. No matter, he held his head high and gloated.

He had the authority to give a media release. Jensen motioned to the faces in his window to move back, and let him out of his vehicle. After a quick look in the mirror to check his teeth and hair, he pushed the door open, and used it as a shield to hold the sharks at bay. Microphones shot at him like quills from a porcupine. All the cameras were pointed in his direction as he was lambasted with questions.

He held his palms up in the air to calm the crowd.

"I'm Corporal Henry Jensen...the officer in charge of this investigation."

A few impatient reporters assaulted him with questions. He raised his hands again, and waited for the noise to die down.

"I can only make a brief statement at this time, and I cannot answer any questions, as the investigation is in its early stages. We exhumed a body here earlier today, and I've returned now on information that they've found a second one. I..."

Someone shouted a question, cutting Jensen off. "What about the body found in the garage on Third Avenue and the suspect you have in custody?"

"As I was saying...the investigation is in its early stages. I can confirm that there was another body in a garage on Third Ave., but I cannot say at this time if there is any link to the other victims, or that the suspect in custody is responsible for any of these crimes.

Identities of all the victims is not yet known and any that are, will be withheld until their families have been notified. The task force commander, Inspector Nickerson, will brief all media later today. That is all for now."

The news vultures peppered Jensen with more questions. Some of them pushed forward, almost crushing him with his door. He fell back into his SUV, catching and tearing the right sleeve of his suit coat. He was pissed off, and laid on the horn to move the crowd out of his way.

Near the main cattle building, the barnyard looked like an active anthill—numerous holes in the ground, surrounded by loose dirt, cops scurrying around, collecting evidence.

Jensen stepped out of his SUV, and drew a deep breath in through his nose. He caught the smell of death in the air. It gave him a rush—the same a crack addict, after taking a hit off the pipe.

A uniformed cop approached him. "Sir, the coroner is done examining the bodies, and wants to take them to the morgue. Do you need anything else before he goes?"

"Yes. Tell him he can't take the second body anywhere until I have a look at it—I'm in charge here. It's pretty easy for him to say their dead, they've been buried."

"It's the same as the other one, sir."

"Really. Are you a homicide expert, constable?"

"I'm just saying..."

"Maybe you should go and do some crowd control at the front gate, so the coroner doesn't run anyone over after I let him leave."

The coroner stood by the open grave with his arms folded, waiting. Jensen briefly looked at the second body, made a few notes, then gave the coroner a cursory nod to take the body away.

He rolled his eyes at Jensen, then got on with the removal.

Including the one in the garage, they had found three bodies in various stages of decomposition, posed and probably killed in the same manner. Dee Reynolds appeared to be the most recent victim. Jensen took in the grizzly scene, proud that he was the one who discovered the suspect, John Alan Lewis. He drew another deep breath, closed his eyes and exhaled. A transformation took place.

Jensen was a different man when he drove away from the scene—he ignored the media at the front gate. He was in a another place...somewhere dark, in his own mind. It was a different time, in his past—he saw his mother's face. Why couldn't he forget the image. It was her death stare, it haunted him always.

It was his mother who taught him about love, or sex—he thought they were one in the same. He thought it was his right of passage to manhood. The interaction was pleasurable, but instinct told him it was wrong. Young Heinrich accepted her lessons physically, but emotionally, it was just another chore.

That all changed when he met a girl who he was sexually attracted to. His mother was livid when she found the two of them together. She banished the girl from his life, then, in desperation, tried to seduce him again. He wasn't interested.

Her consternation turned to anger and she attacked him. He tried to grab her arms as she slapped and punched him in the face. In a fit of rage, his mother's eyes bulged and she frothed at the mouth. He smelled alcohol on her breath.

Heinrich's loving mother was out of control, she tried to gouge his eyes out. He grabbed her by the throat, but she kept punching him. He squeezed harder and her eyes looked like they were going to pop out of her head. Her mouth was agape but no sound escaped from it. The punches grew softer and her arms fell limp at her sides. She became dead weight in his arms when her legs buckled.

Heinrich held his grip when she collapsed. He lowered her to the floor and knelt over her, staring into her eyes. The look of rage was gone, she seemed at peace. He was puzzled for a moment, but realized she was dead. Although happy that she couldn't use him anymore, sorrow and guilt consumed him.

He bent over and kissed her on the forehead. Tears fell from his cheeks into her lifeless eyes. Heinrich collapsed on top of his mother and cried like a baby.

A horn snapped Jensen out of the daydream—the traffic light was green. He looked in the mirror, and willed the thoughts from his mind. He loosened his tie and accelerated. Normally, Jensen never perspired. Strangely, he was soaked. He chalked it up to his memories, and the cloud of death that hung over him.

When Jensen pulled into the detachment parking lot he was amazed at how big the media circus had grown. Then he noticed that many in the crowd were not holding microphones or cameras. They held photos of their loved ones who were missing. They shouted and chanted: "Bring them home—we want justice! Bring them home—we want justice!"

Crying mothers stuck photographs in his face as he made his way to the door. Jensen kept his head down, and pushed through the crowd. The victim's families caught him completely off guard.

Inside the detachment, the only cop who acknowledged him was a rookie working the front desk. He had anticipated accolades, congratulations, and pats on the back. The truth was the patrol cops didn't much care for prima donnas like Jensen, or many of the other investigators assigned to the task force. It was a slap in the face, saying they weren't doing their jobs. Unfortunately, it was true.

Jensen ignored the shroud of silence, and headed back to the interview rooms. He stepped into the observation room, next to interview room A, where John Alan Lewis was being held. A uniformed officer was stationed there, watching Lewis through the glass.

"You can go now, I'll take it from here."

The officer looked at his watch, and noted the time in his memo book. Jensen eyeballed Lewis, who was seated alone in the interview room. He had his head down on his arms, which were folded in front of him, on the table. He appeared to be sleeping. It was a textbook sign of guilt.

Jensen thought about his plan of attack, while he set up both video recorders and then tested them. It was standard procedure to make two recordings in case one of the machines failed. Any competent investigator knew enough to test both machines. It would be embarrassing if someone gave a full confession, and there was no recording of it. His mind raced while he thought about the questions he wanted to ask.

With the recorders rolling, he looked at his faint reflection in the two-way glass. He patted his hair and checked his teeth,

The Highway of Tears

then straightened his tie, and examined his suit for lint. Grabbing the torn sleeve, he puffed and tucked the jagged edge in. Jensen pulled a container of breath mints from his pocket, and popped one in his mouth. He was ready to go head to head with a serial killer.

In an odd way, he felt like Lewis was an old childhood friend—someone he could relate to. He was anxious to hear the sordid details of each and every one of his kills. He considered Lewis' m.o., and wondered what deep and dark secret in the man's past led him to kill and pose his women in such a way. What was the root of his evil?

Looking frazzled, and a bit disheveled, Inspector Nickerson walked into the observation room. "Ah, Jensen...I'm glad you made it through the crazy mob outside."

"Yes, sir. I was just about to interview Lewis. Did you want to sit in?"

"No, Corporal, I know you're more than capable. I'll observe from here. That way I'll be able to monitor my phone—it hasn't stopped ringing since seven this morning. Off you go...don't let me hold you up. Good luck."

Lewis didn't even acknowledge Jensen when he walked into the room, and sat down. He purposely cleared his throat to get the man's attention. The Corporal placed his briefcase strategically in front of himself. He simultaneously flipped open the two latches and lifted the lid so that it concealed him from Lewis.

He had to let the suspect know who was in charge. Lewis would have to sit up straight, and crane his neck to see over the top, who was across the table from him. It was a game of chess, and Jensen made the first move.

He watched as Lewis slowly sat up, but all he could see were arms and the top of a man's head, behind the black leather briefcase. Jensen saw that he had the suspect's attention. He spoke from behind the attaché. "Am I disturbing you, Mr. Lewis?"

"Yeah...it's been hours...who are you?"

Jensen smirked as Lewis craned his neck up and from side to side, in an attempt to see who was speaking to him. He removed a pen and writing pad, then closed the briefcase. He slid it to one side and neatly placed the pen and pad directly in front of him.

He greeted Lewis with a cold stare. That was Jensen's second move—looking him straight in the eyes. The eyes don't lie, and can say a lot to the trained observer.

Lewis had light brown eyes, with a one-inch scar over the left one that suggested he might have zigged when he should have zagged. His crooked nose hinted that he probably stuck it in someone else's business. The shortness of his black hair hid the fact that it hadn't been combed in a while, and he had a three-day beard. Sitting, he appeared similar in height to Jensen, but thinner.

The Corporal knew that a good investigator never assumes what the suspect may or may not have heard, or been told, prior to the interrogation. Canadian law states that police must tell a person of interest or suspect, why they are being detained or questioned. It also says if the investigator has made up his/her mind to charge a person with a criminal offence, they must first advise that person of their legal rights.

Many suspects will clam up as soon as they are read their rights, but Jensen knew he had to go by the book in such a high profile case. He was also aware he was being recorded, and that his boss was watching, so he went slowly, one step at a time, obtaining the tombstone information first.

Corporal Jensen introduced himself, then asked the suspect for his full name, date of birth, address and place of employment—all for the record. Surprised that Lewis hadn't

The Highway of Tears

asked yet, Jensen told him why he was there. And before Lewis could answer, Jensen informed him of his constitutional rights. A standard police caution was delivered. It basically told Lewis he didn't have to say anything, and could call a lawyer.

Lewis responded to the legal mumbo jumbo. "Yeah, I know my rights...do I look stupid? Why don't you tell me what you think you got on me, and I'll tell you if I want a lawyer?"

"As you wish, sir. We've un-earthed some bodies where you work and live, Mr. Lewis...and we think you know all about it."

"What makes you *think* I killed those women?"

"Who said that the bodies were women's?"

"Everybody knows—it's those crackhead whores who are disappearing like pine trees. Maybe beetles are killing them too."

"I don't think beetles buried the two young women we found on the farm, where you work."

"A lot of people work there."

"And how would you explain the young woman we found under the garage floor, where your taxi was parked, at your residence?"

The suspect sat back in his chair and crossed his arms. "How would I know what was under the floor...I only rent there."

"We searched the garage, your taxi, and your residence. We recovered evidence..."

"Like fuck—what evidence?"

Inspector Nickerson listened intently, from the next room. He hadn't heard of any incriminating evidence being recovered from the house, and figured Jensen was only bluffing Lewis to provoke a reaction. It is a technique that police can lawfully use during an interrogation.

"We have your souvenirs...you know, the pieces of jewellery you took as mementos from the women you killed."

The two of them were eye-locked in a staring contest, each man trying to read the other, until that point.

Nickerson noticed Lewis's eyes narrow and he looked up to the right; he was thinking or trying to remember. He was stiff in his chair with his hands folded on the table in front of him.

"Yeah, I got a box of junk jewellery—I've had that shit for years, so what?"

"What about the silver feather earring?"

The corners of Lewis' mouth relaxed, almost as if he was about to smile. He glared at Jensen, and pushed himself back from the table, as though he'd just been hit with a blast of cold air.

Jensen and Nickerson were both startled by the reaction.

Lewis knew Jensen was bluffing. Nickerson wondered why he referred to that one specific piece of jewellery.

"What about the earring, officer?"

The Corporal hesitated before he answered, the bluff was a fatal mistake. "Did it come from one of your victims...a souvenir perhaps?"

"If there was a silver feather earring in that box, someone musta planted it there, officer."

Nickerson became concerned. He never liked to hear such allegations when it came to his people. He thought about the earring for a second, but was distracted by a phone call.

Jensen changed his tactics before Lewis changed his mind, and asked for a lawyer. "We have a witness who saw you pick up one of the victims in your taxi—which isn't licensed as such...by the way."

"I use it to make a few bucks between big jobs—so what if I pick up the odd crack whore and trade a blowjob for a ride."

"Now you're saying you're having sex with prostitutes. I thought you used the taxi to make money?"

"I got needs...don't you, officer? Lewis chuckled. "I've seen you out there too...checkin 'em out. You don't fool me."

Corporal Jensen was taken aback. Not only had he lost the upper hand in the interrogation, Lewis had called his bluff, and was accusing him of picking up prostitutes—in front of his boss and whomever else that might be listening. The neck of his shirt felt tighter and his face started to redden.

Lewis leaned forward, and peered into Jensen's eyes. "We all have secrets, don't we, officer?"

Jensen was flabbergasted, he lost his train of thought, and had no idea what to ask next. There was a knock on the door—Jensen tried to compose himself, before answering it. Nickerson was there.

"Could I speak to you for a minute, Corporal?"

Jensen could tell his boss was upset, he normally called him by his last name. He joined the Inspector in the viewing room, and stared at Lewis behind the glass.

"He's not going to tell you anything, Corporal. I thought he would have asked for a lawyer by now, but he obviously knows we have nothing to tie him to the bodies."

"You know forensics will prove differently, sir."

"You're probably right on that, but he's accusing you of planting evidence and who knows what else. I think it's time to back off, until we get DNA or something else concrete. He's obviously smarter than he looks. Kick him loose, but get surveillance on him before you do. Maybe he'll do something stupid."

"But I..." Nickerson raised his hand. "Yes, Inspector. I'm sorry—I really thought I could get something out of him."

"I thought so too, Corporal. Maybe you weren't prepared enough...he caught you off guard and even embarrassed you in there. Frankly, I expected more from you."

The Inspector's phone rang again. He grabbed it from his belt, and walked away. Jensen dropped his chin to his chest, pouting like a little boy who just had his water pistol taken away. He turned and put his face up to the two-way glass. Sporting a mischievous grin, Lewis stared directly at him, even though he couldn't see through the mirrored glass.

Gloat all you want John Allen Lewis...you'll get yours!

37

Swap Meet

Carol stood in front of the stove, cooking breakfast. "How do you like your eggs, Norm?"

He took a bottle of water from the fridge. She couldn't have known he wasn't a morning person, and he didn't want to insult her. She and Sal had gone above and beyond since he met them and was adopted into the family. They had also welcomed Bozena and Two Snakes into their home, with no questions asked.

"Cooked, Carol—whatever's easier for you."

She laughed. Norm saw Sal and Two Snakes outside on the deck, sipping their coffee in silence, taking in the beauty of the mountain scenery. A chipmunk was perched on the railing, munching on a peanut that Sal offered it for breakfast. American gold finches fluttered around the feeder in the yard.

Norm slid open the glass patio door. "Looks like you guys are watching the nature channel out here."

Two Snakes nodded and Sal chortled. "Guess you don't get much of this in the city eh, Norm?"

"Nope. The biggest hills around the area I live are old garbage dumps that have been buried and turned into toboggan runs."

Sal laughed out loud.

"Nothing more natural than skiing on a garbage dump eh, Two Snakes?"

He nodded again. His eyes were fixed on the Twin Sisters. Norm filled his lungs with the crisp air. Autumn wasn't too far off.

"Busy day ahead of us, Tonto. Today is the day we find Hope."

Sal chimed in, "How long has she been missing, Norm?"

"I don't know...what day it is today? I think it's about two weeks—give or take."

"Probably seems like two months to her." Two Snakes added. "So, what's the plan, Kemosabe?"

"I told Strickland nine, but I'd like to get there before him to scope the place out and find somewhere for you to hide, so you can back me up."

"I wish I had one of my hunting rifles that I removed from the truck before you borrowed it. It's better to be prepared—how well do you know this Strickland guy?"

Sal left the deck, and went into the house.

"Not well. I've never seen him with any weapons, but that doesn't mean he has none. And I agree with you about being prepared."

Carol came out of the house with a tray loaded with breakfast goodies. Norm smelled the bacon, his stomach gurgled in anticipation. Sal returned with a scoped hunting rifle and handed it to Two Snakes. "This should work for you."

Two Snakes had his coffee cup in one hand, and was reaching for a piece of toast with the other. He eyed the gun and then the food. Like a kid in a candy store, he didn't know which to take first.

Carol placed everything in the center of the table: scrambled eggs, fried eggs, home fries, toast, sausage, and bacon. Norm usually didn't eat until he was wide awake, but there was no way he'd pass up a feast like that. Breakfast was his favorite meal of the day.

Carol waved her hand over the offering. "Don't wait for me guys, dig in."

Norm glanced at the rifle, but was more interested in the grub. Two Snakes stuffed a half a slice of toast into his mouth before he took the rifle from Sal. It was a .30-06 caliber, bolt action, with a scope. He checked the action, put a piece of bacon in his mouth then pointed the weapon into the bush. After looking through the scope he nodded his approval to Sal.

Two Snakes put the rifle down. Carol asked if anyone needed a coffee refill, before she sat down. Sal had his mouth full, but held his cup out to Carol. Norm tapped her arm just before she made it back into the house. "Where's Bozena? Isn't she joining us for breakfast?"

"The poor thing was exhausted so I let her sleep in. I put aside a plate for her."

"Are you sure you and Sal are okay with keeping an eye on her while we go looking for Hope? If we find her we can turn over both girls and the bad guys to the Mounties at the same time. Hopefully, I can get back to my original plan of visiting my sister, and then get home before the snow starts to fly."

Sal answered before Carol could. "It's not a problem, Norm. It's the least we can do for her—don't you worry. And you're right to be concerned about the weather in these parts, especially in the mountains. Do you have snow tires on the bike?"

Sal laughed at his own question. Norm shook his head. He was busy chewing and trying to beat Two Snakes to the last piece of bacon. Besides, his mother had taught him it was impolite to talk with his mouth full. He checked the clock on his cell phone, and gave Two Snakes a look.

He nodded, knowing Norm was signaling him it was time to go.

On the way to the lumber yard Two Snakes took the handful of bullets that Sal had given him out of his pants pocket. He looked them over, chose one and loaded it into the rifle. The sound of the bolt snapping back into place caused Norm's heart to skip a beat.

"Ever shoot anyone, Tonto?"

He answered with a question. "You?"

"Nope. Had my gun out plenty of times, and pointed it at a few bad guys, but I never had to pull the trigger. I was a pretty good shot at paper targets, but always wondered how I'd do under fire."

"A lot of guys mess themselves."

Norm stared ahead at the road, nodding silently.

"Did you?"

"No, but it don't mean I wasn't scared shitless. I hunted and killed all kinds of animals, but they don't shoot back at you, and try to blow you out of your socks with grenades."

"I thought about the military before I became a cop, but someone had to stay home to protect the women and children. The more I hear about it, the more I know I made the right decision. You still think about it much?"

"I try not too."

"I hear ya. There's the lumber yard up on the left. We're early so we can check the area before the fat man gets here. I don't know if he'll bring any backup. Do you want to look for high ground to set up, or lay in the back of the truck?"

"High ground is always good—maybe the roof of that shack, near the front gates. It'll give me a clear view of the gate and the entire yard. You can drop me off on the way in, then park out in the open where I'll have a clear field of vision."

Norm headed that way.

"That tree beside the shack should keep me hidden from the road."

He glanced down to the bag of weed on the floor beside Two Snakes' feet.

"You should be able to see the trade though your scope. If he gives me Hope's location I'll adjust the left mirror. If I don't like the way things are going, I'll tap on the roof with my hand. After the deal goes down I'll let Strickland leave first, then pick you up on the way out. If things go sideways, do what you have to."

"Is this a bad time to tell you that I suffer from PTSD?"

"Are you fucking with me?"

"No, really, I do—but it doesn't happen very often—just when I'm stressed or upset."

"Should I tell you a good joke, or show you some naked pictures before we do this?"

"We're here—looks quiet inside. Drive close to the shack and I'll jump out quick. Don't worry about me, I'll be fine."

"Yeah, okay—think happy thoughts up there."

Norm parked in the middle of the empty lot, facing the road and Two Snakes. He wasn't sure if the tightness in his chest was excitement or nervousness. He was anxious to find Hope, but didn't trust Strickland as far as he could roll him. Two Snakes gave Norm a wave that said he was ready and that someone was coming. It was the puke-green pickup truck.

By the way the truck leaned on the driver's side, it appeared Humpty Dale was alone. He drove into the lumber yard slowly, eyeballing Norm, and giving him a wide berth. He circled around Norm's truck and stopped about ten feet from the driver's side, their doors lined up.

He took a long haul off his cigarette then flicked it out his open window. "You got my weed, man?"

Norm held up the bag so Strickland could see it. The fat man opened his door and started to get out of his truck.

Norm barked. "What are you doing?"

"Relax, man. I got a map to give ya...it's too hard to explain where to go."

Wally-walrus waddled over to Norm's truck. He held his palms up in front of him to show he wasn't carrying anything, except the piece of paper. Norm reached out the window and Strickland handed him the map.

"My weed?"

Norm handed him the shopping bag and Strickland peered inside. He looked relieved. "So when do I get Little Bo Peep back?"

"As soon as I get Hope back—and I'd better not see any marks on her."

"Hey, man...I got no control over that."

"So tell me about the guy, your buddy, is he gonna give me any trouble?"

"Bear. His name's Bear and he's a little bigger than you. He's a mountain man and he keeps guns in the house. Hope was locked in a bedroom in his cabin, last time I was there. He ain't gonna give her up without a fight."

Norm adjusted the mirror.

"You can go now, Dale."

Strickland hesitated for a moment, while he lit up a smoke.

"So when do I get my girl back?"

"We'll let you know. I guess it'll depend on your buddy."

"What do you mean, we?"

"I have a buddy too, Dale. See the guy with the rifle, up on the roof of the shack behind you?"

Strickland turned and saw Two Snakes. He coughed the cigarette right out of his mouth and ran back to his truck. Never seeing such a fat man move so fast, Norm laughed out loud. Strickland jumped in his truck, fired up the engine, and spun the tires in the loose gravel. He yelled out the window as he left. "You're fuckin crazy, man!"

38

Getting the Girl

"Can you drive your own truck, Tonto? I need to catch up on some phone calls."

"Sure, Kemosabe. I hope you didn't ruin Geraldine, she and I have been together a long time."

"Probably longer than your wives, huh?"

"Let's just say she's been more dependable, and a lot cheaper to run."

Two Snakes put the rifle behind the seat, and the two men headed towards Kispoix. Norm's first call was to Laurie. He felt badly that he hadn't spoken to her in a couple days, but he was hoping to call her with good news.

He caught her at home. "Hey good-looking, it's Norm...I have some good news."

"Oh my God, Norm, I've been dying to hear from you. What's going on?"

"I think I know where Hope is..."

"She's alive?"

"I believe so. The trucker she hitched a ride with gave me a location where a mountain man is keeping her—up near Kispoix. We're heading there now."

"We? Are you with the police?"

"No, I haven't called them yet. I thought I'd wait until we get closer, and call them for backup. I want to check things out before they storm in."

"I've been worried to death about Hope, but I'm concerned about you too...now that we..."

"Thanks for caring, Laurie—I've joined forces with a local guy whose niece is missing too."

"I'm sorry to hear that—it's just crazy around here, with all those missing and murdered girls. I'm just relieved that Hope is okay. Bring her home, Norm. Do you think I should tell Charitee the news?"

"No, let's wait and see what happens...if and when we get her back. There's no use getting her all excited if we can't pull this off. Who knows what the weirdo has waiting for us up there. You'll be my first call, once she's safe."

"Okay, Norm. You be careful...I've come to miss you since your little visit. Do you think you'll be coming by again, when this is all over?"

"Uh...I'm not sure what I'll be doing, Laurie, we can talk more about it later. You take care—ciao for now."

Norm didn't realize he was smiling when he hung up. Two Snakes was staring, when he looked over at him.

"What was that all about, Kemosabe—did you rescue another damsel in distress?"

"Not quite...it's not like we planned it."

Two Snakes laughed out loud. "Yeah—you never plan it."

"She's Hope's friend...I just..."

"You don't have to explain nothing to me, Kemosabe. Good for you."

"I have to make a couple more calls—don't' you have some driving to do?"

Norm called the task force office next and left a message for Jensen to call him back. He was about to try his cell phone, when he felt Two Snakes staring at him again.

"What now, Tonto?"

"I think we need to talk about that guy."

"Jensen? Why have you got such a hard-on for that guy?"

"I just think he's no good..."

"Hold that thought—I want to check in with his boss and sick the cops on Strickland before he dumps that weed."

"Remind me to stay on your good side."

Norm called Inspector Nickerson and looked out the window while the phone rang.

"Hello, Norm, I'm glad you called...what's going on?"

"I've got good information on where Hope Lachance is being held."

"She's alive?"

"I believe so. I tried Jensen's line and left a message on his voice mail."

"Yeah, I gave him a few days off...he caught a serial killer. We've recovered three bodies so far."

"That's great...I mean, not for the victims...but you caught their killer. Anyway, I was wondering if you want to pick up Dale Strickland—he's in possession of two pounds of marihuana, right now. He has it with him in his truck and he's on the way home from Smithers.

When your guys seize his rig, you should have forensics check for DNA in the secret compartment in the back. I'm sure they can find something to put Bozena there and maybe even some other missing girls."

"I can do that. What do you need from us, to recover the Lachance woman?"

"I'm not sure yet, but I'd like to have the Calvary somewhere close by, if and when we need them. My tracker friend, Two Snakes, and I are gonna do a recon of the place where she's being held, before we make any attempt to rescue her. It's near Kispoix—we should be there in an hour or so. Can you give your guys there a head's up as to who we are and what we're up to?"

"Consider it done, Norm. Don't take any unnecessary chances, that's what we're here for."

"I hear you, Inspector. I'll keep you posted...oh, I almost forgot, you can send someone to pick up Bozena too. There's no use us keeping her from her family any longer, I'm sure she's anxious to go home."

Norm gave him the address, then hung up and called Sal and Carol's place to give them the head's up. They wished him luck in finding Hope. He reached down and grabbed the Tim Horton's bag off the floor, by his feet. He pulled out one of the chicken salad sandwiches and asked Two Snakes if he wanted the other one. He shook his head.

"Okay, Tonto. You talk...I'll listen and eat."

"I know he's a fellow cop and all, but things don't look good for your boy, Jensen."

Norm mumbled with his mouth full, "They gave him a few days off...his reward for catching a serial killer, I guess. They got three bodies so far."

"Yeah—one of them was my niece's friend, Dee Reynolds. I saw pictures of her in a grave on the farm, where they found her. I didn't tell you about the other girl from the group home where they stayed. I can't remember her name, but she knew Dakota too...says they were all turning tricks. Apparently they were saving their money to run off to Calgary.

Anyway, this other girl says one of their John's has a dark colored SUV. That's what's been bothering me for a while now. I keep seeing blue and black SUV's. I saw one at the cabin near the graveyard I told you about and Jensen..."

"Drives a dark blue Ford Explorer—I know, I've been in it." Norm laughed. "You remember the night we met at the bar?"

"Yeah, why?"

Norm swallowed the last bite of his sandwich, and washed it down with his Diet Pepsi. He turned to Two Snakes.

"Jensen gave me a lift home that night—picked me up stumbling through the parking lot. I guess I butt-dialed him or something. Anyway, I had a bit of a buzz on..."

"Yeah, that's fair to say."

"It was your fault—so he was driving me home and I heard a thud in the cargo area—I asked him if he had a bowling ball in the back." Norm snorted. "So maybe it was a body, eh?"

Two Snakes shook his head.

"I'm serious, Norm, the dude fits the profile...cop or not. He's a loner, the right age, has the means, and he's wound so tight that his ass squeaks when he walks."

"I dunno, buddy. But you know...now that I think about it, he had a shoe scuff on the dashboard, in his otherwise pristine vehicle. Hey—he also had what I assumed was a shaving nick on his neck. Guess I wasn't that drunk after all."

"See...think about it, Norm. It fits. The cabin I saw could be his, with his parents buried there, in the grave yard. Maybe he was adopted. We need to check the land registry office."

"I thought you were going to do that?"

Norm's phone rang.

It was Inspector Nickerson. "Hey, Norm. I have a quick question for you."

"Shoot, Inspector."

"I'm just going over some files and pictures, and wanted to clear something up. Do you remember being here one day and dropping something on the floor, that came from Jensen's drawer—maybe a piece of jewellery?"

"Ah...yeah, a silver earring...looked like a little feather."

"I thought so. Where are you at now?"

"I dunno...Tonto, how far are we from Kispoix?"

"The town is up that last road we passed. According to your directions we should be coming to the private logging road. What was that about a silver feather earring? My niece, Dakota...Holy Shit!!!"

39

Little Things

Henry Jensen was a man of routine; he was surprised when he rolled over and saw the time on his alarm clock. It was the best night's sleep he'd had in as long as he could remember—probably because he'd slept in his own bed, and not in a motel room. Working with the task force and on the Lewis case meant that he practically lived at the Ramada. It made sense for work reasons, but he was never comfortable there.

After climbing out of bed, and relieving himself, he stood naked in front of the full-length mirror on the back of the bathroom door. He held his head high, patted his stomach and gave his Johnston a grope before he put on his bathrobe.

The smell of fresh coffee brewing caught his attention—he'd set the timer before retiring for the night. His lips allowed a little smile when he felt the warmth of the pot. Jensen poured himself a cup and sat down at the kitchen table to read the newspaper. *My name will surely be in here today.*

Savoring a sip of the bean, he gazed around the cabin; it hadn't changed much over the years. The original logs were still visible in the open ceiling, but the walls had been insulated, covered with paneling and painted a peach color—his mother's favorite. The floor was wood planked, with a few throw rugs. There were no family pictures adorning the walls, only photos of himself and some RCMP memorabilia—he loved their red colors.

The cabin sat empty for years after his parents died, and he moved away. When he did return, he updated the plumbing, electrical, and appliances. Except for his parent's bed, he kept most of the rustic furniture. He considered those, the comforts of home.

Something crawled onto his bare foot, a carpenter ant— probably from the trap door under the table. It gave access to an old root cellar that had been used for cold storage. Occasionally, Jensen used it as his own personal morgue, prior to burying his victims. The room was also accessible from a grade entrance at the back of the cabin, but he disguised it with the wood pile, to deter intruders.

A photograph of the cattle farm where the bodies were found, covered the top half of the front page. He took another sip of coffee, and read the headlines: 'Missing Girls Found Buried on Farm.' The story started with the body count, as usual, but no names were being released until the next of kin were notified. It was the usual journalistic crap...Jensen skimmed down to where he saw his name:

Corporal Henry Jensen, of the Royal Canadian Mounted Police's task force, confirmed to this reporter that a total of three bodies have been recovered so far. Two bodies were discovered on the farm and a third in a garage on Third Avenue. Police sources revealed that a man who resided at that residence, John Alan Lewis, was taken into police custody for questioning.

Corporal Jensen would not confirm that the three bodies were connected or if Lewis was responsible in any way. He said that the investigation was in its early stages. At a later news briefing, Inspector Harold Nickerson reiterated the above facts and confirmed that Lewis was in police custody. He would not elaborate if any charges were to be laid. When asked how

The Highway of Tears

police got the information on Lewis and the bodies the Inspector declined to comment.

Jensen guffawed and flipped the page hard enough to tear it at the top. *They'd have no bodies and no suspect if it wasn't for me. Lewis...who does he think he is...trying to outsmart me? He'll get his.* He thought about the interview. He'd screwed up, and he knew it. Lewis was sharper than he'd anticipated, he wouldn't underestimate him again.

I shouldn't have assumed he took jewellery for souvenirs, like I do, but I needed leverage to question him about other victims...surely there are more. I deserve another run at Lewis. I can't believe Nickerson sent me home...what was he thinking, sending his best investigator home at a time like this?

He reached for his coffee, but his thumb hit the handle and knocked the cup over, spilling the contents all over the paper. *Crap! I wanted to save the article.* Jensen jumped up to get a rag. *I need to clear my head.* He cleaned up the mess, then went to the kitchen sink. Gawking out the window he thought to himself. *Looks like a nice day to go trolling.*

* * *

Harold Nickerson loosened his tie and rolled up his sleeves. He wondered how many innocent trees had given their lives to contribute to the stack of paperwork on his desk. Reports were still coming in from various Investigators and Forensic Specialists. It was his responsibility to make sure all the files were in order.

While multi-tasking, he thought about Jensen. It was his demeanor that concerned him. *Sure, the man was dog tired, but he was way off his game and he blew the interview with Lewis. And what was that crap about an earring?* Nickerson's phone rang and disrupted his train of thought. He let it go to voicemail.

Finding Hope

The press release hadn't gone well for the Inspector—as usual. Whenever the police had a good suspect, the media tended to jump to all sorts of conclusions. John Alan Lewis was their only suspect for the murders of the two women found at the farm and the one in his garage, but there wasn't any physical evidence against him yet. Nickerson felt it would come in time, and he could always be arrested and charged then.

As the Inspector perused the paperwork in front of him, he knew that some of the pieces needed to complete the puzzle were in the files, but it would take many more man hours to build a prima facie case. There were witnesses to talk to and DNA samples to process, the latter could take months. The bodies had to be shipped all the way to Vancouver to be meticulously examined by expert pathologists.

Jensen popped back into his mind...something was nagging at him. He took a break from the case files and pulled the Corporal's personnel file from his lower desk drawer. Nickerson had it handy, since he'd thought about promoting Jensen to Sergeant. The task force was mostly made up of Constables, with a few Corporals, and he was looking for someone to be his right-hand man. With Jensen's seniority, experience and good work in discovering the recent bodies, he was a good candidate.

The Inspector had the personnel file sent to him, thinking that he'd rubber stamp a recommendation for promotion, but he became apprehensive and thought he'd research Jensen's background so that he could make an informed decision. In telling him to take a couple days off, he hoped to make that decision before Jensen returned to work.

Looking through the file, he realized just how little he really knew about the man. They had never worked together per say, but had crossed paths during investigations or seminars, in the past. The decision to transfer Jensen to the task force was made by someone above Nickerson's pay grade.

He noted Jensen was never married and his current address was there, at the Ramada. That wasn't too unusual, considering that no one knew how long they'd be assigned to the task force or how long it would operate.

The Inspector was surprised to see that Jensen resided in Prince George when he was hired, but then he moved around the country quite a bit. He looked over his original application and saw that he had legally changed his name before being hired. His birth name was Heinrich Johan Johansen. *Not a big deal,* Nickerson thought, *he probably had his reasons with a name like Heinrich.* Under next of kin, there were none listed.

The file contained various letters of commendation from past supervisors, but no formal complaints. There was a short note attached to one of Jensen's transfers. The supervisor felt that the officer was too close to certain women who worked the streets. Jensen explained that they were informants, after he was seen with one woman in his work vehicle.

It appeared that Jensen had requested the other moves himself. Again, that wasn't unusual in the RCMP, where some officers moved around until they found their niche. There was one comment that caught Nickerson's attention—it was made by a supervisor upon Jensen's promotion to Corporal. He thought that the candidate had leadership potential, but his arrogance and aloofness were a bit bothersome. He wasn't always a team player, especially when working with female officers.

Nickerson sat back in his chair and placed his reading glasses on the personnel file. He replayed the interview with Lewis in his head and remembered how Jensen had control at the beginning, but then lost it when called on his bluff about the jewellery. *I forgot about that—why is it bugging me?*

He reached over to the corner of his desk and flipped through the case files until he found Jensen's report from the search at Lewis' house. Nickerson skimmed the report until he got to the list of property seized. According to the report another officer seized a handful of assorted jewellery from the bedroom.

So what's the connection—was there something there that belonged to one of the victims? It doesn't say here and he never mentioned it to me. He should have, it would be a big piece of the puzzle...enough to charge Lewis with possession of stolen property, for starters.

The Inspector picked up the list of seized jewellery, got up from his desk and walked over to the bulletin boards where photos of the victims were posted. He scanned the before and after pictures of the young women, but didn't notice anything unusual. He yawned and rubbed his eyes, then put the file down on the table by the coffee maker. He poured himself a cup, and turned back to the victims.

He stood in front of their pictures, studying the face of each missing woman. Something caught his eye—one of the girls wore a pair of silver ear rings. He put his coffee down and picked up the file, scanning the list of jewellery again. *Well I'll be dammed, what do we have here?* On the list of items seized from Lewis' residence was: one silver feather ear ring. He looked back to the board and at a picture of a girl named Dakota. She wore a pair of silver feather ear rings.

Nickerson stared at the photograph. *That's no coincidence.* He turned and walked to the back of the room where the temporary evidence lockers were lined up along the wall. Being the officer in charge, he had a set of keys. After removing the evidence bag that contained the jewellery, he went back to the picture of Dakota. He located the silver feather in the plastic bag and held it up to the photo. It hit him like a Mack Truck.

The Inspector took the evidence bag and report back to his desk and called Norm Strom. He asked him if he remembered the item from Jensen's drawer that fell on the floor when he was in his office that one day. Norm remembered and said it was a silver feather earring, but then someone yelled, "Holy Shit!" There was nothing but garbled sounds and static after that, then his phone went dead.

40

Finding Hope

"Life is like riding a bicycle. To keep your balance, you must keep moving."
—Albert Einstein

Hope caught a glimpse of the highway ahead, through the trees. She smelled the fresh scent of pine in the air, probably from the logging trucks that regularly passed by. It was so thick she could almost taste it—the flavor of freedom. After the last bend in the laneway the main road came into full view; it was a beautiful sight.

She heard the roar of a truck's engine and she started to yell, even though she knew the driver would probably never hear her. Hope waved her arms in the air as she neared the highway, but no truck was visible yet. The noise grew louder—it came from behind her. It was Bear, in his pickup. He barreled toward her and she recognized his scowl, his face was covered in blood.

Hope reached the highway and ran out onto the pavement directly into the path of another pickup truck. It swerved at the last second, crossing over into the oncoming lane. Bear's truck roared off the laneway to where she was standing, frozen it time. Sheer will helped her to leap out of the way. Bear was so focused he didn't see the other vehicle and ploughed into it, broadside.

The Highway of Tears

The force of the collision rolled the other truck over and it landed in the ditch on the far side of the highway. Down on all fours, Hope stared at Bear's stalled truck; she prayed he wouldn't get out. She looked to the other truck for help, but there were no signs of life. Smoke poured from under the hood of Bear's truck and drifted over her like a blanket of fog. In a daze, she still heard the sound of a roaring engine, but it wasn't coming from either of the crashed pickup trucks.

The pitch of the sound changed, she searched for it—screeching tires and the unmistakable machine gun noise from a Jake Brake. A jack-knifed logging truck was skidding sideways across both lanes of the highway, in her direction. Terrified and still on all fours, Hope crawled off the shoulder of the highway and rolled down into the ditch.

The logging truck slammed into Bear's pickup and swallowed it like a whale gathering dinner. The chains holding the logs in place on the trailer snapped and timber rolled over top of Bear's truck and down the highway. The screeching and crunching of rubber and metal was deafening. With her hands over her head, Hope lay face down in the bottom of the ditch, afraid to move or look up.

It seemed like an hour had passed when she heard a man's voice. "Miss, are you okay?"

She rolled over and looked up at a dark haired man, wearing a green tee shirt and jeans. He stepped down and held out a hand to help her from the ditch. "Are you okay? I need some help—there are two men trapped in their truck, in the other ditch. I already called 911."

The smoke had cleared, but Hope was still in a fog—it was like the end of a bad dream. She saw what was left of Bear's truck; it was completely crushed. She turned her head, knowing that he was still in there, somewhere.

"I'm sorry miss, he's a gonner—he came out of nowhere. There was nothing I could do. Did you know him?"

"Uh...no, I don't know who he is."

Hope and the trucker ran over to the pickup in the opposite ditch. It was upside down, and the driver was trying to climb out of the window on his side. His left arm was bleeding, and he had a few small cuts on the same side of his face. The trucker helped the Aboriginal man out of his truck and to his feet. He leaned on his vehicle for support.

His long hair was matted with the blood on the side of his face. He gently prodded the gash on his arm, then brushed broken glass from his shirt. "Wow, I'm still alive. Can you help me get my friend out? I think he's unconscious—his door got smashed in. Norm, can you hear me?"

The good Samaritan and Two Snakes tried to pull the driver's door open, but it was jammed. Hope watched, not sure what to do. She took off the blouse that she wore over a tank top and wrapped it around the wound on Two Snakes' arm. The trucker crawled through the driver's window far enough to grab Norm's arm, but he was still buckled in. The tug on his arm was enough to bring him around.

He saw that Norm was dazed, but understood what the man was trying to do. He motioned for him to release the seat belt. After righting himself, he crawled to the window, where the truck driver helped him climb out. He staggered to his feet and saw Two Snakes, standing beside a woman.

He was smiling. "How you doing, Kemosabe?'

"I'm a little banged up, but everything seems to be working. My ribs are pretty sore—what the hell hit us? I remember being on the phone...then the rest is a blur. Hope, is that you?"

She was still in shock and looked puzzled. "Do I know you?"

"Not really...we met briefly in Jasper. We were supposed to meet again in Hyder, but...never mind. I know you've been through a lot, we can talk more later. I'm Norm Strom."

Hope stepped closer. "Kind blue eyes, friendly smile...the retired cop. I remember."

Norm blushed, he wasn't sure why. "That's me, I've been looking for you since you went missing—as a favor to your friend, Laurie. And I met your daughter—she's a cutie, just like her mom."

"Charitee...is she okay? My ex was here and said that he'd seen her. I..."

"She's fine, Hope. I talked to Laurie earlier today and everything's good. Your ex...you mean Robert? He was here?"

"Yeah, he came to the cabin, then him and Bear fought and he got his leg stuck in a trap and I ran and..."

"Bear, the guy who kidnapped you? Where is he?"

"He's over there under that truck, somewhere."

Norm looked at the trucker. He shook his head and Norm grimaced. "Has anyone called for help?"

The wail of sirens answered his question; the cops and paramedics were there in another two minutes. Before long, other vehicles had stopped on the road, and gawkers moved in, adding to the chaos and confusion. After the police taped off the accident scene, Norm talked to one of them, and found out that Inspector Nickerson had dispatched them to the area.

He looked around for Hope. She was in the back of a cruiser, talking to Charitee on the phone and balling her eyes out. He left her alone.

Two Snakes came up behind him and put a hand on his shoulder. "How's your girlfriend?"

"She's good. How's the wing, Tonto?"

"Just a scratch—I could really use a beer."

"I hear ya. Hey, where'd you get off to?"

"Hope said that her ex got caught in a trap near the cabin she was being held in, down that laneway."

"Yeah, I caught that..."

"Me and one of the Mounties went for a look-see and only found his left leg—it was still in the trap."

"What?"

"Yeah, go figure. The cop thought that he tore himself free of the trap, then crawled off somewhere and died in the bush. We lost the blood trail along the stream."

"And you don't buy that?"

"This ain't the city, Kemosabe, I've seen it before. One hungry animal takes advantage of another wounded animal—it's the law of nature."

Norm laughed out loud, then winced and held his ribs. "Well, that's street justice...or nature...whatever. Are they gonna look again for the rest of him?"

"I dunno. Not our problem...is it?"

"Nope. You're funny, I like your style. Hey, have you seen my phone?"

"Oh, yeah—I forgot. I found it on the road, near our wreck. It must have flown out your window." Two Snakes laughed out loud when he handed it to Norm. "It's a little banged up."

"A little banged up? The screen is all smashed and there's buttons missing..."

"Don't worry, Kemosabe, the Mounties are covering your expenses...remember? Wait until they get the bill for my new truck. Hey, by the way, do you know who's minivan that is with the big log sticking through the middle of it."

Norm turned and started laughing again. He held his ribs, trying to suppress the pain. "Stop making me laugh. That belongs to the one-legged psycho who is now bear food. I've seen it before—the plate matches the one that Jensen gave me."

"Speaking of psycho's, why ain't he here?"

The Highway of Tears

"I dunno, he's been MIA for a while."

"Hey, Norm, how the hell are we getting home?"

"My cop buddies are taking care of that. When we're done here, they're giving us a ride to the airport and then flying us back to Prince George. First Class."

"Kemosabe, you forget where you're at. First Class here means we'll be stuffed into a four seat bush plane."

"You're probably right. I'm going back to check on Hope."

She was still sitting in the police cruiser, on the phone. She gazed at Norm and smiled. "Yes, Laurie, he's hear now. I'll tell him you said so."

Hope hung up the phone. "Laurie says you're a very sweet guy—that I should be grateful you found me, since the cops did nothing. It sounds like you two got pretty close."

"Uh...maybe, we helped each other out...you know, to try and find you." Norm blushed again.

Hope got out of the car, stood up and wrapped her arms around him. She gave the retired cop a big hug and said, "You're a good man, Norm. Thank you."

41

Loose Ends

Norm suggested to the pilot that he call the Inspector—Hope was not happy about going to Prince George before seeing her daughter. Nickerson said he wanted to debrief everyone at the task force office, but Norm and Two Snakes said they didn't mind the detour to Stewart.

The Inspector sympathized with Hope and told the pilot to adjust his flight plan accordingly. She was quiet and stared off, out the window. Norm let her be and nodded off. He couldn't even imagine what she had gone through. Two Snakes had the best seat, up front with the pilot, where he got to admire the view.

Norm felt the touchdown in Stewart directly in his ribs. He winced. When the plane taxied up to the hanger, Hope's welcoming party was there waiting and waving. Charitee hopped up and down like a Mexican jumping bean. Laurie held on to her arm for fear she would run into the path of the arriving plane.

Norm and Hope disembarked; he told the pilot he'd be back in five minutes. Hope barely had her feet on the tarmac when Charitee leapt into her open arms. Laurie's eyes locked onto Norm's. Her soft smile and penetrating gaze warmed his heart. She hugged him like she never wanted to let go.

His face flushed and Hope looked on in wonderment, but Charitee stole her attention back, chattering like a record on high speed. Hope put her daughter down to give Laurie a hug, then she turned to Norm like she was going say something. She reached up with both hands, cupped his face then said, "I'll never forget you."

Laurie looked puzzled when the pilot called out to Norm; she assumed he was staying. He put up his hand to wave goodbye, and said he had to report to the Mounties in Prince George. She lunged forward, bear-hugged him, and kissed him on the cheek. Teary-eyed, she peered into his eyes and said, "I'll always remember you."

* * *

It was after dark when Norm and Two Snakes walked into the task forced office, in the Ramada. Disheveled hair and puffy eyelids accented by dark rings made Inspector Nickerson look as though he just went a couple rounds with Muhammed Ali. There were a handful of other cops in the room, but the mood was somber.

"Someone die?" Asked Norm, when they stopped at the Inspector's desk.

He surveyed the cuts and bandages on Two Snakes and bruises on Norm's forehead and right arm. "I wasn't told you guys were so banged up...anything serious?"

Norm answered, "We've both been hurt worse, we'll live."

"That's good to hear. Have a seat, gentlemen, we need to talk."

Two Snakes chirped off, "About your man, Jensen?"

Before Nickerson could answer, Norm asked, "Where the hell is—"

"He took some time off...or rather, I told him to take some time off. At first I thought he was just burned out, but..."

Two Snakes interjected, "I think it's more than that, Inspector."

Norm added, "We don't have any actual proof, sir, but we think Jensen might have something to do with the missing women around here. His vehicle matches the description given by witnesses and—"

Two Snakes cut in again. "And there's a graveyard by a cabin up in the Caribou Mountains—"

"Yes, yes, gentlemen. We all need to take a deep breath. I know he's been up to something too, I discovered he planted evidence in John Alan Lewis' house, during the execution of a search warrant—for misdirection, I think."

The Inspector slid the evidence bag, containing the silver leaf earring, across the desk to Two Snakes. "Do you recognize this?"

Two Snakes leaned forward, his eyes grew wide. He stuttered, "Th-that be-belongs to my niece, Dakota...she's missing."

Norm inquired, "Is that the thing you asked me about—the one in Jensen's desk?"

"I'm afraid so, Norm. He hasn't answered for it yet, but as far as I'm concerned, there is no reasonable explanation how it went from his desk to Lewis' house. He was obviously trying to frame the man."

Two Snakes added, "I'd be more interested in how he came to be in possession of it in the first place. Why haven't you questioned him yet?"

"Honestly...I was planning to, but I've been in this business a long time, and I have a very bad feeling in my gut."

"I told you he was evil, Norm." Two Snakes shook his head.

Norm asked, "What are your intentions, Inspector?"

"He does need to be questioned, he has a lot of explaining to do. Earlier today, acting on my gut feeling, I sent a sniper out to his cabin, the place you're talking about—to keep an eye on him. My man has been hiding out there all day, reporting back to me.

Don't worry, this man is ex-military—the type who can live on bear shit and worm juice to survive in the wilderness. Just before you two arrived he saw Jensen standing over a fresh grave in what looks like the family plot."

Nickerson took his reading glasses off and cleaned them with the end of his tie. "Having my own suspicions, I checked his personnel file, and found that he changed his name before he started with us, and the name matches up with the property owner of the cabin. The land registry office confirms the title has never changed hands, and someone's been paying the taxes."

Norm sat back in his chair, folded his arms across his chest, and eyed the Inspector. "I think we're all in agreement here, in regards to Jensen—he's like bad news in a church newspaper. We're all pretty tired. Maybe we can catch up on the Lachance file tomorrow, if that's okay with you, sir?"

"Actually, Norm, I was hoping your friend, Mr. Greene, would help us out when we go out to Jensen's place in the morning. I understand you hunt and fish in the area, and know the lay of the land? I already have a search warrant ready to go, but I'd like to be sure of the map."

Two Snakes answered, "I'd be glad to help—even if it's only to find out what happened to my niece."

"What about you, Norm? You're welcome to come along, as an observer. I think I owe you that."

Norm reached into his pocket, pulled out a wad of crumpled receipts and put them on the Inspector's desk. "Speaking of what you owe me...I kept receipts for all my expenses. And then there's the issue of Mr. Greene's truck that was totaled by Hope's abductor, Daniel Grayson—we'll leave it with you. So what time is the big show tomorrow?"

Finding Hope

The Inspector signed the bottom of a form, and added it to one of the piles on his desk. "I'll be briefing everyone here at 5 am."

Norm shuddered. "Shit, I was afraid you'd say something like that—can I get a wake-up call? Oh yeah...and do you happen to have an extra phone that I can borrow until I leave town? Mine got trashed in the collision."

"Sure, anything else, Norm?"

He grinned. "Well, now that you ask, I'm a little shy on cash, and was hoping to buy my friend here a couple beers and maybe some wings—you're quite welcome to come along, Inspector."

Nickerson opened his desk drawer, pulled out the petty cash box and handed Norm a C note. "This should be enough to quench your thirst."

Two Snakes snickered. "You haven't seen him drink, have you?"

"Sorry, but I'll have to pass on your invitation so I can prep for the raid."

The cold beer soothed their parched throats, boggled minds, and tender wounds. It had been a rough couple of days. Norm and Two Snakes sat at the bar at Billy's and stared up at the television as if it was the first time they'd ever seen one.

Norm broke the silence. "Do you really think that Jensen is a psycho serial killer who preys on young women?"

"I have no doubt in my mind, Kemosabe. I told you what I thought the night we met—remember the Fox?"

"So what else does your medicine tell you?"

"I'm afraid to say."

"Why? You can tell me...you're like my brother from another mother."

"That's funny. It's just...I think the evil bastard killed Dakota."

"Why do you think that? There's obviously more than one killer around here and who says she's dead? Maybe she's in Calgary, with her friends."

"I don't think so, I saw her in a dream. She was climbing a white mountain that was surrounded by dead trees, trying to reach the spirit horse so it could carry her into the afterlife."

Norm sucked in his lower lip, and scratched his beard. "And that means she's dead?"

"Yes, Kemosabe. I've seen the place...it's the graveyard near Jensen's cabin."

"Holy shit—I'd be afraid to go to sleep if I had dreams like that."

Two Snakes raised his mug and took a sip of beer. Norm studied the tattoo on his upper arm. "Hey, you never did tell me the story behind your name and that tattoo."

"Two Snakes? It's from a parable about *the two snakes*."

"A what?"

"A parable...from the Manichaean Scriptures, my grandfather was into that kind of stuff. It's a story about the two snakes, *Heavy to Carry* and *Light to Carry* and their bodies, souls and pitfalls..."

Norm lost his focus and all he heard was blah, blah, blah. His weary mind drifted off. He thought about the first time he met Hope and how much had happened since, how her life had changed, forever. She might be tough enough to get past it, but there'd be deep scars, for the rest of her life. He wondered if they'd find the rest of her ex, Robbie...but he really didn't care if they did.

His gaze landed on the barmaid's derriere, when she unknowingly offered him a clear view of her shapely backside. Then he thought of Laurie.

Two Snakes cleared his throat. "And the two snakes lived happily ever after."

"Huh?"

"You didn't hear a damn word of my story, did you?"

"I'm sorry, Tonto. I'm fried...my mind is elsewhere. Hey, how are we gonna get home? We don't have any wheels. Shit! I forgot to call Loretta to see if I can crash there tonight."

"I got couch space."

"No offence, brother, but she's a lot better looking than you...and she feeds me. I'm gonna call her and then take a cab— I need some sleep."

"I'll see you in the morning, Kemosabe. It should be an interesting day."

42

Crispy Killer

His wrinkled suit, unshaven face and bloodshot eyes, suggested Harold Nickerson spent the night in the office. His alertness and fast speech said that he'd injected several cups of highly caffeinated coffee into his bloodstream. The ERT guys were just as pumped; two of them shoved Timbits into their mouths like coins into a slot machine.

Norm nodded to the Inspector as he passed by his desk, and joined Two Snakes, who was seated near the back of the room, by himself. Nickerson was busy on the phone.

"Mornin, Kemosabe—no coffee or donuts, like the rest of your buddies?"

"First of all, mister Two Snakes parable, they're not my buddies—they're Canada's finest and I'm only a retired city cop. Secondly, I've never drank coffee, and I prefer a healthier breakfast—like bacon and eggs. And lastly, it's too fucking early in the morning for me to be talking to you."

The Inspector asked for everyone's attention. Norm surveyed the battle-ready group. There were ten heavily-armed ERT guys, four investigators, who were dressed in plain clothes—with Kevlar vests, four uniformed cops, himself, Two Snakes and the Inspector. *Enough manpower and firepower to take down a whole village—I thought they just wanted to question Jensen.*

Nickerson pointed to a map on one of the bulletin boards, and went over the raid plan one last time. Two Snakes leaned over to Norm and whispered, "How do you like my map?"

"Nice. I love the cute little log cabin. Who are all the little stick people in the back yard?"

"Shut up...that's the graveyard."

Norm saw the Inspector staring at him and Two Snakes, and thought he was going to get shushed, but he waved them over. The rest of the raid team picked up their gear and headed out to the parking lot.

"Norm, you and Mr. Greene can ride with me. We'll be bringing up the rear, where I can keep you out of the line of fire."

"Fine by me, Inspector, I hate guns."

"What? Didn't you carry one on the job?"

"When I didn't forget in the drawer or glove box. I don't mean to be critical, Inspector, but isn't this overkill—I thought you only wanted to question Jensen?"

"That's the plan, Norm, but I like to be prepared. I've been trying to reach him by phone and he's not responding. I'll try again when we get to the cabin, he deserves a chance to surrender peacefully."

After turning off the Highway of Tears, at the devil's pitchfork, Nickerson checked in with his sniper, who was still babysitting Jensen. According to him, Jensen was in the cabin all night and still there. He was keeping an eye on the front door until they arrived.

As per the raid plan, the team parked their vehicles, and split up at the fork in the logging road where they wouldn't be heard and could remain out of sight. One half of the team walked through the bush on the north side of the cabin, and the other half approached from the south, where the graveyard was.

Once everyone was in place Nickerson received confirmation over the radio. That was his signal to call Jensen and ask him to come out.

The Inspector made the call to Jensen's cell phone but there was no answer; it went to voicemail. He left a message to call him back ASAP, then waited three minutes and called again. He got the same result. Nickerson updated the entry team then waved Norm and Two Snakes up closer, where they could watch the action.

The early morning sun beamed through the trees casting shadows that made the cops look ten feet tall. The chirping and singing sounds of birds was replaced by the thumping of boots on the ground and the crunching of leaves and twigs beneath them.

Norm took cover behind a tree, which was thick enough to shield him and far enough away to be out of the line of any stray bullets. Two Snakes lay on the ground about six feet away, watching through binoculars. He pulled a piece of jerky from his pocket. Feeling Norm staring, he tossed it to him without removing his eyes from the lenses.

According to the recon done by Two Snakes and verified by the sniper, there was only one entrance to the cabin—the front door. There were windows on the front and sides, but none at the back. A vehicle under a tarp was parked in the driveway out front, about fifty feet away from the front porch.

Norm watched the five man entry team approach the front of the house. They crouched down and went in low under the windows, stacking up to the right side of the door, where the handle was.

Just when the lead man reached for the door handle, the window in the front door exploded, sending shards of glass flying into the air. Before the team could react the two front windows on either side of the door also shattered, showering the team with debris.

The cops on both sides of the house reacted to the gunfire at the front door and fired rounds into the other windows. From his position in the trees, Norm found the sound of the gunfire deafening. Two Snakes dropped his binoculars, and used his hands to cover his ears. They must have shot a hundred rounds into the cabin, before Nickerson shouted for everyone to cease fire.

There was no echo, the thunderous noise was swallowed by the forest. Silence hung in the air. Before the Inspector could utter another word, the cops at the front of the cabin lobbed two tear gas canisters through the open windows.

Norm had seen tear gas used before and didn't remember it being smoky. He was a bit puzzled seeing grey-white clouds spilling out the windows and drifting up and into the trees. The entry team had their gas masks on and were about to breach the front door when someone shouted, "Fire!"

Nickerson gave the order to hold positions. Two Snakes turned to Norm, wide-eyed. Norm shrugged. If the bullets and gas didn't chase Jensen out, maybe Nickerson thought a fire would. They waited and watched as the inside of the cabin started to glow like a jack-o-lantern. The dry timbers caught fire quickly. Flames, gasping for oxygen, crawled out the windows, and up the cabin walls like burning tentacles.

Norm had seen plenty of fires and burned bodies during his stint as an Arson Investigator, but he never stood by and watched anyone burn to death. He remembered the warehouse fire, where he would have died if Johnny Eagle hadn't pulled him to safety. Being trapped in a burning building was horrifying.

The Inspector held the radio microphone to his mouth, but no words were uttered. He just stood there, in awe of the fire, knowing it was too late to do anything. If Jensen hadn't been killed by a police bullet, he would surely perish in the raging inferno.

Norm approached Nickerson; he was on his phone, calling for fire and paramedics. The other cops backed further into the forest to escape the heat.

Two Snakes came up along Norm's side. He guffawed. "Maybe they can try to save the forest from burning down—good thing there's no wind today. Want some more jerky?"

Norm grinned and couldn't resist the comeback. "Somehow, I think hotdogs would be more appropriate."

Nickerson glared at Norm. "Do I have to remind you that a police officer is in there. At the least, he deserved a fair trial."

Two Snakes snapped back at the Inspector. "He got it—trial by fire. I'm going to check the graveyard. Maybe you'll change your opinion of the man after I find what I think is buried there."

Norm shielded his face from the heat of the fire, the cabin was fully engulfed and a portion of the roof caved in. Two Snakes started walking toward the graveyard. Norm looked at the Inspector, shrugged, then followed his friend.

They followed a path from the cabin to a clearing on a hill. The giant boulder caught Norm's attention first, then the decrepit picket fence and dead fruit trees. The graveyard looked sinister, even in the daylight.

Two Snakes stopped in front of a mound in the tall grass and kicked at it with the toe of his boot. "You see this...it's a fresh grave. Take a look around, there are more of them."

Norm wandered, then stopped in front of the tombstone and read the inscription. He leaned in closer. The carved letters of the woman's name were darker and shiny around the edges, compared to the man's. The grass was trampled around the marker. Norm peeked behind it and saw a shovel hidden between the monument and a tall shrub.

He brought it to Two Snakes. "Here, it will be easier with this."

Two Snakes took the shovel, but didn't reply. His thoughts were elsewhere—a place that Norm didn't care to visit with him. Leaving his friend to dig, Norm walked the path back to the fire.

There was nothing left to the cabin, but partial walls and half of a collapsed roof. A tanker truck was parked on the front lawn. A man sprayed water on any parts of the structure that were still smoldering. A sign on the truck's door read, Highway Mobile Wash. *Just as good as a fire truck.* Norm thought. He walked up to the Nickerson, who was talking to some of the other cops.

"Any sign of Jensen yet, Inspector?"

"One of the guys saw a body in the kitchen. We were just about to go in, but we want to make sure the walls aren't going to come down on us when we get in there. The County Building Inspector happened to see the smoke from the highway and came here to see what was burning. We're waiting for him to give us the nod."

"Two Snakes is up on the hill, digging up a fresh grave; he thinks his niece is buried there. Do any of your guys have an extra shovel?"

"How the hell would he know his niece is...never mind, I guess it doesn't matter now. I've got a bunch of cops sitting around here with nothing to do—I was going to send some back home. I'll see what equipment they have and send a few of them up to the graveyard. It's included in the search warrant."

While Nickerson barked some orders into his radio, the Building Inspector joined the group. He eyeballed Norm, trying to figure how a guy in a Harley shirt and jeans fit into the equation.

The Building Inspector spoke up when Nickerson was off the radio. "The corners of the walls are still intact and holding what's left. I see the body in the kitchen, under some debris...you should be safe getting it out. Just stay away from the back wall, it took more heat because of the wood pile. I can knock it down if you want."

"No, thanks. I don't want to mess up the scene anymore than we have already." Nickerson turned to Norm, "You've got some expertise in this area; do you want to come for a look?"

"No need, Inspector, I've seen enough crispy critters. I'm just an observer, remember? And technically, if I go in there, you'll have to include me on your search warrant-return to the Judge. I'm gonna go back up the hill and check on my friend."

When Norm reached the graveyard, Two Snakes was standing by himself, among the dead and withered fruit trees. Norm saw the open grave with an un-zipped body bag in it. The young girl was not familiar to him, but she had a silver feather earring in one ear. Two Snakes was right about Jensen. Norm could not imagine his friend's pain.

The ERT cops had shed their gear and were busy digging up the other graves in the Johansen family plot. It was a macabre scene. Norm walked over to Two Snakes and put a hand on his shoulder. "I'm really sorry about your niece. You wanna get out of here?"

"Yeah, I'm gonna have to go tell my sister. That oughta be fun."

Back at the cabin, Inspector Nickerson was standing near the front porch, talking to another cop who was holding a plastic evidence bag. It contained a scorched and partially melted RCMP badge.

"This was still clipped onto his belt." The cop was showing it to the Inspector, as Norm and Two Snakes stepped up beside him.

"Jensen's?" Norm asked.

The cop answered, "Yeah, he's burnt to a crisp, but we found a bullet hole right between his eyes—one of our guys must have shot him before the fire started. There's a shot gun on the floor, near the front door and his service pistol is still in his hand. We're trying to recover it now without tearing his hand off."

Nickerson said, "That's lovely. At least he didn't burn to death."

Norm noticed Two Snakes, checking out the Ford Explorer in the driveway. Someone had pulled the tarp off, before the heat melted it to the SUV. It was Jensen's work vehicle.

Two Snakes shouted over to Nickerson. "Hey, any sign of the other one?" Then walked back to him.

"What other one?"

"There was an older, darker colored Explorer, parked in the same spot the last time I was here."

"I don't know anything about that."

"What are you doing with this one?"

"I'll have one of my guys drive it back...if we can find the keys."

"They're in the ignition. Can Norm and I drive it back to town? My truck is in the junkyard and I haven't had a chance to call the insurance company yet."

"I...uh..."

Norm tapped the Inspector's elbow with the back of his hand.

"I guess it would be okay, for now?"

Two Snakes opened the driver's door. "You coming, Kemosabe? I gotta go see me sister."

"Yeah. You can drop me off at the Ramada—I owe the Inspector a pile of paperwork."

Norm got into the Explorer with Two Snakes. Red and watery eyes revealed the pain he was feeling. Two Snakes drove back out the laneway and turned onto the other fork, leading away from the highway.

"Where you going, Tonto?"

"'I wanna show you my fishing spot. I used to bring Dakota there—it's where we bonded."

Norm saw the lake, just past the clearing at the end of the road. It was serene and not another person or building was in sight. Pine trees ringed the lake as far as the eye could see. A charcoal streak ran through the powder blue sky, smoke from the cabin fire. Two Snakes parked near a stone fire pit, surrounded by four stumps.

"Hmm, that's weird...my canoe is gone. I keep it in those tall weeds over there."

"Maybe someone borrowed it."

"There's no one else around here, but it's happened before. I figured it was just kids...there's another logging road on the other side of the lake. That's where I found it. I'll have to drive around the other side next time I'm up here."

Two Snakes walked to the water's edge and took a handful of dirt from his pants pocket. He tossed the dirt out over the lake and uttered some words in his native tongue. Norm stood in silence and watched his friend send Dakota off to the spirit world.

43

New Horizons

Loretta and Mark listened in awe as Norm told them the whole story—about a truck driver who kidnapped Hope, and the mountain man who held her captive. And about a Mountie who was also a serial killer. Mark had questions Norm couldn't answer, things that other people would be asking themselves for years to come. Loretta said she felt sick to her stomach, and thought she'd probably have nightmares.

Mark shook his head in disbelief. Loretta gave Norm a hug then said, "I know it's all sick and twisted, Norm, but maybe you should write a book about it some day."

"Yeah, maybe then people will believe what's going on around here, and do something about it."

As before, they told him he was welcome back anytime, he was considered part of the family. Norm was grateful, but it was time to move on—his sister was expecting him in Vancouver, later the next day. It was too distant and too scenic of a drive to cover in one day. He was in no hurry.

He'd called Laurie to say hey, but really to ask how Hope was doing. She said Hope was as well as could be expected, considering everything that had happened. Charitee didn't know any better, and was happy to have her mommy home. Laurie asked Norm to stay in touch, but he knew he never would.

Norm also called Sal and Carole and brought them up to date. He thanked them again for all their help, and told them they'd be welcome at his place in Windsor, any time.

The Highway of Tears

Having said goodbye to Loretta at breakfast, Norm had Mark drop him off at Two Snakes' place. His bike was still in the garage there. Two Snakes was in the driveway polishing the blue bomber when Norm got there.

"That's a nice ride—sorry I never got to take it for a spin."

"Maybe next time, Kemosabe, as long as we're not hunting psychos."

Norm saw his bike in front of the muscle car. It was as clean and shiny as the day he bought it. He smiled and turned back to Two Snakes who said, "It was filthy—I'd be embarrassed to ride it in that condition."

"It's just gonna get dirty again on the highway, but thanks man. Hey, what's the insurance company say about your truck?"

"They're replacing it—seems a high-ranking officer in the RCMP made me out to be some kind of hero...said I helped to capture a kidnapper and serial killer."

"Imagine that. Maybe you can work with them again some day."

"Not likely, I don't want to press my luck."

"Yeah...Tonto, I'd say we got lucky all the way around. I just want you to know..."

"I know, I know, my friend. I'm glad it all worked out for you and your girlfriend—think you'll ever see her again?"

"Doubt it. I've already been down that road, and I don't like to backtrack. I'm looking for new horizons...paths I haven't travelled. Think we'll ever hook up again...maybe you can make a trip east some day?"

"Any good fishing holes there?"

"I don't fish much, but I know some good watering holes."

Two Snakes extended his hand. "You're a good man, Norm Strom. You are a credit to your people."

"Likewise, my brother. Give me a shout if you have any more dreams that might concern me."

Two Snakes smiled. Norm secured his travel bag, and mounted his iron horse.

"Hey, hang on a minute. Can you drop something off at the Ramada for me?"

He retrieved a pair of binoculars from the garage and handed them to Norm.

"Aren't those...?"

"Yeah, I forgot to give them back...but being a hero and all..."

Norm laughed. "Sure, no problem. It'll give me a chance to say goodbye to Inspector Nickerson." He looked over his shoulder at the old lady's house. "Should I rev it a few times to keep you in good with the neighbors?"

Two Snakes chuckled and shook his head. Norm rolled down the driveway, dropped the engine in gear, and rumbled off.

The task force office was quiet, but everyone was busy. All the cops seemed confined to their desks, buried in paperwork.

"Hey, Norm, I thought you'd have been halfway across the country by now. You must be anxious to get back home."

Nickerson looked like he's aged five years since the day Norm met him.

"Not really, Inspector...nothing but an empty house waiting for me. I'm going to Vancouver to visit my sister, then I'll head back through the northern states. Anyway, I'm dropping off these binoculars for Two Snakes—I guess he forgot to give them back to you."

"Uh-huh, I bet he did. How'd he make out with his insurance company?"

"Good. They're gonna replace the truck...seems someone here put in a good word for him."

The Highway of Tears

Nickerson smiled. "It's the least I could do for him...and you Norm? You're still a young man...maybe you'd be interested in some contract work with the task force?"

Norm's face cracked and he chortled. "No thank-you, sir. I did have a little fun, but I don't miss this shit—not one bit."

"That's too bad, you do good work...in an old-school kind of way." Nickerson stood and shook Norm's hand. "Let me walk you out, I'd like to see that bike of yours."

When Norm got to the office door he turned to the Inspector.

"You never told me how you made out with the fat man."

"Mr. Strickland. He's keeping two of my Investigators busy full-time. We found the weed you told us about, and more of it in his home, along with some un-registered firearms and a bunch of prescription pills that didn't belong to him. He sang like a soprano, and gave up everyone he knew to save his own bacon...the boat captain, a weed dealer, and another trucker who runs stolen goods."

Norm grinned and nodded his head up and down.

"Besides the guns and drugs, he was also charged with kidnapping and unlawful confinement. Forensics took all kinds of samples from his truck, but we won't get anything back on those for some time. You did good getting that asshole off the street, Norm."

On the way through the lobby, Norm caught a glimpse of a familiar pretty face. It was Melanie. Her smile reminded him of what was missing in his life. He returned the facial gesture and waved. In the parking lot, Nickerson checked out the bike, while Norm got on and checked the gauges.

"Hey, Inspector...what ever happened to that serial killer that Jensen caught? I read in the paper that you found two more bodies that you think he was responsible for?"

"Funny you should ask, Norm. His name is John Alan Lewis. We've put together a solid forensics case, the two investigators who took over for Jensen found the other bodies. We think there are more, but we'll never know for sure."

"Can't you offer him a deal...the number of bodies is really a moot point now, isn't it?"

"That's the thing, Norm. We'd love to offer him a deal, but no one has seen him since the interview with Jensen. It's like he's disappeared from the face of the earth."

Norm scrunched his face and thought about it for a moment. He shrugged and switched on the ignition, then revved the engine, letting the exhaust pipes roar for effect. He shouted over the noise, "Really? Good luck with that."

He drove off and glanced into the lobby, passing by the front doors. Melanie was all red hair and white teeth.

As Norm cruised south, out of town, he thought the stratus clouds looked like layers of white cotton candy. When he looked up the wind whispered in his ears, *"Beware of the fox."* He guffawed and drove past a young girl, hitchhiking. She flashed a big smile. Norm used the mirror to adjust his sunglasses and saw that she had turned around and was looking his way. A dark colored SUV pulled off the road and stopped behind her.

Previous Books by Edmond Gagnon

"A Casual Traveler"

"If you want a great vacation go to an all-inclusive resort, If you want a great travel experience go anywhere else."

Ed's first book is a fun collection of short stories inspired by his travels around the world. His chronicled adventures and misadventures take you to faraway places like Cambodia, Viet Nam, Thailand, Peru, Chile, Argentina, Belize, Guatemala and Mexico. He also shares his motorcycle trips across Canada and the United States.

The Black & White Crimes Series with Norm Strom:

"Rat"

Police Informants exist in a netherworld that very few other people dare venture into. They reach out from the darkness to the police, shedding light on the worst of crimes and criminals. Their anonymity is crucial to their success and survival. "Rat" tells the story of how one cop rises through the ranks using his arsenal of police informants as his own secret weapon in his fight against crime.

"Bloody Friday"

Two best friends from Belfast share a common dream of a better life elsewhere. In their quest to discover the world they choose two completely different paths. Jimmy Flynn gets involved with the IRA, becoming a gun and drug smuggler. Patrick Kelly joins the military, doing a tour in Viet Nam as a sniper. From there he joins the Toronto Police and becomes a drug cop.

The story moves from Belfast, through Viet Nam, to Boston, Toronto and Detroit. Across the border in Windsor, drug cop Norm Strom uses his police informants to combat the war on drugs. Drugs, guns and women are the common denominator that draws all three men together. In their endeavors to either fight crime, or profit from it, one of them will have to pay the ultimate price.

"Torch"

Arson Detective Norm Strom is always one step behind a serial arsonist who is responsible for burning several buildings in the city. He tracks down known arsonist Johnny Eagle and turns him into his informant, hoping to use one torch to catch another.

Eagle tells all, revealing the pleasure and satisfaction he gets from setting and watching a raging inferno. Detective Strom relies on Eagle and his other informants to help him discover the true identity of the serial arsonist.

To keep the cops off his back, Johnny Eagle rats on his own friends. Is he playing both sides of the fence? Detective

The Highway of Tears

Strom and Johnny Eagle each tell the story, putting the reader in the middle of a game of cat and rat.

"In policing, uniforms and cars are black and white. On the street, in real life, nothing is black and white."

Author Bio

Edmond Gagnon is a retired Police Detective, who worked the streets of Windsor, Ontario, for over thirty-one years. He spent time in narcotics, morality, property crimes, fraud, and arson. As a result of his numerous criminal investigations and arrests, he learned how to *write a good story* and put the bad guys behind bars.

After retiring, he travelled the world and chronicled his adventures. To share his tales, Ed wrote and self-published a book of short travel stories called, "A Casual Traveler."

Inspired by his personal experiences in policing, Ed created his Black & White crime fiction series and wrote his first novel, **Rat**, to give readers a behind-the-scenes look at police informants and their contribution to law enforcement.

Bloody Friday and **Torch** are the next two novels in the series that tell individual stories involving Detective Norm Strom. In Ed's latest novel, **Finding Hope**, the newly retired Detective gets involved in the search for a missing woman along the infamous *Highway of Tears*.

Ed continues to write and travel the world with his wife, Cathryn. They share their travel stories along with restaurant, movie and book reviews on their blog:

foodtravelmovies.wordpress.com

All of Ed's books can be found online, through the usual retail outlets. They can be purchased locally, through Ed and some Windsor book stores.

www.edmondgagnon.com

CPSIA information can be obtained at www.ICGtesting.com
Printed in the USA
LVOW11s2307050616

491263LV00001B/5/P

9 781634 914086